PERSISTENCE

Marc Costanzo

1

"Sir, I'm going to need you to calm down."

Officer Celia Miller stood inside the cramped one-story residence, one hand on her hip, the other on her holster. Not the gun holster, not at this juncture, and it really didn't even seem like the type of situation that would escalate to that. No, her right hand was on a holster that contained mace she would spray into this bastard's eyes if he continued to be belligerent.

That was one thing that surprised her when she became a cop. They hand you a gun and a baton, but it's the mace you get the most use out of. Stings like a prick from a cactus in your eye. She hadn't experienced it firsthand yet. Didn't really want to. She had become a cop so that she wouldn't have to be one of those cowering victims spraying a puny silly-string of habanero pepper into the eyes of an attacker, and yet the moment she got her badge, she got her mace.

"Sir, please acknowledge that you understand what I'm asking you."

"Bitch, you come into my house, I'm just trying to watch my programs."

"They's my programs," called a voice from the kitchen. "It's my unemployment check that done paid for the Deeveearr!"

"Shila, you know I put this roof over your head. You know I did!"

They never teach you how stupid some of the conversations you overhear will be, how ridiculous the situations you'll be put into are. 90% of the job is talking to people like this in houses just like this one: borderline hoarders, newspapers and old pizza boxes and football videogame cartridges scattered about, a rusty fan providing the only air despite the fact it's 108 degrees outside. Blinds that aren't blinds but X-Men blankets that haven't covered a sleeping child since three rounds of probation ago. And a red-skinned white guy with as many dollars to his name as he has teeth, wearing a beater and a pair of acid-washed jeans covering his skinny chicken legs. His arms with barbed-wire ink, preventing the escape of any muscles that might dare try to elude the prison of his emaciated frame. And, yelling from the other room, the wife, or the girlfriend, or the baby mama, wearing a long shirt in place of a nightgown, a cigarette in one hand and a yowling baby in the other, a baby with eyes too blue and too innocent for this home.

Welcome to Ravencourt.

"Sir, please lower your voice."

"Who are you to tell me to lower my voice? I'm an American citizen. You seen them Mexicans loitering around the other end of town, go bother them, they ain't even got papers."

"This isn't about them, I'm just trying to get a sense of—"

"Sense of what? Way I see it you ain't got any sense in that pretty blonde head of yours. You got colored folk in masks robbin' and carousin' throughout the town, but instead of doing some actual police work, you disturb an honest, hard-working American."

She had to repress a flash of anger. If this were anyone else on the force, something tells her that hair color would not be used as a descriptor. Nor would the word *bitch*.

"Your wife called us and said..."

"She ain't my wife."

"Your acquaintance said you had been drinking..."

"I can't drink in my own home?"

"And that you slapped her when she went in to feed the baby."

"She feeds that baby too much, it's gonna be as fat as she is."

Celia sighed. "So you do admit to slapping her? That's assault."

"I ain't admitting to a goddam thing. I know my rights."

"Apparently you know how to use a left, too."

"Miller," said a voice from the other side of the room, at the door frame of the kitchen. An edge to the word, an authority, even though she and her partner were at the same pay grade and she had a year and a half on him in seniority.

Celia turned toward the voice and the man it belonged to. Officer

Donald Wilson, about as cop a name as you can get. The face still too youthful to be all that intimidating, try as he might. Wilson had the athletic build of a local boy who was great at football in high school and not much else, with wide brown eyes that took nothing too seriously.

He also had sandy blond hair. But fuck if you'll hear this yokel throw it in his face.

"What is it, Officer Wilson?"

"Why don't you let me talk to him for a second? You can speak with Miss Jessups."

"I've got this."

"I know you do, I just thought maybe I could calm down Mr. Jessups."

"Mr. Marsh," said Mr. Marsh.

"Sorry. Mr. Marsh, I mean," said Wilson, locking eyes with the man, a shared understanding between the two that she'll never have with this asshole. A playfulness was in Wilson's eyes that shouldn't be there in a cop, a playfulness that suggested this is all just a joke and I'll get things straightened out for you.

"I think I can handle the questioning."

"Of course you can. I just thought maybe Mister…"

"Marsh."

"Marsh and I could sit down, have a drink, get this taken care of."

"Finally, a cop that speaks my language," said the man in the beater, sitting down on a tattered couch that smelled faintly of dog pee and pepperoni pizza.

Wilson winked at Celia, who returned the favor by staring coldly back. Wilson shuffled toward a chair and Celia walked briskly past him, not bothering to meet his gaze. She could hear the groans of a chair creak as he sat.

As the two gentlemen, one a cop and one a lowlife, began to converse, Celia entered the kitchen to find Miss Jessups halfway through her third cigarette. The pudgy arm carrying the pudgy baby balanced a Terrible's Casino ashtray on a hand two decades younger than the woman's eyes.

The woman blew the smoke up toward a ceiling fan that looked precariously close to flying off its preordained circular path.

"Whatchoo want now?" she asked.

The baby, who was crying before, now just looked on the verge, a lip quivering as he gazed at Celia with those bright blue eyes.

"Can you tell me what happened? The way you told the 911 operator on the phone?"

"Ain't nothing happened."

"What do you mean?" asked Celia.

"Just what I said. I got all mixed up, thought I felt something when I didn't. Must've gone and ran into the refrigerator again. Sometimes all this smoke gets to my head."

"Ma'am, if he hit you, then it would behoove…"

Miss Jessups laughed. "Be who the what now?"

"It would be in your best interest and that of your child to let us know. We need to press charges."

"It's his fourth offense," said Miss Jessups.

"Exactly."

"So what, you're gonna cart him to jail on th'other side of the state? What am I gonna do when I need a sitter? When I wanna hit up the Tumbleweed? Take Erique along with me? My girlfriends don't wanna party with no baby."

"Keeping your child, Eric, is it?… in a safe environment is far more important than the Tumbleweed."

"Says you with your perky tits and your hips that ain't birthed no two kids. I can't go finding me no better man if I'm dragging a squealer along. I gotta make myself look presentable. What are you, 22?"

"I'm twent…ma'am, my age doesn't matter."

"You got some learning to do about how the world works. I'm 35. You gonna be calling and asking my advice in a couple years, 'specially when them men that think you so cute now instead just see an icy old twat who got but one thing to do with that police baton."

Celia grimaced. 35? Jesus, this woman was only seven years older than she was. But her eyes were decades.

There was no point staying here any longer.

"If you change your mind and would like to press charges, please let us know."

Celia nodded in Miss Jessups's direction, and much to her surprise, Erique laughed. His big blue eyes regarded Celia with something like curiosity, wondering how this heretofore unseen pretty woman in the tan uniform and the shiny badge came to enter his raggedy world, like a '65 Camaro just passing through a junkyard.

Celia smiled at the child, and he returned the smile. She stared into those big blue eyes and thought that oases really can exist in any desert.

And then the mother blew smoke into the air, and the fan wafted it right into the boy's face. He began to cry anew, his screams reverberating through the house.

"Shut that baby up!" yelled Mr. Marsh.

The oasis was gone as quickly as it appeared.

2

Celia tried her best not to slam the ramshackle front door of the house, but to no avail. She was surprised the rickety wooden bastard didn't swing right off its hinges after it clattered to the chipped wall.

At least she wasn't the first into the squad car. That would be even more embarrassing. No, she walked out through the sweltering heat, watching the invisible tidal waves wash upward from the concrete of the derelict driveway. She leaned against the car and put a hand above her eyes to shield the sun. Every house on this block was ratty in the way that only government housing that no longer draws government assistance can be. The type of neighborhood where kids in diapers would wander outdoors aimlessly if the desert didn't keep them inside.

Celia stood there while Officer Wilson ended the chat with the charming gentleman inside the house, even shaking his hand and telling him to have a good day. Telling the perpetrator of the goddamn domestic abuse case to have a good day. As Wilson strode back to the car, the look on his face concealing the smugness made him look even more smug than he would have otherwise.

"You've just gotta know how to talk to them, Miller," he said. "You'll pick it up eventually."

Celia didn't say a word. Wilson stood at the driver's side, looking at her from behind his sunglasses. She didn't wear hers, preferring to meet his concealed eyes with her own blue ones from between squinted lids. He considered her without having a right to, then shrugged and opened his door. She got in after he did and succeeded in failing to not slam another door.

Wilson started up the 2004 Crown Vic and pulled out of the driveway as, from the speakers, Toby Keith started a lilting soliloquy about beer. Celia stared out the window as the low-income housing gave way to low income liquor stores. Theirs wasn't a big town, but it was large enough to have its amenities. In the richer part of town (or street of town, as was more apt), they had their Italian restaurants with their $22 steaks and $45 pinot (the most expensive in the city). In this part of town they had their liquor stores with wines from the most recent calendar year. You would not be surprised to find out the wine in each location was from the same truck.

The whole of Ravencourt could be contained within that section of the Vegas strip that extends from Caesars to the Stratosphere. Those are the types of measurements that pass muster in towns that rest just two and a half hours north of the City of Sin and an hour and a half from anything approaching a tourist venue. A couple decades ago, Ravencourt received some little notoriety among UFO nuts for a purported crash. As a result, the town had a disproportionate number of tacky t-shirt shops and novelty stores selling all manner of alien paraphernalia.

Ravencourt's only other brush with fame occurred just a few years ago, when FBI agents had nabbed a serial killer nicknamed John the Face Eater on the furthest outskirts of town. You could still hear officers at the Tumbleweed or the Rude Awakening clinking their glasses to that fine day when they had assisted with cordoning off the area and traffic duty.

Otherwise, Ravencourt stayed largely off the map, unless that map offered quite a bit of detail. A population of just over or under 11,000 depending on the carnal proclivities and health woes of its citizens in that particular year. A drive-in movie theater on one side of town, a throwback that locals still bragged about. A smattering of fast food restaurants, a shopping mall, the rich on one side, the poor on the other, the commercial district smack dab in the middle. Oil money kept the community sticking around, even if the wells nowadays were far drier than the bottles in the bars. Good people, staunchly but not unanimously Republican, conservative, a faith in God but a love for its people, a welcoming hand to strangers. A local drink concoction called Cactus Punch that would knock you on your ass with just one sip if you had never ventured this way before.

This was Celia's Ravencourt, and now the small city large town was passing her by. Or rather, she was passing it by.

"You didn't file the report," she said, still looking out the window.

"I figured you would do that while I drove," Wilson said.

"Why would you figure that?"

"Look, I'm not looking to…"

"Standard protocol is to fill out the report and initial notes upon reentering the vehicle while the details are fresh in your mind."

"Jesus, Celia, we went to the same academy."

"We didn't get the same grade, though, did we?" She finally pulled her focus from the town and turned to Donald, eyes wide open without the sun to lessen their impact.

"What do you want from me?" he asked, turning the wheel to the left so he could navigate down a street that would bring them to the station.

"To take the job seriously."

"What's there to take seriously? White trash, he hits her, she calls us, she denies calling us, he hits her again, lather rinse repeat."

"You talked to him like he was the victim."

"If she doesn't report him, what the hell are we supposed to do? I can't exactly beat a confession out of the guy."

She shook her head. This was useless. They'd done this song and dance before.

He pulled into the parking lot of the station. The squat, ranch-style structure was once home to the town's visitor's center. With such a thing proving unnecessary and the police requiring more space than their previous one-room, one-cell operation in order to better crack down on the burgeoning meth trade that had become Ravencourt's chief export, the PD moved in and made the domicile its own.

A little expansion went a little way. They added a garage that could house a half dozen squad cars, a couple cells in the back, and knocked down a wall here and there for offices, cubicle space, and a locker room. Voila, you got yourself a police station.

Wilson parked the car. It let out a groan as he did so. The Vic had seen better days, but there wasn't enough money for all officers to get new vehicles. Surprise, surprise Celia drew that short straw.

Wilson pulled the white report pad out from its spot in the dashboard. The newer vehicles had computers that could upload the reports automatically. Their ride: not so much.

Wilson scrawled on the paper.

"What are you doing?" Celia asked.

"Well, you made such a big deal about the goddamn report."

"Don't leave out details."

"Would you rather do it?"

This was the definition of a no-win proposition, something that Celia had been dealing with for a few years now. If she said no, Wilson gets the shit-eating satisfaction of having a confirmation that his "partner" of the past couple months remains a complete and utter bitch. If she said yes, his opinion of her lightens somewhat but she has to do the work while he gets to go inside and grab lunch with the rest of the boys in blue.

"You do the fucking thing," she said and stepped out of the vehicle. Let him think she's a bitch.

This time she doesn't slam the door as she strides toward the front of the station.

3

Celia opened the set of glass double doors and was greeted by Judith the receptionist and an otherwise empty welcome area. Potted cactuses and plaques on the wall spelled the history of the station, the plaques detailing the names, badge numbers, and term of service of every chief in the town's barely 100-year history, and the cactus that had been here since the Eisenhower administration had seen more perps than anyone currently on the force.

Judith was divided from the general public by way of a piece of sliding plexiglass. A metal door to her right could be unlocked by either Judith buzzing you through or a key that you had to work from side to side just to turn in the lock.

Celia had attempted to get the force to take some of their budget from last year to upgrade the door lock system to an RFID scanner. She had been voted down. They opted instead for a squad car that could go 120 mph in 5.5 seconds and that had a protective shell that could withstand any shot short of a tank shell. In Ravencourt. Where you don't often see tanks.

"Hi, Judith," said Celia as she entered the foyer. Judith, the department's 70-something receptionist, pecked at a sandwich laid out in front of her, peeling off pieces of bread and PB & J instead of picking the whole thing up to take a bite.

"Chief wants to see you," she said.

When she first started on the force, Celia thought that she and Judith Burkschneider would develop a camaraderie seeing as how they were the only two women on staff. That thought went out the sliding plexiglass window once one unfortunate lunch break made it abundantly clear to Celia that Judith felt nothing but disdain for the young cadet.

Judith, whose husband left the force six years earlier yet still came in every Wednesday night to play poker with the guys, was the type to fuss over her man's collar and *tsk tsk* when he belched, to play pinochle with the other women while the menfolk watched the game at police parties. Celia's appearance on the force was an affront to the standard order of things. Judith, used to facilitating the phone calls, paperwork, and other minutiae of police work for officers without prodding, did not speak to Celia unless required to and seemed to provide a disdainful smirk whenever the young officer asked for something that fell well within the purview of Judith's support role.

The first and only real incident between the two women occurred at lunch on one of Celia's first weeks on the force. Celia, attempting to extend the olive branch, invited Judith out to a local eatery, a new place around the corner that had all the locals raving, going by the fancy name of Arby's. Or Arbé's if you insisted on calling it by its original French pronunciation.

Judith demurred, explaining that she had already brought her lunch, brought in her lunch for the entire rest of the week in fact. Celia, still trying to make a good impression in those initial days returning to Ravencourt from UNLV, persisted, asking and asking until she was able to wrestle a free day out of her the following Thursday.

So they went to Arby's, Celia ready to have a woman-to-woman conversation, get to know some of the intricacies of the system, the little tics of the boy's club that it takes any rookie a good couple of years to sink into. Celia had ordered a roast beef sandwich, Judith had dutifully brought along her everyday Peanut Butter with a Yogurt.

They sat facing each other in the booth.

"So how's Hank like retirement?" Celia asked.

"Just fine," replied Judith as she placed little pieces of bread into the pinhole of her pinched lips.

"Really? That's great. I hear it's really hard to adjust for some people."

"He has his programs."

"Oh yeah, what do you guys like to watch?" Celia had asked.

"What are you doing?" asked Judith.

Celia had thought she was referring to the way she sort of chewed on straws when taking a drink from her cup. Slightly embarrassed, she covered her mouth and laughed.

"Oh, sorry, you know what they say about old habits."

"You're too young for old habits," said Judith. "What are you doing in that station?"

"I guess I don't..."

"The last thing those men need when they come back out from the field for a bit of a shit-shooting session is a pair of tits causing them undue stress."

A piece of roast beef fell out of Celia's mouth and onto the table as her jaw fell. She was too stunned to even say anything for a minute. She swallowed the rest of her bite of fancy roast beef.

"I think the boys can handle..."

"You don't know what those boys can handle, sweetheart. Now I always loved your daddy, he was a good man, but he wasn't right in the head if he encouraged you down this path."

"I guess I don't understand the problem," said Celia.

"That _is_ the problem. The men in this precinct, they need someone they can trust to have their back when they're deep in the mud. With you around, their minds, they get all hazy. I hate to think what would happen to you sometime when that low-cut uniform catches one of those boys' eyes when they haven't been getting any," (and here she lowered her voice, as if this was the offending portion of the diatribe) "_marital relations_ from their wives. What if they can't control themselves, sweetheart?"

This was the first time in her life that Celia had been told that she was asking for it. She had not expected the suggestion to come from a matronly desk clerk in essence saying that it's not a man's fault if his predilections get the better of him.

At the time, Celia had jumped up and run to the bathroom. She slammed the door behind her and turned the lock, barely able to do so in time before the tears welled up. Not giant, racking sobs, Celia wasn't the type, but the type of cry where your tears well up and get right to the verge of breaking the dam.

She had expected some piss-poor treatment, had been dealing with little backhanded comments in some form or another since she started on the force. But the boys played around the edges, catching themselves asking but actually telling her to make copies for them in the guise of it's the rookie's job, lobbing in the occasional comment about the considerable heat she was packing, har har har.

The last person she expected to come out and so overtly belittle her, make her feel like hell, was the only other X chromosome in the Ravencourt PD.

All of a sudden it had all caught up to her at once, the comments, the jibes, the office duties that no other cop would be expected to do, and she felt the tears coming harder.

But then she clutched the wet, grimy counter of the Arby's bathroom sink, tightening her grip until her wrist hurt and she was forced to focus on the pain rather than the tears and the words. She made herself look up, to see just how stupid she looked, the face of someone brought so low by a person so insignificant they had to resort to shit shoveling just to make themselves feel better about their own low lot in life.

She saw a face she didn't like and didn't want to see again, not in a mirror or in her own thoughts. Right then and there she banished that person, the girl who could be brought down by a snide comment, to a recess of her mind. Not banished entirely, for can we ever banish those weaker versions of ourselves we hide from the world? But buried in a spot that she could access when it was safe. A prisoner in maximum security solitary confinement that would only get visiting hours every couple months or so, far from the prying eyes of other prisoners. Or cops.

She wiped her eyes and threw the paper towel in the wastebasket, never looking away from her own eyes. Celia might hear that prisoner calling to her at times, asking to be let out. But that girl was deeper now, and Celia thought that she would not come to the surface anytime soon.

Celia walked out of the bathroom, ready to tell Judith that she'd see her back at the station, not curse her out, but take the high road and let it be known that she would not shirk from the path laid out before her. She would tolerate the woman. She saw now that she did not have to and would not ever be friends with her.

But Judith's side of the booth was already empty.

That's how little she thinks of you, whispered the voice of the prisoner inside of Celia.

Celia slammed her mind's prison cell in the little girl's face and sat down to finish her Roast Beef and Cheese.

And now here Celia was, nearly a year later, Judith telling her that the Chief wanted to see her.

Celia smiled at Judith. "Thank you. Any other messages?"

Judith swallowed her bite of sandwich and wiped her mouth properly. "I would tell you if there were."

"Always a pleasure."

Celia shook her head and headed to the door. It didn't open right away. Judith hesitated another moment, giving herself time to swallow a nibble of sandwich, before buzzing her in. Celia opened the door and entered the hive of inactivity that was the command center of the Ravencourt Police Department.

4

The bullpen. The guys to a one hadn't approached a baseball diamond for anything but interleague softball since high school, yet insisted on calling the array of desks and cubicles where they spent most of their time "the bullpen."

It wasn't much to look at, nor were many of Ravencourt's finest, currently engaged in a game of catch with an orange magic marker. There were three cops there at that point: Mikey Hilcox, who everybody except for Celia called Foxy Coxy; Jared Smalls, who everybody called Little Red, despite the fact that he was 6 foot 4 if he was an inch; and David Appleby, whom everyone called David.

Each wore the standard tan button-up shirt and greenish gray pants that signified the uniform of the Ravencourt Police Department. They also wore the unofficial uniform of Ravencourt PD, a penciled mustache and a shit-eating grin. Hilcox still struggled to get more than a few strays to perk up above his upper lip, while Little Red's mustache on his massive dome would have looked like a beard on any of the smaller men. Smalls's close-cropped mustache matched the hair on each of their heads.

They barely spared Celia a glance as she walked in. She watched as Mikey about spilled over in his chair trying to catch an errant throw of the marker. The other two laughed as Mikey righted himself and shambled over to pick it up near Celia's feet.

Mikey scooped up the marker and gave a little salute to Celia.

"Hiya, C," he said.

This was a nickname given to her when she started on the force, and she had wondered then as she still did now if it didn't have an ulterior definition hidden behind the simple shortening of her first name.

Of course it does, whispered the voice before Celia clanged her mental nightstick on the bars of her interior cell.

"Officer Hilcox," she said in acknowledgment. He scooped up the marker and flung it back at Red, who easily picked it off before it had a chance to hit its mark. Hilcox sauntered back over to his desk.

Celia took a look around the room and had time to notice that — amid all the cubicles, amid the posters with pictures of a perp with a gun in his belt as he's being pushed down into a squad car (the caption on this reading "Look Before You Book"), amid the random paraphernalia of an office, the paperwork, the halogen lights, the OSHA checklists on the walls, the series of empty chairs — one particular chair stood empty when it shouldn't have been. The 911 officer's station.

Most precincts have an employee dedicated to that particular task, but Ravencourt wasn't what you would call a high traffic area, and the duties of the 911 operator typically fell to whoever happened to be next up in a rotation. The calls that came in would range from a cat in a tree to the far more exciting meth addict in a tree, with the methods needing to be applied to each situation remaining relatively the same (hoist up a ladder, use a soothing tone of voice, watch out for claws and the smell of cat piss).

"Who's manning 911?" asked Celia.

Hilcox caught the marker then tossed it to Officer Appleby. Appleby tapped the marker against the side of his head, which Celia now saw had a headset attached to it.

"I'll trade if you want a break from patrol," said Appleby.

"Oh, that's ok, Appleby, you get your rest."

Celia walked through the tangle of cubicles toward the left, where a hallway branched off and led to the Chief's office. The request she had just fielded was a fairly common one. For the past few months, Celia had been able to note an uptick in the amount of trade offers. It was as if the other officers were not so subtly trying to steer her into a 911 operator's role. She suspected that such ideas had even been brought to the Chief's attention. No doubt the officers were convinced that they were helping her out by getting her off the streets and into an air-conditioned precinct where she could be comfortable.

Left unmentioned during such musings was that the officers,

herself included, loathed the 911 shift. The role was supposed to be filled not by officers but by trained civilians, but the dedicated 911 operators had been excised a few months back because of budget cuts.

As a result, the remaining members of the Ravencourt Police Department had to alternate 911 duties. You don't sign up for the force because you want to sit at a desk all day, even in Ravencourt where that desk might be your only respite from triple digit heat.

When the other officers spent time at the 911 desk, they generally goofed around and visited any number of websites that collected humorous photos and selfies of women tugging on their clothes. They didn't worry about anything much other than lunch and when they could get off the spot for another two weeks. When Celia rotated in, which seemed to happen far more frequently than it did to others, she was casually handed paperwork and "asked" to do things like make copies or check schedules or inquire with the ammo depot as to whether they had a surplus of any piece of equipment.

Judith jobs. Not cop jobs.

Celia entered a stubby hallway lined with photos of chiefs, plaques of officer names, and more photos of teams lined up for softball games. "The Ravencourt Carrion" their team was called, a moniker popularly adopted some 25 years ago after the local fire department made a crack about how all the police in that town were expected to do was pick dead animal carcasses off the ground. A chief took it and ran with it and a softball team name was born.

The outfield's green on the photos of the softball diamond was the only color like that both along the walls of this grey hallway and in the current view from the window of Ravencourt in general. Like much in Nevada, the city was seemingly built on hardscrabble and a whole lot of gumption in the middle of a parched environment. The town was founded just above an underground stream with a source somewhere up in the nearby mountains, running down below the town and providing the sustenance needed to allow the color green to grow in spots. Wells were positioned throughout, drawing the water needed to allow survival. The town didn't have much, but they had water.

Celia approached the Chief's door, which was open today as it was on most days.

He's going to ask you why you have to be so combative to the boys.

"They don't mean nothing by it. It's just their way."

Celia shook her head and turned the corner as she knocked on the frame.

Henry Burton was on the phone, but he motioned Celia in with a wave of his finger, rolling his kind, gray eyes at some foolish statement said by whoever was on the other end of the phone.

"And you're sure?" he asked in a deep but assuring voice, the type of cadence that could take command but that could also remain collected and even fatherly when the situation warranted. As it had nearly two years ago when her father had died — what brought her back to this town in the first place.

Whatever the person said on the other end of the line must have satisfied Chief Burton.

"Alright, I'll get it right over to you," he said as he placed the phone back in its cradle. He fixed her with his eyes and a kind smile turned up the corners of his lips. "Officer Miller."

"Chief Burton," she said, then thrust a thumb back behind her shoulder. "Judith said you wanted to see me. Is this a 'shut the door' type of conversation?"

"I sure hope not," he said. "Have a seat."

Celia shut the door and took a seat. The Chief may have thought it was a conversation that didn't have to be private. But Celia knew better. She knew the scoffs and the jokes made behind her back about the Chief. That he had protected her, that if not for him she wouldn't have made it onto the force, that they were sleeping together (which they weren't, in case you were wondering). She didn't want to give ammunition to them with anything that was said in a meeting with the boss, no matter the content.

And the truth is that you wouldn't be on the force if not for him.

It <u>was</u> true, try as Celia might to silence the sentiment. She told herself that she had made it onto the team through sheer force of will, that she worked harder than anyone and scored better on tests than anyone and followed protocol in a way that would make any bureaucrat smile if such a thing was possible.

But that didn't do justice to the situation, which caused Celia a certain amount of chagrin. The Chief had shielded her. He had protected her during moments of jocularity gone too far, of good-natured ribbing that turned to bad-natured screaming, of undisclosed moments at smoky bars where the other officers had threatened to go on strike if Celia didn't leave the force.

This last bit Celia could never be sure took place, but her interior voice insisted that such a thing was real, and it tended to be right about these things.

And now the kind eyes of this 65-year-old friend and superior were looking at her with an all too common mixture of joviality and worry. He was a man turned gray by the force and red by the sun, and even approaching retirement the way he was, he showed no signs of slowing down.

No one doubted the Chief's control, accused him of slipping in his old age. And without being in the good graces of such a man, Celia didn't know if she would have lasted this long.

"How are things going out there today, Officer?"

"Responded to a domestic dispute in the 400 block. The accuser refused to press charges, despite our urgings."

"How did Officer Wilson handle himself?"

"Adequately, sir."

"Adequately?"

"He's filling out the report now, I'm sure he'll do an adequate job detailing the situation."

"Celia," and here Chief Burton ran a hand through his gray hair and looked around at the many plaques and honors that adorned his walls. "You and I both know that adequate is far too polite of a way to describe the abilities of one Officer Donald Wilson. Why weren't you able to get an arrest? Because of something he did?"

"The suspect was noncompliant when questioned by myself, and Officer Wilson took over questioning using a different tactic."

"A dumbass to dumbass sort of conversation?"

"Your words, sir, not mine."

"And what words were used to address the victim?"

"Words that get nowhere because this particular victim doesn't know how to be anything but."

Celia took a breath, caught herself.

"Sorry for speaking out of line, sir."

"Please," he said, and stood up. Then sat down again, not knowing how to carry himself. "I wish you spoke out of line more. It's your most ingratiating quality."

"Outside of work, maybe," she said. "I just want to do my job to the utmost while I'm here, sir."

"And drop the sir," he sighed. "I've known you since you were days old. Sammy couldn't wait to bring you by the station to show the boys. I should have known we were in trouble when the first thing you did when you were carried in was take your little fingers and grab at my badge."

"You're lucky I didn't go for the gun."

"That came not long after. Celia, you know I'm not gonna be here much longer. I'm on my way out and I'll need to pick a new Chief."

"What are you saying?" she asked, her voice higher than she would have liked, betraying a hint of anticipation that she would have preferred remain hidden.

"That I won't be able to keep the dogs away much longer," he said. "Whoever takes over will be one of the boys in these ranks. And you're too smart not to realize that they're not your biggest fans. I get more complaints about you than all other officers combined."

And what did you think, Celia? That he was getting ready to offer you the job of Ravencourt Chief of Police? A 28-year old girl as Chief? Even if you are the most qualified in this station.

"With all due respect, Chief, I don't need your protection."

"Maybe not," he said. "But I hate to think what would happen without it."

"I may get complaints, but I go by the book with everything I do. So you tell me if I'm doing something that falls outside the rules."

"Falls outside the rules? Are you kidding me? You're a chief's dream! I wish the rest of these vultures had half the brain cells that you do. Your police reports read like dissertations. I've had traffic tickets come in with Thank You notes on them. But you have to make more of an effort to be a team player."

"A team player."

"Go to the bar with the crew. Bust their balls. Let them bust yours."

"Are you telling me to be less stuck up?"

"No. That's not what I mean. But you can't pretend to let it wash over you."

"Excuse me?"

"You're stronger than everyone here. You're a threat to their order. And as long as they perceive you that way, you can never get in. Don't pretend to be stronger than you are, than they are. Be—"

"A girl?"

"A helping hand. You don't have to let anyone walk over you, that's not what I'm saying. But there are ways to get ahead without

     PERSISTENCE

turning everyone against you.”

Celia nodded, biting her lip.

“Now, that said, I need you on 911.”

“Are you fucking kidding me?”

“We need someone to go up to The Rocks and check on our parolees. And you know how that went last time.”

“So just because they’re afraid I’m going to crack them in the balls with a nightstick, Appleby gets to go out on patrol while I man phones like a secretary?”

“It’s not a secretarial job, you know everyone has to do it. C’mon with that. I send you out there, the addicts and lowlifes will get all riled up and someone’s parole is going to be revoked. I got enough on my plate with the State Police breathing down my back. Just cool your jets for today, I’ll have you back on regular rotation next weekend.”

Celia sighed. The Chief had made up his mind, a thing he didn’t do lightly. Although she had a unique power to convince him of many things, she got the sense this wouldn’t be one of them. Mostly because, in this regard, he was almost certainly right.

“Fine. But I’m having lunch first,” she said as she stood up to leave.

Chief Burton grimaced, clenching his teeth in an apologetic manner. Celia’s demeanor sank further.

“Seriously?” she asked.

“No time. Haddock wants to talk to you about what happened out at the Rocks. He thinks it could be tied to the alien investigation. I think he’s grasping at straws, but apparently my rank doesn’t count for much with the state.”

She sighed. “Fine.”

“Remember: be cooperative but don’t speculate. He isn’t one of us. It’s strange really...”

“What’s that, sir?”

“Guy like that, bigshot from Carson City, coming down here. Why? Because he happened to make a connection on an internet search?”

“Some weird stuff has been going on, Chief.”

“And we’ve got it handled just fine. It seems odd that, the moment we start investigating, this mystery man pops up looking into everything. Be on your guard, Celia. If my hunch is right, this recent string of...*activities* could go higher up than we thought. Last thing we need is a media circus and even more state troopers who don't belong coming into our town. God forbid, the FBI will be next."

"I'll be perfectly pleasant, sir."

Just like they always want you to be, she thought.

"Thank you, Officer Miller."

Celia opened the door and turned to leave.

"And Celia?"

She looked back. The Chief smiled.

"Good work out there with the domestic call. Others might not, but I see the work you're doing. Keep it up."

Celia smiled and closed the door behind her on the way out.

5

"Come in, Officer Miller."

In an ordinary situation, meetings between two officers would not be taking place in an interrogation room, but seeing as how Ravencourt PD rarely had reason to interrogate suspects (meth-heads and tweaker armed robbers being notoriously un-Machiavellian when it comes to their plots and machinations), the little-used storage area-turned-interrogation chamber was the perfect place to stick an unwanted guest.

That guest was Sergeant Dwayne Haddock of the Nevada State Police, acting liaison with Ravencourt PD in an ongoing matter of interest. The broad-shouldered man with gray at his temples filled the cluttered space yet had a gracefulness about him that somehow kept him from knocking into the boxes of files and impromptu computer equipment he'd dragged in to surround his desk.

Celia pulled out the chair to sit but then saw that it was covered in different binders.

"Um…"

"Oh, sorry about that," he said. "Let me."

He moved his way around the table before Celia had a chance to stop him, picking up the binders and sitting them precariously on a nearby filing cabinet. The spines of each binder featured an assortment of names you wouldn't expect to see heaped together in one pile: "UFO sightings 1956 – 2017," "Opioid Trends Across Demographics and Geographic Strata," "A History of Nevada Mafia Activity."

Celia sat down as Haddock stepped over an old desk chair that

had been retired to the room well before this investigation had begun.

"Chief Burton told me this is your lunch break. Sorry about that."

"Who needs a ham sandwich, right?"

"I'll try to be brief," he said, pulling out the desk chair and wincing as its metal legs squealed across the concrete floor. "I'm trying
to gain a deeper understanding of what happened when you had
your…*incident* out there on the outskirts of town. What do they call
it around here, it's got a funny name?"

"The Rocks."

"The Rocks. Clever."

He looked at a message buzzing in from his phone, which he had
leaned on the circular piece of metal normally reserved for cuffing
uncooperative perps. Whatever was there didn't interest him, as he
swiped the screen like someone being particularly dismissive of a
Tinder profile.

"You think it's connected to what's been going on with The Illegals."

He grimaced. "I'd prefer if the officers in this department would
stop referring to this group of masked criminals with the borderline
offensive name they themselves seem to have bestowed upon the
outfit."

"Sorry about that. But you have to admit it's catchier than 'Novelty Mask Persons of Interest'."

Despite Burton's trepidation, Celia liked Haddock. He had a low
tolerance for bullshit and, unlike even the Chief, seemed discontent
with the thinly veiled racism that was par for the course among the
department and in the town as a whole.

"Whatever they're called, I want to catch them so I can get out of
here and get back to Carson City. And I'm hoping you can help me
with that."

"I'll do what I can, sir," she said. "But quite honestly, I'm not sure
what connection there is. No alien masks at the scene, no obvious
connection to a low-rent crime outfit."

"They stopped being low-rent when they committed two murders
and robbed a casino."

Celia took a breath.

"What do you want to know about the incident?"

"Everything," said Sergeant Haddock. "Start at the start."

     Persistence

6

The incident Haddock referred to played out about a month ago, in the unaffectionately nicknamed section of Ravencourt known as The Rocks.

The Rocks were the beginnings of a mountain on the outskirts of Ravencourt. You followed a winding road upwards through a bunch of, well, rocks, until you suddenly emerged on a circular plateau festooned with cacti and trailers. A rather rough area, a combination of trailers, tents, and lean-tos. Many a trailer were said to house a healthy supply of marijuana or a meth lab. The streets were dirt and the Chief liked to say that the people were too.

The Rocks drew in a certain set of people like a magnet. Wannabe drug dealers, not-so-wannabe sex offenders, and the coup de grace, parolees. Housing laws in Ravencourt weren't what you would call overly concerned with staying in the bounds of Constitutional rights. In Ravencourt and similarly unscrutinized towns on the middle fringes of the United States, Mayors and City Councils protected their citizens, and if that meant passing a law saying that the aforementioned lowlifes couldn't live within 500 feet of a church, a school, or a public institution, so be it. And if that eliminated most everywhere within the city limits, so be that too.

And so The Rocks had sprung up like a weed at the edge of town, and try as they might to kill it, the City Council never could. The dregs had to migrate somewhere, and better for everyone if they collected in one spot the police could keep tabs on.

Every month, Ravencourt PD conducted drop-ins to make sure that crime (drug dealing, prostitution, illegal weapons) was at least kept indoors instead of flagrantly out in the open. Even this mild threshold for escaping arrest regularly failed to be met by the citizens of The Rocks.

One duty that the police had inherited from the recently vacated Parole Office was to visit those on release from the penitentiary a couple hours away and make sure they were obeying the terms of their release. Much slack was given.

But not by Celia.

Last month she had gone up to the Rocks, by herself. The job used to be pursued two to a squad car, but as with most things in life, budget cutbacks took their toll, and the already stretched-thin Ravencourt Police Department had other matters to attend to.

So she followed the winding trail up to the not-so-stunning vista that was The Rocks. Weeds choked the road the closer you got to the top, and every once in a while you would see a pair of eyes or multiple pairs of eyes staring at you from shaded rock embankments along the side of the road. An animal would skitter across the road occasionally; if it got hit it would be dinner for a gaggle of lucky residents.

Celia crested the hill as the sun began to retreat from the trailer-laden patch of elevated ground. She wanted to get in and out quick; it was common knowledge that the Rocks wasn't a place you wanted to be at night. Badge or no, things could quickly get as ugly as the assorted sex offenders and drug abusers.

Celia parked and looked around at the tired scenery laid out before her. She began her run of the trailers by weaving between abandoned tires and abandoned people, dogs that snapped at the ends of their chains, and people who peered out not from curtains but from blankets embroidered with imagery from children's cartoons.

She had a half dozen stops to make, nothing out of the ordinary. A sex offender who had a proclivity for showing up at Ravencourt Elementary and lying on top of the monkey bars with his dick in his hand. A meth addict whose attempts to create his own product had singed off a pair of eyebrows which struggled to grow back two years hence. A seventy-six-year-old man who had gotten out of prison five years ago after serving time for a double murder and who now had nowhere else to go.

The day was uneventful. They answered what was asked of them and no more. Celia jotted down her notes and did quick inspections of their hovels.

With one trailer left to check, way on the other side of The Rocks, she decided she'd had enough walking. The sun had had about enough of The Rocks as she had, and if she could get out of there five minutes sooner, she would. So she drove to the farthest edge of the gathering of trailers, toward an embankment that provided a rather stunning view of Ravencourt down below. A trailer was perched feet away from that edge.

She pulled her squad car in near the double-wide with a children's wading pool below its eaves. A woman who a day after a bad flu would weigh upwards of 400 pounds was sitting in the pool, drinking a Coors Light and letting the sun bake her skin to parchment.

"Is Billy Relman here, ma'am?"

The bulbous woman looked up, the skin of her arm slapping the water as she lowered her beer.

"BILLY!" the woman yelled in the general direction of the trailer. She turned back to Celia and took a swig of Coors.

Celia waited a few seconds until a woman with a shaved head who couldn't have weighed more than 90 pounds pushed the door open with force.

"What'choo fuckin' want mamma?" she asked before seeing Celia standing there. "Oh great, the fuckin' law."

Celia took note of the track marks running down the woman's skinny arms. As if sensing Celia's gaze, the woman began to scratch the pustules. She would have been pretty if her face wasn't sunken in and the teeth in her head weren't rotted yellow. She wore a pair of cutoff acid-washed jean shorts and a Black Sabbath tank top without a bra.

"Is there a Mr. Relman?" asked Celia.

"I'm Billy. Ain't been no goddamn Mr. Relman since my daddy stuck his head in the oven. Nearly burnt the damn house down but couldn't asphyxiate himself worth a shit. He had to borrow a gun off of Funkedelic to finish the job."

I don't even know where to begin with that one, Celia thought.

"I suppose it's you I'm supposed to talk to, then. You mind if I come in?"

"I'd prefer that you didn't."

"As a stipulation of your parole I'm afraid I have to insist."

And so Billy led her into the trailer, where Celia ran a check of things to make sure there were no obvious signs of drug paraphernalia or, in Billy's case, prostitution. There weren't. Clothes strewn about everywhere, a hand-carved rocking horse lying in the sink, and a Chihuahua shaking as it stood on top of a microwave, looking out the window. An air conditioner sputtered out gusts of stagnancy to keep the trailer somewhat cool.

She asked Billy the requisite questions about if she had been seeking legitimate work, if she had avoided contact with her previous "manager," if she had any gentleman callers dropping by the trailer. Billy gave perfunctory answers, as they all did when questioned.

Finally the day seemed at an end.

But those arms.

Billy couldn't help but scratch at the track marks. The whole interview, she would scratch when asked a question and, when Celia would take notice, she would stop and dig her fingernails into the uncovered mattress that sat beneath her.

Let it go. She's in for prostitution, not drug abuse.

"May I ask where you got those marks on your arms?" asked Celia.

"They're nothing. Just a rash. Allergies from this shit-ass dog. Muffin, go lay down."

Muffin didn't move from atop the microwave. His pupils were the size of dimes.

"You sure they're not from syringes?"

"Do I look like a goddamn diabetic? I didn't go to jail for sugar shit."

"You know what I'm saying," said Celia.

"Aren't you done? It's time for you to leave."

Her eyes had darted to the microwave. Not the dog, but the microwave. Celia picked up on the movement.

It's not your job to find out what's in the microwave. You don't even have a warrant.

I don't need one, she argued to herself.

You're asking for trouble again. Trouble you don't need.

"Did you make dinner?" asked Celia.

"Excuse me?" said Billy, her pointed nose scrunched up.

"The microwave. You seem in a rush to get me out of here. I thought maybe you warmed up some food."

"Don't you worry about what I'm eating," said Billy, now scratching at her arms feverishly as she raised her voice.

"You alright in there, Billy?" asked Mama from the wading pool.

"Shut up, Mama. Go bother Hoyt and leave me alone."

Celia stepped toward the microwave.

"Don't you open that," said Billy.

"I don't mean to be rude," said Celia, reaching for the microwave's handle. "I'm just famished from being out here all day and could use a bite to…"

Celia opened the microwave door. The Chihuahua leapt away and hid beneath the mattress. Celia peered inside.

Cash and crystal meth lined the inside of the microwave in nearly equal amounts. Celia's hand went to the gun at her hip.

"You mind telling me what you're doing with this?" asked Celia.

Billy stared at the floor, shaking her head. "You shouldn't have done that. Hoyt's gonna be pissed."

"Who's Hoyt? Where did you get this kind of product?"

Billy continued to shake, not just her head but her whole body. Tears filled her eyes.

"If you don't want to talk I think I'll just make myself a meal."

Celia shut the door of the microwave and keyed in 2-0-0. Billy's eyes widened as she heard the beeps of the keypad.

"No, what are you doing, you can't!" she yelled.

"Tell me where this came from."

"Please!" Billy stood up and with uncanny speed leapt toward Celia's side of the trailer, meaning to grab for the microwave door. Celia easily pushed her away, but Billy wouldn't stop yelling all the while.

"You can't, please, do you know what will happen? They'll kill me, he'll kill me!"

"Who?" asked Celia, her finger over the microwave start button. "Who's going to kill you? Hoyt?"

"Please!"

"Why would Hoyt want to kill you?"

"You don't know what you're doing. It's not Hoyt I'm worried about. It's *him*. It's *them*."

And that's when a shotgun blast tore a hole through the front door of the trailer.

"Get your ass out here, woman!" yelled a voice from outside.

I think I just met Hoyt, she thought.

Celia lunged toward a filthy mattress at the aft end of the trailer. With one hand she grabbed at the furthest edge of the fabric and lifted up, and with another she unholstered her pistol. She was relieved to see that the mattress was a box spring, which actually has quite a bit of stopping power against bullets. She heaved the mattress's bulk forward and pressed it diagonally against the door.

Another blast from a shotgun tore through the mattress.

Celia covered her head and pulled a cabinet down in front of her.

Billy had skittered the other way and gingerly pushed a dual dog food and water dish lying on the floor off to the side. She grasped at the floorboards until Celia noticed her finger catch a metal ring. Billy pulled up on the hatch and then dove down beneath the trailer. The dog followed her.

Well fuck. I went the wrong way.

Celia looked around. Not many options. And she didn't really feel like killing a redneck today. Well, she did, she pretty much always did, but it probably wouldn't sit well with the department.

"Ravencourt Police Department!" Celia yelled. "Put down your weapon."

Instead of complying, Hoyt tried to push in the trailer door. But with the mattress propped up against it, the door wouldn't budge. The mattress buckled at an awkward angle, giving a bit. Celia extended her foot and the mattress held steady.

"You get out here right now," said Hoyt. "This here is my property. You're the trespasser."

Celia pulled out her walkie.

"Base, this if Officer Miller, shots fired out at the Rocks. Requesting immediate backup."

The radio crackled.

"Holy shit, Celia, are you fucking kidding me?" said a staticky voice Celia pegged for Officer Wilson.

"Goddamnit, Donald, just send the backup."

She placed the radio back in its place and called out to Hoyt.

"Officers are on their way," she said. "You can make my life a lot easier and yours a lot longer if you put your hands behind your back now."

"Why don't you get your ass out here and see where I put my hands."

The door rattled in its hinges as Hoyt first pushed and then barreled into the door. The ratty mattress with the myriad fluid stains wasn't going to hold out much longer.

"What you doing there, Hoyt?"

Another male voice from outside. This one seemed older.

"I've got a lady cop inside going through my shit illegally. That dumb cunt Billy let her in, Dirnt."

"You got a cop in there? Are you out of your mind?"

"Listen to your friend," Celia said. "Vandalism is one thing, assaulting an officer is another."

"The product's in there," Hoyt said to the other man, whose name was apparently Dirnt. "Boss will have our balls."

"Well, shit. I'll get my gun."

Footsteps padded off.

"I'll tell you what, sweetheart," said Hoyt. "You hand over what I know you already seen, you can walk out of here no worse for wear."

"You mean the meth or the cash?"

"Oh. Um. Fucking both."

Celia's eyes moved toward the microwave. She let herself see through to the meth inside. The display still read 2:00 from where Celia had keyed it in when threatening Billy.

Interesting.

"You win, Hoyt," she said as she approached the microwave. "I'm coming out."

Her hand moved toward the Enter key. Then she hesitated. This hadn't exactly come up in chemistry class. She didn't know the damage it would cause.

Do it. Show them not to fuck with you.

Celia bit her lip. Thought about it, lifted her finger…

And then walked away. If she blew up the trailer, Hoyt might die. But so might the obese woman, the dog, and Billy. She'd be kicked off the force.

Desperate times called for desperate measures. They didn't call for stupidity.

"You best not be stalling, bitch," said Hoyt.

Celia aimed her gun toward the door.

It would be so easy. To blow his brains out. From right here. You could walk through the door and be home in minutes.

Her finger hovered over the trigger. If she fired, the whole Rocks would be on her. She could already sense them watching the incident.

The truth was Celia had to be smarter than the other officers. Follow protocol. The moment she didn't was the moment that she showed a chink in the armor, that everyone jumped on her for not going by the book, for making a mistake.

    Persistence

Plus the paperwork for discharging a firearm would be a bitch.

She lowered the gun and approached the flung mattress. She moved it from the door and positioned her hand on the door handle.

"I'm coming out, Hoyt" said Celia. "I've got your product."

"Prove it. Shove it through the door hole."

"It's my only leverage. I do that, you'll blow my head off."

"I will not."

"You will."

"Well, fuck then."

"I tell you what," said Celia, now leaning up against the wall of the trailer. "You stick your head in and I'll show it to you."

"Then you'll blow <u>my</u> head off."

"I'm a cop. That's illegal, Hoyt."

"Are you lying to me?"

"No, sir. That's illegal too."

There was silence from the other end as Hoyt thought about it.

"Shit, well alright. I'll stick my head in, you set the meth and shit in a pile so I can see it. Then you can open the door and go."

"Sounds good," said Celia.

"I'm coming in."

Celia heard Hoyt shuffle forward. One hand still firmly wrapped around her gun, she dropped the other to her other holster. She unlatched the other weapon that never left her hip.

Hoyt stuck his head in the basketball-sized hole he had shot open in the door. He had curly hair, a bulbous nose, and in his brown eyes the look of a man who spent too much time in an altered state. He looked up toward Celia.

"Where's the…"

But that was all he got out when Celia let loose with the pepper spray in her hand. Hoyt yelled and tried to get away, but only succeeded in cracking his head against the scuffed metal of the trailer.

Celia shoved the door open, causing Hoyt to lose his balance and topple backward. But with his head still caught in the hole, Hoyt's neck snagged and put all of his weight on the door, which came off its hinges and landed on top of him. He dropped his shotgun as he dropped on his ass in an awkward, forward-pitching sitting position. Hoyt tried to rub his eyes but the width of the door made it impossible.

Celia gave the door a push with her toe and Hoyt toppled backward, cursing and rolling from side to side like a turtle on its back.

She finally had time to look around. Sure enough, the citizens of The Rocks had descended, watching with interested disinterest. Some had beers in their hands. One kid held a stuffed zebra wearing a pair of sunglasses.

A scrawny man with scraggly blond hair materialized out of the crowd, his eyes looking down, muttering to himself. In one hand he dragged a shotgun through the dirt. Celia raised her pistol and pointed it in his direction. The man, who Celia assumed was Dirnt, didn't even notice the gun aimed at him until he was steps away.

"Goddamn Hoyt I told you not to go off half-cocked, rotten, son of a good for nothing..."

He finally tripped on the trailer door and looked up and into the barrel of Celia's gun.

"Can I help you with something, sir?" asked Celia.

"Nope," said Dirnt, dropping his shotgun and muttering as he walked away.

Celia heard sirens from a couple miles off. The backup making its ascent up the cragged mountain.

About fucking time.

* * *

Later, after Hoyt had been hauled into the back of a squad car and Celia had showered the grime from the experience off of her, she had knocked on the door to Chief Burton's office.

"You did good today, Officer," said the Chief. "We got the meth and cash in evidence. Don't know where it came from, but you can be damn sure we're going to find out."

"Thank you, sir," said Celia. "But I actually had one request."

"Hmmm," said Chief Burton.

"The girl. Billy. It was her place I busted into."

"Oh yeah. Revocation of parole. Nice work."

"Actually, sir, I was wondering if that would be necessary."

"Why is that? She had possession of methamphetamine and cash likely derived from the sale of such," asked Burton, truly curious.

"But her parole wasn't conditional on meth. And there's no evidence she was using."

"What were those track marks on her arms?"

"Okay, she was using something, but not that. But she was scared, Henry."

Henry shuffled in his seat. Celia knew that using Chief's first

Persistence

name always got to him. It was her indicator that this was important.

"She was like a dog with a vacuum cleaner. She was scared of someone."

"And you put his head through a door."

"I don't think that's the one she was scared of. She mentioned someone…else. And we weren't able to arrest that someone."

The Chief leaned back in his chair and rubbed his eyes. "You get a name out of her?"

Celia shook her head. "I think if you put her back in she's just going to be broken by the system. With nothing hanging over her, though, I don't know, maybe she has a chance."

"We enforce the laws, Celia, we don't write 'em."

Celia sighed. There had been something *so sad* about Billy. Celia didn't sense malice with her. Just sadness. And fear.

But she had a dog. And its food bowl and water dish were filled. Celia had a soft spot for people who would take care of animals, especially if they couldn't even be bothered to take care of themselves.

"Hoyt said it was his residence," said Celia, an idea coming to her. "What if his name's on the property?"

"Well…"

"Then we can get him with the possession charge. *Only* him. He goes away, she gets her mind right."

Burton sighed. "I'll look into it."

"Thank you, sir."

Celia had left the office. That had been last month. Billy had in fact gotten out.

But due to jail overcrowding, a lack of priors, and the aid of a lawyer far outside of his price range, so did Hoyt. His eyes were still rimmed red from the pepper spray when he walked out of his cell.

* * *

"You stuck your neck out for the girl," said Sergeant Haddock as he finished jotting notes on his pad of paper. "You didn't need to do that."

"Chief usually listens to me on these sorts of things," said Celia. "She wasn't bothering anybody. He sees that."

"In your personal opinion, do you see a connection between what transpired out at The Rocks and the gang activity that's been taking place over the last six months?"

Celia bit her lip, a habit she had been trying to kick for years without luck. "That would be speculation."

"Maybe. But maybe I'd appreciate some speculation from the one person in this department who doesn't seem to have their head in the sand when it comes to what's been going on in this town."

Do I tell him? About the off-the-clock investigation?

You mean the investigation that's turned up nothing but guess-work?

Maybe it will help.

He doesn't believe in you. None of them do.

Celia took a deep breath. "I've been checking into..."

There was a knock on the door. Officer Appleby entered the cramped room, the mic and earpiece for the 911 desk still wrapped around his ear.

"Sorry to interrupt," he said.

"We're in the middle of something," said Haddock.

"My shift's wrapping up. You need to take over 911 for me."

Not "can you take over 911 for me?" Or "when you're finished up here..."

An order. From someone who had no business interrupting or telling her what to do.

"We can talk later," said Haddock, sliding his card across the table for Celia to take. She placed it in her palm as she stood.

Appleby now stood there with his hand held out and the earpiece dangling below.

Celia pretended like she didn't see his outstretched hand, walking past him and out the door. She could almost hear his eyes rolling as he turned to follow after her.

7

"911, what's your emergency?"

Celia sat at her desk in the bullpen, having taken the place of Officer Appleby, who had happily scurried away to take over the patrol duties that should have been hers.

"Yeah, uh, it's my mom. She's having trouble breathing."

"What's your address?"

The boy, who had the squeaky voice of a teenager, told Celia the address. While keeping the line open, she calmly got on the comm system and dispatched a unit to the location, along with an ambulance and a fire truck as was standard procedure.

"What's your name?"

"Danny."

"Alright, Danny, is your mother still conscious?"

"Yes."

"Okay, good, as long as she stays that way I just need you to stay by her side. Hold her hand for me, okay?"

"Okay."

"Now," said Celia, "the ambulance will be there in a minute or two. You stay on the line with me and tell me if she stops breathing or goes to sleep. Can you do that?"

"Yes, ma'am."

She didn't go to sleep or stop breathing. Responders arrived on the scene to discover that the woman had had a particularly bad asthma attack. She didn't even need to be transported to Saint Michael's. Still, it was the most excitement Celia had had since her four-hour purgatory had begun.

Instead of her normal uniform, Celia now wore a pair of jeans and a plaid t-shirt. After her talk with the Chief, she had headed toward the locker room to change into something other than a uniform. No sense wearing sweaty clothing when all she was going to do for the remainder of the day was take calls.

On her way to the lockers, the Chief had passed her and patted her on the shoulder. He smiled, a sad smile, and walked away, leaving Celia to get ready for her 911 shift.

Celia had entered the one and only locker room and approached her locker, tossing only a slight glance toward her "facilities": a shower which had been stuck in the corner and separated by a curtain from the men, the thought being that an ugly beige curtain would give her the same amount of privacy as having a dedicated women's locker room. No separate facilities here. When Celia had come on, the Chief had made vague statements about installing a women's locker room once the budget came through for next year. That had been last year.

Celia might sneak back there to change in peace, but a nice cold shower was usually out of the question; she didn't want every other officer in the department trying to ogle her through the part in the curtain. On days when it was dead at the department, say holidays, she might hustle in and take a quick shower. Usually she waited until she arrived back home.

As Celia had changed into her casual clothes, she removed a bullet and the chain it hung on from around her neck, worked it around her hair, and placed it on a small shelf made by the tile in the shower. Her father had given the bullet to her when she was seven. He had been pinned down by gunfire at a convenience store robbery gone south. It had even made the national news.

Darryl Miller hadn't had to fire a shot. He had holstered his weapon and calmly walked toward the storefront. The robber, with two dead men behind him and swimming in deep water with no surface in sight, pointed the gun at him. Officer Miller had walked up to the front doors of the convenience store and only looked at the man. He didn't look at the scared people cowering behind him or the other officers with weapons pointed toward his position.

"It's time to end this, son," said Officer Miller.

He extended his hand then, toward the man. The man, with tears in his eyes, dropped the gun, took Officer Miller's hand, and dropped to his knees weeping. Miller patted him on the back. Chief

Burton, then just Lieutenant Burton, said he'd never seen such a brave stupid fucking thing in his life.

That night, after hours of questioning and paperwork, Darryl Miller had come home, where a supposed-to-be-in-bed Celia was still very much awake. Celia had watched the news with her mother even though her mother had banished her to her room. Celia had peeked around the corner and sat transfixed as she watched footage of the incident play out on their old tube television.

After hugging his wife deeply and reassuring her that he would never do such a thing again, Darryl Miller approached Celia's room. He gently opened his daughter's door and walked in to place a good night kiss upon her brow. He smiled when he saw that Celia's eyes were wide open.

"You're supposed to be in bed," he said in a deep voice that sank even lower from the exhaustion he must have felt.

"I am in bed," said Celia.

Miller smiled. "Asleep I mean."

"Were you scared today?"

"Yeah, maybe a little. Okay, probably a lot. Were you scared?"

Celia nodded her head *yes*.

"That's okay. We all get scared sometimes. Brave people are just the ones who do a better job at hiding it."

"Why didn't you shoot that man, daddy?"

Miller thought about it. Took his time too. Celia grew impatient as most seven-year-olds are wont to do, and was about to pipe up when Miller spoke.

"The most important bullet is the one you don't have to fire."

He ruffled Celia's hair and left the room. Celia watched him go, then noticed in the light from her Little Mermaid alarm clock that he had left a pristine, unspent bullet on her nightstand. She hadn't even noticed the movement, but there it was.

The next day Celia had begged her mom to take her to the mall to get it looped into a necklace. Her mother had protested that a bullet necklace wasn't anything that a seven-year-old should wear to school, that it would send the wrong idea. But with her husband on Celia's side, Cynthia Miller knew she had a losing battle on her hands. She had insisted that the gunpowder be removed, a request that seemed reasonable to Celia. A small hole had been popped into the base of the bullet and a gold chain had been strung through. Celia had worn it ever since.

It was probably then that she had decided to become a cop.

Her thoughts of that day were broken up by the laughing of three other officers who had entered the locker room. Celia buttoned her shirt over a sports bra and stood behind the shower curtain listening, running the bullet back around her neck as she did. She couldn't tell who was talking.

"So they're in the desert, right, and the blonde's boyfriend says, 'I've got a snakebite on my dick.' So the blonde says, 'Well what should I do?' and he says, 'You've gotta suck out the venom.'

"So she goes down on him and she's sucking and sucking, and eventually he comes, right? And it goes like right in her eye, I mean, just fuckin—"

He must have made some kind of gesticulation at that point, because the other officers had chuckled. Celia bit her lip.

"...So the blonde is wiping her face and she looks up at the boyfriend and is like, 'Oh, no, the snake venom! You have to suck it out of my eye.'

"And the boyfriend zips up his pants and says, 'Not until you brush your teeth, bitch!'"

The men roared with laughter. As they did, Celia had pushed the curtain aside and walked past Officers Hilcox, Smalls, and Appleby, who was changing from his uniform into his civvies. The men stopped laughing, looking sheepish.

"Hey, Miller, sorry about the 911 break," said Appleby.

"That's okay. At least I don't have to worry about snake bites."

Celia exited the locker room, slamming the door perhaps a bit too forcefully.

8

The clock ticked down the last few seconds of the day as Celia twirled her cellphone in her hand. She was just glad that she didn't have to wait for someone to relieve her; the county took over 911 calls at six o'clock, with the department taking back over at six the next morning.

6:00 p.m. finally rolled around and Celia took off her headset. She clicked out of a spirited game of Angry Birds on her phone and stood up. She stretched and cracked her back. The Chief had left a couple minutes ago with a nod and a wave of the hand, talking on the phone with his wife about what was being had for dinner. Meatloaf seemed to be the consensus.

A flood of activity overtook the station. This was the time of the day when shifts were ending and beginning. As such, officers were headed in and out of the locker room, going in in t-shirts and khaki shorts and coming out with uniforms and vice versa.

Celia shut down her computer and looked up to see a smiling face standing in front of her. Reddish skin made even darker by a year-round farmer's tan that hadn't yet taken its toll and turned to leather. He had the build of a college athlete who had still taken the time to take care of himself. In total, he was the kind of guy that "badge bunnies" flocked to in droves.

Celia sighed. She would give him this much: the man knew how to fill out a uniform.

"Officer Martinez," she said.

"Would you cut it out with that Martinez shit, Celia?"

"Fine. Jason. What's up?"

"Are you headed to the Bronco tonight?"

The Bronco was the closest thing that Ravencourt had to a police bar. On a Friday night like tonight, it would be packed with current and retired officers congregating to shoot pool, throw darts, and knock back beers. Joining them would be an assortment of towns-folk who didn't mind throwing back with the local law. Everyone else would typically head to one of the half dozen or so additional bars along Main Street.

Celia had no desire to go to the Bronco or really anywhere else tonight. Her Netflix Watchlist had gotten rather stacked and she wanted to take it easy.

"I think you're on your own, Jay."

"Oh, c'mon, you always say no. Is it me?"

Yes, she thought.

"No," she said out loud. Just not in the mood." She wrapped her purse around her neck and fixed her hair in a scrunchy.

"How about someplace else then? We could hit up the Tumble-weed, rough it for the night."

"I don't think the Tumbleweed would take too kindly to a couple cops," she said.

"Who cares? That's the beauty of being cops. An all access pass to anywhere and anything."

"Good night, Jason."

Celia headed toward the parking lot, pushing the glass door open and heading out into the bright Nevada sun. 6:00 p. m. in the desert is no different from noon really. She put on a pair of sunglasses and hit the fob on her car. A battered Jeep Liberty in lipstick red lit up three spots down. Celia walked across the baked concrete and opened the door.

A muscular arm pushed it closed. She turned to see that Jason had followed her. He hadn't bothered to use sunglasses to block the sun from his eyes.

"When are you going to talk to me?" he asked.

"I think I was talking to you a minute ago."

"You know what I mean. I mean talk about us."

"We've had that conversation," she said.

"You had that conversation. It was more like a speech. I didn't get very much say in the matter."

"Do we have to do this here, Jason? Again?"

"You're right. Let's go in my Challenger. The A/C's like a freezer."

"I don't want to talk in the department's Challenger."

"Then here, in the sun. Whatever. I just want to talk to you."

"Not here either," she said, exasperated. "Nowhere. We're done. We haven't been together for years."

"So last Christmas, that meant what? That meant nothing to you?"

Oh, Jesus. That drunken decision had turned out to be one of the poorest of her life.

She and Jason had been high school sweethearts. It was all very classic Americana. Jason had been not the star quarterback but the star kicker, while Celia was a starter for the soccer and volleyball teams. Everyone had expected the two of them to end up together. It led to no end of gossip when they also turned out to be the only two people who had left Ravencourt to go elsewhere.

Celia's travels had taken her to the University of Nevada-Las Vegas, not crazy far in the grand scheme of things, but miles away from the reserved small-town nature of Ravencourt. Jason had taken a different route, opting to enlist with the Marines.

The problem was that Celia had never considered the relationship serious the way that Jason had. The dating pool in a town like Ravencourt was rather small and Celia knew almost from the start that it was a relationship she had just fallen into. No small amount of "I love you's" had been said, but they were said in the high school "groping for real emotion" way, not the real "know it when you feel it" way. To Celia they had only seemed like the right words to say to someone when you'd been with them for two months or so.

She had looked at college with a sort of relief. There had been a time when Jason had toyed with the idea of following her to UNLV, and it was probably the pit in Celia's stomach as he was considering this option that confirmed for her that she didn't love him. She encouraged him to follow his dream of joining up, hoping that it would save her the trouble of a painful breakup.

It did. Things ended amicably, with both agreeing to keep in touch yet understanding that there was no place in each other's lives at the moment. Before she moved back to Ravencourt, Celia still looked upon her time with Jason with fondness, the thought of their final night of lovemaking in Jason's car before Celia was to go to college still bringing a smile to her face. She considered it less an epic goodbye and more just one of those things you should do in that situation. It's your last night before a split, you put out a little.

And all in all, it was a good night.

Jason had felt differently. He had carried that night around with him like a weight around his neck. Jason had attempted to keep up contact at a level far beyond that of Celia's. Many a phone call and a text message were placed, even if it trailed off when he went to Basic.

But even in a loveblind state, Celia knew he couldn't fail to see that her texts back to him were becoming more and more irregular. Also less informative. A *How r u* was more likely to return *Good* or nothing at all than anything of substance. And so they had drifted apart.

Still, as if it had a gravitational pull, Ravencourt had brought them back together again. After Celia had gone on to get her Master's degree in Criminal Justice and Jason had shipped out for two tours of duty in Iraq, the two found themselves back in Ravencourt under vastly different circumstances. Celia thought it would be a brief stop to see her father before his health took a real turn, yet found herself feeling an urgent need to carry on his torch by signing up for the very police force he had quit just two short years prior. Jason had always been in it for the long run; he had grown up in Ravencourt and saw himself dying there an old man.

When Celia came back into the picture, he pictured her right next to him.

After Celia had moved back to town, just a couple months after Jason himself had come back to the force, he attempted to pick up where they had left off, calling her the most beautiful, worldly person in this small town Shitburg (he was a poet to be sure) and pestering her with voicemails and texts at all hours of the night.

Celia had warded off these advances until the department's annual Christmas party at the Bronco. She had had a bit too much to drink, had been feeling lonely, and was actively talking about a desire to purchase a cat to anyone who would listen. Jason had picked up on this cocktail of desperation and Celia gave in during a moment of weakness under the mistletoe. And goddamn his arms were strong and he kissed like he did back when they were in high school, and for a second it was like his hands had never left her body.

She had woken up with a hangover and the smell of eggs wafting in through Jason's kitchen. She had gotten out of there as fast as she could.

"I don't want to talk about the Christmas party," Celia said, pushing away the memory of that night and the subsequent morning.

"Because you know how it felt. You know that I'm right."

"Jason, stop. I don't want to be mean to you, but you're relentless. I can't do this every time you decide I belong with you. We have a friendly, professional relationship brought about by our joint enrollment in the Ravencourt Police Department. I do not have to hang out with you outside of work functions if I choose not to. I am not going to the Bronco tonight."

"But Celia…"

"Have a wonderful night, Officer Martinez."

Celia got into her car and turned the key in the ignition. For a moment she worried that it wouldn't catch, a problem that had been happening more frequently, but it started without a hitch and Celia drove out of the parking lot.

Jason watched her go, glaring against the sun.

"Bitch," he said.

9

Celia perused the aisles of the supermarket, throwing items that could potentially be used to cook a dinner into her basket. She had opted to cruise right past the produce aisle, knowing full well that she would just end up tossing out the moldy fruit and vegetables in a couple of weeks anyway.

Tonight she set her sights on the frozen section, picking up a smattering of sodium-filled pasta dishes whose contents looked not a smidge like the lovely display of primavera on the box. After that she moved one aisle over, avoiding a group of teenagers and a mother whose two-year-old child kept licking the handle of the grocery cart from her perch in the seat. Celia opened up a freezer filled with ice cream. She glanced at the boxes just enough to bemoan the state of a world that allowed a product called Kim Kandyashian Krunch to exist on store shelves. Then she put it in her basket anyway because it had pretzels and chocolate and that shit's delicious.

Dinner in hand, Celia moved three aisles over to hit up the booze. She grabbed some Strongbow hard ciders and a bottle of Jack to brush her teeth with.

That done, she headed to her last stop, the pet food aisle, picking up a ten-pound bag of cat food.

Fuck you, she thought to no one in particular. *So I bought a cat and it's Friday night and I'm getting food for that cat. Mind your own business.*

Celia walked past a husband who was scratching at his head as he examined a crumpled-up grocery list. Other than him and a few other aimless wanderers, Wheel-Loo Grocery was pretty vacant.

As the sun got ready to make its descent, Celia approached a register and swiped her credit card before the gawky teen named Melvin had a chance to ask her how her day was. Defeated, the teen didn't say anything, just smiled and stole a glance at her chest.

"Paper or plastic, ma'am?" asked a voice. Celia looked up and locked eyes with the bagger. Recognition dawned.

"Plastic is great, Wilfred."

"You got it, Celia. How's the station? They hanging in there without my mug around?"

I can't escape goddamn cops in this goddamn town.

"Oh, we get by. Miss those oatmeal cookies you'd always bring in."

"I'm having too many of those cookies now. Laura's got me festively plump."

Wilfred patted his stomach and then sighed. He placed Celia's groceries in her bag.

Probably resentful that you got to keep your job while he was pushed out. To work at the Wheel-Loo.

When budget cuts hit, staff like Wilfred were the first to go. Lifers without desire to retire or move up particularly high on the force. Wilfred and three or four others didn't need to pass the detective's test or put in for transfers or promotions. Oh, sure, their wives would pester them once money got tight every couple years or so, or an old car needed to be replaced by a new model, or a bathroom had to be redone. The men would go in and dutifully talk to the chief and ask to take the detective's exam, and then they'd take home some registration paperwork and it would either never get filled out or the test would be failed but by that time the wives had forgotten and it was back to normalcy.

Wilfred and his ilk were content seeing to traffic duty when red lights went out, patrolling the haughtier parts of Ravencourt, having their stead and nothing more. They were satisfied being cops, overweight cops whose belt sizes increased to match their guts and whose speed decreased to do the same.

There wasn't room for satisfaction during cutbacks at the Ravencourt PD. Today's satisfied employee is tomorrow's grocery bagger. The economy hit hard and it hit people like Wilfred the hardest. The newest recruits, like Celia, the department could afford to keep around because they didn't have to pay them much, while the brass—well, the brass is usually safe in most economic situations.

Wilfred finished packing Celia's groceries and handed her the bags. Celia took her receipt and another chest glance from the cashier and then took her and her cat's weekend reserves from the paunchy, 60-some-year-old man.

"You have a good evening. Tell the boys I said hello."

"Will do. And you tell that wife of yours I said hello."

Celia walked on, her focus already shifting, when from behind her...

"You should smile more, Celia. It's not all bad."

This. The polite suggestion Celia had dealt with at numerous points throughout her life. The idea that she had to put aside whatever emotional state she was in to provide an aesthetic boost to some rando because her resting bitch face wasn't good enough for them.

She turned back to Wilfred with her biggest, toothiest, faux-cheeriest 'Fuck you' smile, then walked out of the store, the façade crumbling instantly.

10

Celia sat on her couch watching a movie wherein the partner of a cop who was *this close* to retirement was taking on a gang of Yakuza to avenge his buddy's death. Celia marveled at the various inaccuracies depicted on the screen, such as the number of bullets in the main character's gun, the difficulty of pulling off a shot through a sniper scope when moving in a Mini Cooper at 60 miles per hour, and the size of the breasts of the avenging cop's female partner (always relegated to assistance with maps and door codes with her trusty computer).

Murray the Cat meowed at her feet and then crawled up next to the bowl of popcorn balanced on her lap. Celia moved the popcorn and Murray took his place. Celia stroked his fur and he meowed anew.

"You're the only man I need in my life, aren't you Murray?"

That sentence snapped her out of it.

Holy shit I just crossed some kind of bridge.

Celia looked around at her disheveled apartment, at the stack of laundry in the corner, at the refrigerator that concealed far too many beers and not enough vegetables, at the pictures of a cat who was just as at home underneath a bed in the darkness as he was on the lap of his owner.

As if sensing her sudden need to get out of her apartment and do something more than sit inside avoiding cops, old high school friends, and human contact in general, her phone vibrated. She looked at the name on the text. Brian B.

A smile crept across her face. *Now we're getting somewhere.*

She slid her finger across the face of the phone and read the message: "What's up."

Her thumbs danced along the phone's screen: "Watching Flix of the Net. U?"

"Just thinking about u…You wanna meet up at T's in 15?"

Celia sat up. Now that was unexpected.

Brian B., as her phone named him, was Brian Burke, a student at UNLV that Celia had met at a college party (not on the Strip; college parties in Vegas were almost never on the Strip). He had been an environmental studies major, she had been tipsy, and they had shared a furious make-out session that ended with an exchange of phone numbers.

They had met toward the end of Celia's college tenure but the beginning of Brian's own Master's program and had seen each other a few times, with only a couple of those few turning physical in any manner. They hadn't even technically slept together. It was all very far from official, but Brian was a good guy to talk to. When Celia's father's health took a turn and she came back to Ravencourt, they had kept in touch with the occasional text, the regular email, and the intermittent phone call.

Up until now, he had only visited twice: once last summer around the Fourth of July and once this past March over spring break, making a detour to Ravencourt to see her. She had thought that was sweet until he showed up at the truck stop meet-up with three buddies with liquor on their breath, yelling at him to hurry it up already. They had chatted occasionally since then, but it hadn't been the same. She had worked up the courage to surprise-visit him on a whim during the middle of a week in March when she had some time off, but that voice…

You're going to walk in and there's going to be some freshman on his couch and that will be that and you'll have to drive all the way back like an idiot

…had caused her to think twice. She ended up aborting the mission before she'd even left the city.

But now this. Intriguing.

"You're in town?" she texted.

No response for a couple minutes. Celia vacillated between putting the phone away and texting again when her phone chimed.

"Yup. Just tonite. Cmon id like to see u."

She already had a pair of jeans on in place of her sweats when

PERSISTENCE

she texted back: "Idk…I'm already in bed." She had a pair of boots on by the time she hit send.

"Oh then I could come to u ;)."

Celia was headed out the door. "Your such a boy. I'll be there in 15."

11

She was there in 10. T's was a diner on the edge of Ravencourt proper, not far from where the highway passed by. No doubt Brian had dropped in because it was close to the interstate. But had his visit been to see Celia specifically or come about on his way to somewhere else?

No matter. T's wasn't someplace Celia's tastes would typically run, being a glorified truck stop diner and all, but Celia didn't have to worry about cops here. That much was for sure. Which meant all she had to worry over (a pleasant worry) was what Brian was doing in town.

She walked into the diner, festooned as it was with license plates and stucco, deer heads and linoleum, a rather unpleasant and contradictory set of themes. Celia spotted Brian immediately, sitting alone at a booth pointed toward the door. He looked up from the menu and grinned.

"Celia Miller. As I live and breathe."

He adjusted his glasses and stood up as she walked toward the booth. Celia hoped she was able to contain her smile to no more than a slight upward tilt of the lips but felt like she was maybe failing in that but was okay with failing in that. And was that a flick of his eyes downward toward the unbuttoned top button of her flannel shirt? She thought it was.

They hugged, awkwardly, and sat down across from one another. Celia acted like she didn't catch the waitress looking away quickly after staring with judgment at a white girl hugging a black man.

"How have you been, Bri Guy?"

          PERSISTENCE

Bri Guy? Ugh.

He laughed, not in a condescending way but in a genuinely amused way. "I'm good, Celia. You?"

"I've been okay. Work and shit."

Silence.

Well, this is going well.

"I'm gonna get right to the point," Brian said, suddenly serious. "I need money."

Celia's heart dropped for a second, until Brian smiled again, that smile that was going to get her in trouble.

"You're fucking with me," she said.

"A little bit, yeah."

"Goddamnit, Brian."

From then on, it wasn't so awkward. Chisel in hand, ice broken. They ordered food and chatted.

"What are you doing in town?" Celia asked.

"I'm not really sure," he said. "I quit college..."

"You quit college?"

"And suddenly I realized I was driving and I realized I was driving north and then I realized I was driving to Ravencourt and then I realized I was driving to you."

Suddenly it didn't seem so important why he had left college.

"Well," she said, taking a breath, "I'm glad you came by."

"I've wanted to see you."

"Yeah. Me too."

They smiled at each other, a good smile, and Celia didn't even hear the jangling bell behind her indicating that someone had entered the restaurant. Didn't hear the boots approach the table. It wasn't until she saw Brian's eyes move away from hers and upwards that she herself looked up and let her smile turn to a look of disdain.

Jason Fucking Martinez.

"Jason Fucking Martinez," she said.

"Friend of yours?" asked Brian.

"He's not," said Celia.

"I am indeed," said Jason, extending his hand toward Brian, his lips curled back in a wolf's smile. He was out of uniform but still had his gun holstered to his hip. "How do you know Celia, buddy?"

"Jason, get the fuck out of here," said Celia.

"Whoa, whoa, whoa, now I was just stopping by to say..."

"Listen, buddy, the lady asked you to leave..."

Before Brian could say another word, the hand that he had put up to ward off Jason was extended painfully behind his back, bent crooked along the backside of the booth. Brian winced as his face was pushed down toward the table. Every head in the restaurant snapped around.

"Word of advice, son," said Jason. "Don't ever reach your arm toward an officer of the law, you hear me?"

"Jason, knock it off," said Celia. She was on her feet, her gaze fixed on Jason, whose eyes burned with momentary hatred.

Then he was letting go of Brian and the look in his eyes was gone. A shit-eating grin appeared on his face.

"Sorry about that, buddy, but you really don't want to go around touching anywhere near an officer's gun." Jason smoothed out his shirt. "Damn, I almost unleashed some of that Special Forces shit on you."

"I bet you put the Special in Special Forces, didn't you?" asked Brian, making a windmill motion with his arm and trying not to let the pain show.

"Get out of here, Jason," Celia said, still standing, not moving her eyes from Jason's.

"Celia," he moved his hands toward her shoulders and she immediately made a bar with each arm and swatted them away.

Pick up the knife from the table and stab him in the heart was the thought that flitted through her head, but Celia thought that a murder charge would be easy to stick in the middle of a diner full of witnesses. Hell, they'd probably try to pin it on Brian given this town's track record of racial profiling. So instead, she just kept looking forward.

"You said you weren't going out tonight," said Jason.

"I said I wasn't going out with you tonight," she shot back.

Jason nodded. Smiled. Turned back to Brian.

"I didn't know they made male badge bunnies," he said, then laughed without an ounce of humor. "Fuckin' A."

Jason walked out, casting Celia one last glance as he brushed by. He picked up speed as he cruised out the door and into his pickup truck. Celia stood in silence until she watched the headlights trail off into the distance.

"Are you alright?" she finally asked, feeling bad the moment she said it because Brian was probably feeling emasculated enough as it was.

"I'm fine. I think maybe I should go."

He was standing up and Celia was nodding.

"Ok."

Brian looked at her, a sad smile, and then started to walk past her.

"You know what," said Celia. "Fuck that. C'mon, let's get out of here. Cancel our orders," she shouted to the kitchen. She took Brian by the hand and led him to the door.

"Where are we going?" asked Brian.

"Just shut up and get in my car," she said.

12

"I take it that guy was some kind of ex?" asked Brian.

"If it's all the same, why don't we discuss anything else in the world but him?" said Celia.

A bartender set two shots of Jameson down in front of them. It was the most high-end whiskey available.

"Better yet," she said, "let's drink."

They toasted to one another and knocked back the drinks.

Celia had dropped into the one place she knew they wouldn't be bothered: the Tumbleweed. Cops wouldn't touch the place on account of it being a general hangout for lowlifes; lowlifes wouldn't touch any cops who did visit on account of not wanting to be arrested. A few dirty looks would be directed her way, but no dirtier or more lascivious than what she received on a daily basis at work or out in the field.

The decor was what Celia liked to think of as Redneck-Chic in that it was probably designed by a redneck chick who didn't know how to spell chick. The piece de resistance was a rattlesnake whose length, a state record at the time it was caught, extended up above the numerous bottles of alcohol the entire length of the bar. All along its scaly surface were lipstick prints. It was a ritual required of any female wanting to get a free Raven's Feather Cocktail (black licorice-flavored vodka over ice, whipped cream, and a black feather of dubious origin on top). They would crawl up on the bar, shake their ass for the beer belly-toting men in attendance, shake some more, show a little cleavage, and plant a smacker on the snake. The menfolk would cheer and the women would get their free drink.

The rest of the bar was dark, lit by red light that seemed to descend from the rafters like a madam at a low-class brothel. A couple pool tables and a dartboard, currently occupied by a man continually scratching his arms and a woman constantly adjusting her bra, sat on one side. Dust seemed to be everywhere, even on the red barstools and the cracked urinals in the bathroom.

The gathered patrons kept looking over at the two of them, their voices dropping as they exchanged no doubt awful dialogue about the pretty cop and the dark-skinned outsider. After some time, they went back to their business of picking one another up and telling all manner of bullshit about exploits no one had been around to witness.

"I meant it when I said it was good to see you," said Brian.

Celia slammed down her shot and pulled Brian toward her. She kissed him on the mouth before giving him a chance to back out (or her to lose her courage).

She pulled away, smiling. Everyone else in the bar glared.

It's been four months since you kissed someone.

Is that true?

Holy shit.

"I think my coming here was a good decision," he said. "What's gotten into you?"

"I get horny when I get angry."

"Are you angry?"

"I'm always angry."

Now his brow furrowed to a look of concern.

Goddamnit Brian Burke, she thought, why do you have to be so fucking serious all the time? Just be a fucking man who wants to get laid for one night!

"Is everything alright? You know, with you. I mean, that guy..."

"Forget the guy. No, nothing's alright, but I'm not in the mood right now, dude."

"I'm sorry, I—"

"You know what it is," she said, feeling herself getting started on a jag that maybe would last awhile, "it's you."

"Who?"

"That's what they always say, right? It's not you, it's me. I don't feel like it is me. I feel like I'm keeping my head down and doing everything right, making all the right fucking decisions, and yet I continue to get shit on. It's not me. It can't be."

"Celia…"

"'Cause if it is me, then that means that I'm the poison. That I'm the venom in that snake up on the wall's fucking teeth, instead of them. And I can't handle thinking that I'm the most poisonous part of this town. But if it's them, and it's not me, then why is it that they seem perfectly content in things and I'm the one…I'm the one who's always been dissatisfied. Who couldn't go with the flow. So maybe I am the problem. Maybe I am the poison."

Oddly, Brian smiled, looking past Celia at nothing in particular.

"I like that," he said.

"Huh?"

"The thought of you. Being the venom in that snake's fangs. Makes you seem kinda badass."

Celia looked down at the bar, tapping her fingers.

"You're forgetting one thing," she said.

"What?"

She looked up at Brian, tears in her eyes.

"Fearsome as it is, a bunch of dumb rednecks found that snake, cut it open, and hung it up on the wall to die. Venom can't compete with the wrath of man, and the smartest, most majestic creature in the world will still lose against a bunch of assholes with a knife."

13

"Bathroom?"

Brian lay next to her in bed, the two of them still catching their breath. It had lasted less time than Celia hoped but not so short as to be noteworthy. At this point, even five minutes was five more minutes than she'd had in far too long.

Celia arched her back and stretched her arms as Brian traced his fingers along her breast. She curled into his body and kissed him on the lips.

"Off to the left there."

He stood up and walked, naked, to the bathroom. Celia looked up at the ceiling fan, pretending not to notice Murray the Cat meowing and pawing on the other side of the bedroom door, clearly upset at being unceremoniously booted from the room he normally slept in.

She sat up and the room spun ever so slightly.

"Whoa," she said.

She'd drank more than anticipated. Not blackout drinking, but enough that she'd better do something fast to avoid being miserable the next morning.

She slowly, very slowly, reached down and patted the ground near her side of the bed, looking for and eventually finding her panties. She kicked her feet up and put them on, followed by the plaid shirt that had gotten tossed across the room. Now on her feet, she steadied herself against the chair and walked to the door.

As she opened it, Murray scurried past her and darted under the bed. She padded down the short hallway to the kitchen and turned on the sink. She let the faucet run, giving the water time to get colder, before reaching to a cupboard and pulling down a glass.

She drank slowly, in small gasps rather than massive gulps.

The lights came on and she squinted in pain, pulling the glass from her lips and wiping her mouth.

"Fuck, dude," she said. "Not cool."

"Sorry," said Brian. "I don't know where anything is. I kept bumping into things." He had put on his boxers and now stood in the entryway to the kitchen, looking that ridiculous but weirdly, casually-sexy way men can when they're bare chested and seem not to care that their bellies have betrayed the lean nature of their youths and now protrude past the hemline of their shorts.

"Looking good," said Celia, rubbing her eyes. She turned back to the sink and refilled her water glass.

He walked up behind her and wrapped his arms around her midsection. She flinched out of habit but then let him draw her closer. She held out the glass of water and he took a drink.

"What's all this?" he asked.

Celia pulled away from him and turned to follow his gaze.

Ah shit.

On the kitchen table was an assortment of random things that Celia had no intention of showing absolutely anyone at the moment. Documents. Library books. An alien mask. A bag of meth and random bottles of OxyContin.

And here was Brian already stepping forward, casting his eyes across the table and picking up a piece of paper without even asking.

"What is all this?"

"It's nothing."

"Did they promote you to detective?"

"Not exactly," she said. "This is more of a side project."

Brian picked up the alien mask and held it up in front of his face.

"Take me to your leader."

He probably thought he was being funny, but Celia was not amused. She snatched the mask back from him and set it on a chair that had been pushed away from the table.

"Whoa," he said. "Sorry. It's late, I'm basically drunk. I didn't know."

"It's okay. It's just, I don't want to talk about it."

"I assume this is about that new gang?"

So much for not talking about it.

Celia nodded.

"They're even talking about that shit down in Vegas," said Brian. "The anchors usually smile and say something like, 'from UFOs to APBs, coming up right after Terry Sunshine brings you the latest forecast.'"

"That's because we've been keeping the worst of it out of the papers. It's easier to do than you might think. Not exactly the Times or the Post out here in the middle of nowhere. Otherwise they wouldn't be laughing."

"What do you mean?"

"The aliens have been committing crimes for months." And then she told Brian everything she knew about the Illegals.

14

It had started six months or so back, with a liquor store robbery gone wrong. The liquor store was in one of the shadier parts of town, as most liquor stores are wont to be. Nothing special about it, certainly nothing to tip someone off to the fact that there would be money worth having inside.

Police got the call around 1:00 a. m. Celia wasn't there, but she had heard about it all the same. There's not much you don't hear about working in a small town like Ravencourt that carries an inordinate level of violent crime.

Celia was able to piece together what happened from viewing the video from the liquor store and an ATM across the street, as well as from picking up bits and pieces from around the police station break area. Although she at first thought that maybe her fellow officers were exaggerating the grizzly nature of the incident, video proved that not to be the case.

Video showed a store clerk named Marcos straightening up a display of Twinkies ("Back and better than you remember!" proclaimed the sign) when his head snaps around. A hooded figure enters the liquor store brandishing a shotgun.

The footage from the ATM revealed that the man had been neither dropped off nor picked up. He simply saunters into the camera's view from the right side of the screen and strides with purpose into the liquor store.

The hooded figure hops the counter, grabbing in one hand the baseball bat slung by the store clerk. Rather than unloading the shotgun at the clerk's head, he turns the gun around like his own bat and swings it at the clerk's knee, his body buckling behind the counter and out of view of the cameras.

While the man busies himself with the cash register, two other men in hoods enter, moving with purpose toward the back of the shop, knocking down bottles along the way.

If the camera would have picked up sound, it would have heard the *boom* of gunshots in the back of the store seconds later. If there would have been other cameras in the store, they may have allowed the police to view footage of 22-year old Matthew Robertson having the left side of his face cleaved away from his skull, the skin around his eye twisting outward as the bullet passed through his cheek and into his brain. They would have captured the look of horror and shock on 14-year old Mindy Conrell's face as her boyfriend's body convulsed on the ground and the shooter raised his weapon at her. It would have picked up the bullet traveling through her neck, causing her to lean awkwardly against the wall. Since she didn't bleed out right away, the camera's all-seeing eye likely would have caught the man who fired the shots cupping the girl's brown head of hair in his left hand as he stuck a knife into her belly with the right.

But the cameras were not there to catch such things, nor were they there to witness whatever else may have transpired in the back room.

What the camera did pick up was the three men walking out of the liquor store six minutes later and parting in opposite directions. One of the men had a black duffle bag slung over his shoulder.

The first man to enter had dispatched the store clerk by that time. As the clerk was positioned behind the counter, the camera did not see the clerk's ultimate fate.

But cops saw the result. It's thought that the masked man had stuck the baseball bat between the teeth of the clerk, lifted it up, and then swung it back down. The man's gums and teeth had been smashed downward, into his throat, and the autopsy (sent away to Vegas and taking six weeks to arrive) revealed that he had choked on their remnants.

The first to enter and the last to leave, the man who perpetrated this assault had turned and looked directly at the camera. His face was covered by a white plastic alien mask.

The incident had made the local papers, but with the most grisly bits held back from public consumption. That included any mention of alien masks. Chief Burton had gotten word that the Channel 7 affiliate was going to send out a reporter to conduct an interview and do a piece about the gruesome murder in an otherwise idyllic town, but it never came to be. Someone had gotten run over on the Strip, and while the driver hadn't been wearing an alien mask, people know the Strip.

There had been no leads, and indeed no real motivation behind the killings. The violence had been quick, brutal, and faded into memory almost as surely as it jumped in.

Two weeks later, a church had burned to the ground. Our Mary The Holy Mother the church was called. Celia was on the scene at that incident, mainly for crowd control. Foul play wasn't suspected at first, as it was assumed that the fire had been electrical, or a gas line, or a dumb kid playing with matches. Buildings burn down.

But when firefighters extinguished the flames, they started to pull bodies out of the rubble. One of those bodies had turned out to be the pastor of Our Mary The Holy Mother, a kindly old man named Father Wallace. His wife was responsible for any number of church bake sales before she had passed away of throat cancer two years previously. Three other bodies were recovered as well. The holiness of these individuals was not assured. Two males and a female, a group of lowlifes whose address out at The Rocks gave away their criminal track records as a sex offender, an OxyContin abuser, and a wife beater (try to pick which is which, the answer might surprise you).

Each of the four people had been chained to a table. Those tables had been set up in the church basement. They were aligned in the shape of a cross.

When the bodies came out, the cops took over. They canvassed the nearby houses, asking neighbors if anyone had seen anything suspicious. Most were honestly able to say that they had not. Some looked shaken when asked, but that was likely not due to the fact that they were hiding something but that they had just found out their pastor had been burnt alive.

Leads went dry. But then there was one neighbor, an elderly woman who couldn't sleep properly because of her husband's sleep apnea and her own arthritis, who had been watching *The 700 Club* (or so she had told the cops; in reality, her DVR had been paused on *Teen Moms*) when she had heard a noise from outside. When she got up to look out the window, the pain in her foot nearly causing her to trip, she spotted two men walking toward the church.

The men were wearing alien masks.

Not wanting to start a panic, Chief Burton had decided to not let that little nugget slip out to the public, and since the entirety of the Ravencourt press consisted of a 75-year old man who still wrote his stories on a typewriter and a 23-year old blogger who dreamed of writing an entire novel in 140-character Tweets, not many questions were asked.

But the cops were informed one day, Chief Burton addressing them in the station's conference room. He had drawn an upside-down-teardrop shaped alien face on the whiteboard.

"Lady and gentlemen," he began, directing a wink Celia's way at the little joke he had developed over the past couple months, "this is the face of a monster from an episode of *The X Files*. But, most recently, people wearing these masks have been responsible for a series of violent acts."

"We should call them the Illegals," said Officer Hilcox aka Foxy Coxy. "Cause they're aliens. Get it?"

Jason had laughed at this, and then the other cops had laughed because the other cops took after Jason.

Celia did not laugh.

"I don't care what you call them so long as you're the only ones calling them anything. As far as the public knows, these men are only linked to the murders at the liquor store. We know that they're responsible for the fire at the church. What we don't know is what else they're responsible for. The sorry state of case closures in the greater southern Nevada area means that these guys may have been active prior to the liquor store."

"Are we talking about serial killers here?" asked Celia. "A mob outfit? Some kind of racket?"

"We don't know, and I really don't like not knowing. So far, you lot have come up with no leads of substance. Where are we on the masks?"

This question was directed at Officer Hilcox, who shrugged. "I checked them out online. They're not exactly unique to the area as much as the Roswell lovers would like them to be. There's about 100 novelty stores between here and Vegas that would carry them. The few I've talked to locally haven't reported anyone buying them lately, in bulk or otherwise."

"As I said, no leads of substance," said Chief Burton. "It goes without saying that I want these bastards caught. What kind of a world do we live in when churches are being targeted as execution sites? That's not my Ravencourt. And if it is then by God I've gotten too old for this job."

He sighed then, as if the weight of the job really had caught up to him. But then the Chief had cleared his throat and looked up from his thoughts.

"We know that this is bad news, but the public doesn't need to know that. We let them know and we'll have high school kids buying these masks just to be goddamn comedians. People will be jumping at their own shadows, and we won't know the difference between the shadows that are harmless and the ones that bite.

"This face," and here Chief Burton had pointed at the alien on the marker board, looking each of them in the eye in turn, "it stays between all of us, in this room." He had swiped an eraser across the face, the alien disappearing.

"Well, what are you waiting for?" asked the Chief. "Get like the Men in Black and put these aliens down."

But a solution hadn't come, and in a few weeks Chief Burton's request for radio silence on all things alien-related came to nothing when the mask-wearing men had gotten in a shootout in Las Vegas and pulled a State Police investigator into the matter.

Not one of them fancy casinos on the strip, mind you. In fact, to call the casino a part of Vegas proper would even be pushing things. In reality, the casino was in a town called Henderson. It was distinguished from The Strip by the presence of Bingo and enough blue-haired old ladies smoking cigarettes to fill a Walk to Fight Lung Cancer charity event.

Although security had been tight at the casino, they stood no match for the alien mask-wearing men, and that's what propelled the story to the big news stations in Vegas and Carson City.

Silver Dollar City made a transfer every day at 2:00 p. m. on the dot, 2:00 p. m. being the slowest time of the afternoon. The early birds to the lunch buffet had left but the early birds to the dinner buffet wouldn't arrive yet. The low amount of foot traffic gave the armored car ample time to back into the casino's loading bay out back and let two overweight, long-on-the-job guards stand by while slightly more intimidating casino personnel walked out a pushcart filled with dufflebags full of money. The head of security, dressed in a suit and carrying a pistol in both his jacket pocket and attached to his ankle, watched over the proceedings.

Video cameras caught the whole ordeal. On an otherwise uneventful Tuesday, the armored truck had backed in as planned. But as the bags of money were being loaded inside under the watchful eyes of casino security and armored fleet security, silent shots rang out.

The casino's head of security is the first to reach for his gun, which is a mistake, because he's also the first one shot, in the chest. The man wheeling out the money is next, dropping the cart and reaching for the pistol at his hip, but he's also taken in the chest and falls like a sack of doughy batteries.

The man in the armored car stays put, as is protocol, and turns out to be the only one left alone. The other two men keeping a watch on things are hit from opposite sides, thrust backwards and into the very armored car they were slated to protect.

With the guards on the ground, four hooded men enter the picture. They grab the bags of money and then turn back, allowing the casino's security cameras to get a glimpse of the face of an alien and not much more. The men are dressed entirely in black, except for one wearing blue jeans.

As with the previous incidents, the men disappeared into the night, no trace of a vehicle or any evidence that could connect them to the previous crimes or even to anyone with a background. Unlike the previous incidents, this heist had occurred in broad daylight.

Also unlike the previous incidents, there had been no casualties. Instead of using baseball bats or lighter fluid or bullets of any kind, the men in the alien masks had deployed beanbag guns. Solid enough to collapse a full grown, even hefty man to his knees, light enough not to inflict serious damage.

The men, and the money, had disappeared. And who turned up? An investigator with the state police, an enterprising sergeant named Haddock whose Google search, of all things, revealed the connection between alien masks in the casino robbery and a liquor store robbery gone wrong some months prior.

15

"And you're working with this investigator?" asked Brian.

It was the first time he'd spoken since Celia began telling the sorry tale of the men in masks who may or may not have been a gang or a cabal of serial murders or a bunch of unconnected dumbasses being given too much credit.

"Not exactly," said Celia. "I was involved in something a few weeks ago. There was a scuffle and lots of drugs and money involved. I thought maybe it was connected. It was a hunch more than anything. Until today when that State Investigator explained to me that he'd been having the same hunch."

"So you know who these guys are?"

"No," she said. "But I started thinking. We've all been too focused on the masks. If they're a bunch of dumb criminals, sure, they leave a calling card. But what if they're smarter?"

"You think you found something even the State Police didn't?"

Brian had that look on his face, the look Celia had gotten her entire life, the one that really pissed her off because it meant *skepticism.* And she was tired of skepticism being directed her way.

"People underestimate me," she said. "When you remove the masks from the equation, the masks that you can get anywhere, the data gets skewed."

"Skewed?"

"Dozens of incidents. Robberies. Drug deals. Small-time crime. No alien masks in sight."

"Okay…"

"Money, taken in small and sometimes shockingly large amounts, but no one's paying attention. The cases are unsolved because they're happening across Nevada and the targets are usually liquor stores, trailer parks, doomsday preppers, self-styled militia men who keep to themselves and don't keep their money insured in banks."

"You're saying there have been dozens of unsolved crimes, all across Nevada, with the same culprit behind all of them? And nobody's noticed except you? That's a reach."

"Because I'm a girl?"

Brian rolled his eyes. "Come on with that. Because it would be noticed. By everyone. There's no proof."

"There might be." She reached over and held out a small bag of meth, a couple ounces at most.

"Oh, fantastic, I left my meth at home. Is it even legal for you to have that?"

"Shut up for a second," she said. "That incident I was involved in, we turned up a bag just like this one."

"Doesn't all meth look alike?"

"For the most part. But they each have a unique chemical signature. Call it a certificate of authenticity for shitheads. This bag comes from a farming community in California. I paid a visit to the department up there on a day off."

"You need to take better vacations."

Celia continued, ignoring the interruption. She was talking fast now, faster than she wanted to, but now that the words spilled out, they felt good. They felt *right.*

"I told them I was working on a related case in Nevada and asked if I could see any case files for recent meth busts. That's when this popped up. I borrowed it, citing an official investigation.

"Then I come back here. Peel off a small sample from the bust at The Rocks, the one I was involved in. Following?"

Brian nodded.

"Now I've got two bags, plus another couple samples scooped from random traffic stops and disorderly conducts. So another day off and I'm able to take them to a friend at the crime lab at UNLV for analysis. You know what she found?"

She was really revved up now, the words pouring out of her faster than she could even catch a breath. She had kept it all to herself for so long that it felt good to tell somebody, anybody, especially someone unconnected to any of it.

"What?"

"They're chemically identical. The meth at the bust I was involved in. That we've pulled off of drunks and parolees. That I got from a small town in *California*."

"What's the big deal with that?"

"They're trafficking across state lines, Brian. Which means FBI, ATF, a real investigation. And then the kicker…"

Celia opened up a manila folder laying on the desk. It had numbers, figures, copies of real estate transactions.

Brian raised an eyebrow. To him they meant nothing. To Celia it could be everything.

"If the meth in that trailer could be tied to outside the state, that means the operation I uncovered could be bigger than anyone anticipated. So I dug in. The trailer I robbed, a couple months ago, it was put up for auction. The previous tenant had been evicted. But rather than be purchased by some other recent prisoner out on parole, it was bought by a holding company."

She pointed at the name.

"Haart of the Sea LLC. So then I cross-referenced it with other properties. Haart of the Sea owns almost half the properties at The Rocks. They've been buying them up for cents on the dollar whenever someone moves or gets busted. Which happens often at The Rocks."

"So who owns it? What do they want with that land?"

"Good question. I can't find any records identifying the owners, and that land is basically worthless. You can't start a development when half the area is filled with former convicts, even if they are trying to turn their lives around. But if they somehow got enough of it? Who knows? A casino, a laundering operation, they could put anything up there."

Brian looked down, across the entire table. He really did look ridiculous standing there with just a pair of shorts in her kitchen. Though she probably looked fairly silly too, talking of a grand criminal conspiracy wearing nothing but a plaid shirt, her foot occasionally brushing against a bowl of cat food on the ground.

"So let's say this is true," said Brian. "Why not tell someone who can do something about it?"

She registered the doubt in his voice. It caused her to deflate completely. Mostly because he asked the same question she'd been asking herself for weeks.

He doesn't believe you. And that's exactly why you won't tell anyone else. Why you haven't told Chief. Or Haddock.

Because they don't believe <u>in</u> you. No one does. They'll laugh at the girl who thought she cracked this thing WIDE OPEN! Look out world! Celia Miller's on the case!

Please. You're pathetic. Grasping at straws. They'll never take you seriously. You don't even take you seriously.

"I need proof," she said weakly, and hated herself immediately for how quiet her voice was.

A man would march into the office and slap all the evidence down on the table. 'Here's what I found! Let's bust some heads. Clean up the streets!' 'I can't authorize an investigation on a hunch, Miller!' 'Dammit, Chief, this is real, I know it in my bones!'

She wasn't that person. And they would never let her be that person either.

Brian took her hand in his. "I believe you."

He said it weakly, his tone conveying the exact opposite. As he pulled her close, she felt him grow hard against her body. He kissed the top of her head, then lifted her chin toward him and kissed her on the lips. She parted her mouth to meet him.

"Sure you do," she said.

She placed the folder back on the kitchen table and let herself be led to the bedroom, where she could simultaneously enjoy her time and hate herself for doing so.

16

Celia woke up to the sound of her phone playing "I Fought the Law and the Law Won." That meant someone from the station was calling. Early. The first rays of sunlight were coming into her bedroom from the east.

She took a second to assess her surroundings and remember the circumstances of last night. She felt drunk-groggy but not quite hangover-sick. She stretched, extending her bare feet over the side of the bed and her arms into the headboard.

It was then that she realized she was alone in the bed. Brian was nowhere to be found.

Did that son of a bitch bail on me?

The second iteration of "I Fought the Law and the Law Won" echoed from her phone. Celia rubbed her eyes and slid her finger across the face of the screen.

"This is Miller."

"It's Chief. Didn't wake you, did I?"

"No."

"You're a terrible liar, Celia. Listen, I hate to do this to you…"

"Then don't do it."

"But Martinez called in sick for his shift. Sounds like he's got the flu something fierce."

More like he's got the morning after hangover something fierce, she thought. *That little shit.*

"And well, you're up on the roster. I can get you your overtime. Mayor and Council'll throw a fit but we need someone out on patrol."

"When do you need me?"

"You be in in an hour?"

She looked around. It didn't look like there was anyone keeping her here. Brian appeared to have snuck off in the night. She had a vague awareness of him putting on his clothes and slipping out the door while the sky was still gray.

"Give me more like two and you're on."

"Hour and a half. See you soon."

He hung up the phone and Celia followed suit.

Murray scratched and meowed to be let out of the room. He would be in a pouty mood having been unceremoniously kicked out of the room for the better part of the night.

Fucking Brian. Fucking Jason. Murray's the only one who doesn't shit all over you and he's the one you kick out.

No, that was cat lady talk, a road Celia didn't want to go down. And in fact she had had a good time last night, whether it was a one-night-stand or Brian was honest about what he said but chicken shat out this morning. And even though she was called in to work, Celia took a perverse pleasure in the idea that Jason had resorted to binge-drinking last night just so he could forget about her. It meant she could still cast a potent spell.

All in all, not a terrible night.

17

Celia showered quickly and got dressed in her uniform, not wanting to hassle with having to change in the locker room. She put on a perfunctory splotch of makeup, fed Murray, and headed out the door. In a way, work would be preferable to sitting around all day, wondering what Brian's deal was and fussing over whether or not she should text or call. While getting ready, she had only glanced at her phone to check for texts two or three times.

As she tapped her fingers impatiently against her kitchen counter, waiting for the Keurig to spit out a cup of awful coffee, she glanced at the kitchen table that acted as the epicenter of her amateur "investigation." A wave of embarrassment washed over her. She had poured her entire thought process onto Brian while he was still half drunk and wondering how he could get her back into bed. He'd reacted exactly as she'd imagined everyone else would (minus the half-staff boner of course, that was unique to him) and now, in the clear light of morning, she realized how ridiculous the whole thing sounded and how she must have looked.

Something's different.

The voice of doubt could sometimes be more observant than even Celia herself. It picked up on everything about her she didn't dare to acknowledge, and right now it was pointing her toward the mess of her kitchen table.

She glanced at the chaos, trying to place what was off. They had rummaged through things last night, so it was all more askew than usual, but something else was different too.

The mask is there. The police reports. The pills...

The pills.

She had a couple bottles of OxyContin that she had delicately "borrowed" before she realized how meth-centric the Illegals' activities seemed to be.

A couple bottles. But now just one.

Had she moved it? No, she hadn't touched it. It was the meth that had been the focus.

He took the fucking pills!

Her one-night-stand was looking like more and more of a disaster by the minute. She looked around the kitchen to see if she forgot something, but sure enough: the bottle was gone.

That son of a bitch. I'm gonna arrest him.

She felt like an idiot. A little girl who'd had a crappy day at work and thought that a sweet guy could take her mind off of things. Yet he had turned out to be just another jerk like the rest of them. Ready to take off in the morning, only now with an added bonus of scoring a bottle he could either sell off or, more likely, spread around at a party when he went back home.

Fuck all of them.

Her Keurig spluttered the last few drops of coffee into the mug. She poured it into a thermos and set off. She'd worry about worrying about Brian later.

* * *

The city was quiet. After leaving her apartment, Celia travelled mostly empty streets with the occasional car. The biggest fount of activity was a farmer's market that had started up about a year ago despite the fact that there were no farmers in the area. Celia pictured her and Brian walking hand in hand through the vendors, goofing around and finding stuff to buy for lunch, then shook the image away as quickly as it came when the phantom version of Brian popped an OxyContin into his mouth.

It wouldn't do to dwell.

She arrived at the station, the parking lot nearly empty. A skeleton crew would be on hand for Saturday. A squad member would act as security at the farmer's market and then two cars would patrol throughout the day. Police presence wouldn't be ratcheted up until night fell and the citizens of Ravencourt made their way to the town's many bars.

Celia was surprised to see that Chief Burton's black Mustang, what he called his mid-life crisis (*better than an 18-year-old mistress*, he would say, and then think about it for a second and follow up with, *okay maybe not*, and then chuckle), was in the parking lot. The Chief must've been backed up with paperwork or his wife's 90-some-year-old in-laws were in town, the only two reasons that typically brought him in to the station on a weekend.

She entered the front door. With no Judith there to buzz her in, she unlocked and then opened the bullpen door. It was empty save for Officer Hilcox sitting at the 911 cubicle playing a game of Candy Crush. He looked up and gave Celia a perfunctory wave of the hand.

She knocked on the Chief's doorframe. He too was playing some kind of game on his computer. Solitaire.

In-laws it is then.

"Oh, hiya, Celia. Sorry again for calling you in. I know you probably had plans."

"Not really. Do you want me to just patrol?"

"Yessum," he said. "We've got quotas met for traffic tickets for the month, so only pull over the real assholes. Drive around, take it easy. Listen to the radio in case we need you for anything. Let fire or med take the lead on any heart attacks and the like."

"Caution tape duty, basically?"

"Basically."

"What are you doing in here, anyway?" she asked. "In-laws in town?"

"Worse," he said. "My sister-in-law. I fear I won't be able to hide out much longer."

"Ok. Well, if I don't see or hear from you have a good…"

"Hey, guys, sorry to interrupt," said Hilcox, having sidled up and now pushing his way in. "Chief, or maybe Celia, you'll know this, but what's the protocol when someone calls in from a callbox?"

"Someone used a *callbox?*" asked Celia. "Did they call from 1987?"

"That's what I thought. Old Mile Marker 19 on Highway 706."

"Holy shit," said the Chief. "I can't believe one of those is still in commission. All the others along the main drag and closer to town got disconnected. Talk about the middle of nowhere: no wonder they had to use a callbox, there wouldn't be a signal up there for miles."

"Do I dispatch it to fire? Or the auto club?"

"What'd they say exactly?" asked Chief Burton.

"It was kinda weird," said Hilcox, scratching his head. "The voice was all scratchy and metallic."

"Could've been the reception out there," said Celia.

"I don't think so. It wasn't like staticky bad. More auto-tuned. The guy just said 'I'm stuck out here. Send help.' I asked him what the nature of his emergency was and all he said was 'You have to help me. Please.' Then he hung up."

"That's it?"

"That's it."

"Can we call it back?" asked Celia.

"Those old callboxes only work one way," said Chief Burton, leaning back in his chair and rubbing his chin between his thumb and forefinger. "I tell you what, Celia, you head out there, see what all the fuss is about. If it's just some guy with a broken-down car, give him and his family a ride into town so they don't die of heat stroke."

"What if it's something more serious?"

"Well, then you use that same callbox and call for backup. Cause you sure as shit won't get reception out that way. Wouldn't even be surprised if your radio didn't work."

Celia nodded her head. Seemed straightforward enough. And at least the drive out there and back would give her a nice break from the monotony of driving through the minimalist streets of Ravencourt.

"Sounds good," she said. "If I don't see you, have a good weekend. And tell Mellie I said hello."

"Will do, will do."

Celia brushed past Hilcox and headed toward the front desk where she could pick out the keys to a squad car. She opened the small wooden box, always unlocked, and saw the half dozen keys left inside. One stuck out more than the others.

Her fingers reached forward and she even looped her thumb into the keyring of the decade-old cruiser she normally drove. But that other key kept calling to her.

Celia smiled and pulled it from the rack.

18

The Challenger. Jason's pride and joy. Although not technically his, considering that it was the department's vehicle, Jason had used his military cachet to insert his control over this one piece of the departmental puzzle. Anyone technically could drive the vehicle, but the last officer who had tried had been the victim of a glass of whiskey mixed with piss. And since the automobile itself was only provided to the department thanks to a Homeland Security grant given to law enforcement agencies that employed honorably discharged military officers, Chief Burton didn't press the point.

Fuck him. Jason's the one who was too hung over to come in to work.

Celia could have asked, should have asked for permission, but it would be Monday before the Chief would even know it was gone. She could even imagine how the conversation would have played out.

"I'm gonna take the Challenger," she would have said.

The Chief, meaning well, would have smiled and shook his head.

"You're going to be the death of me. You know how Jason gets when anyone takes his car."

"It's Ravencourt's car."

"You try telling him that. He'd make everyone's life around here a living hell."

"So just because he's gonna throw a hissy fit we all pay the price?"

"Something like that, yeah."

"Fine."

And that was perhaps the real reason why she didn't ask Chief

Burton. She was afraid that he would have talked her out of it under the guise of going with the flow, not rocking the boat, not upsetting the order of things. And Celia wouldn't have belabored the point because Chief Burton was good to her, was the only one who was good to her, and if he had this one tic, this one remnant of the boys' club that he had to maintain, she would let it slide.

So she took it without asking. Better to ask for forgiveness than to ask for shit you know you won't get.

Celia took it easy on her way out of Ravencourt, but as the pavement from a defunct shopping mall faded and gave way to desert on either side of the highway, she let loose. Almost at once the car's speed shot from 45 to 80. She could have pushed past that easily, but didn't have far to go and didn't want to make it to her destination so quickly that she'd waste a perfectly relaxing jaunt.

The Challenger really was a thing of beauty. Celia didn't consider herself a car kinda girl but this could convert anyone. She didn't know the specs but understood that the Hemi engine would be able to bring her up to 160 miles per hour within a matter of seconds if she just pressed her foot down on the gas.

She can certainly move.

You know what, no, Celia thought, *he. Everyone always calls their cars she. This isn't pretty enough to be a she. And women aren't built like this. This is a tank, but fast too, like a sexy tank, this is the Channing Tatum of cars.*

Celia grinned, amused at her description of the car, likely brought about by her rewatching of *Magic Mike* twice last week. Fine, three times last week.

Channing. I like it. I'm gonna name you Channing, and then I'm going to tell Jason that his car is named Channing and it will piss him off to no end.

Celia laughed out loud at this last part, genuinely enjoying herself.

And the car *was* a tank, sexy sleek but solid. Bulletproof everything, fender and doors designed to withstand a battering ram, a roll cage that would protect an occupant from danger in anything but a crash with a semi trailer.

Contrary to popular belief, most police cruisers are nothing more than glorified sedans with a slight tune-up. They are not bulletproof, the tires are not puncture-proof, and they offer no additional protection during a crash. This is due to the simple fact that police departments have to bid on vehicles, just like any other city institution, and when it comes time to trim the budget, it's hard for any city, let alone one as out of the way as Ravencourt, to justify the purchase of steel plating capable of shielding the President. Most cop cars are lucky to get a trunk full of hardware and a hard plastic partition between the perps in back and the driver in front.

Thanks to one helluva grant, though, Ravencourt got to participate in a pilot program in which they got to test drive a car that could stop anything short of a rocket launcher.

This was in combination with the armor and weaponry that currently sat in the trunk thanks to the Department of Defense Excess Property Program, otherwise known as DOD 1033 (which sounds like a tax form but will fuck up your shit even faster than the IRS).

When there's a war, all sorts of exotic, state-of-the-art implements of destruction are commissioned for use overseas. Weapons contractors and the DOD get creative when cash is limitless. But when those wars come to an end, the country is left with a surplus (in assets, certainly not in cash).

Rather than just destroying the leftovers, the guns are handed over to police departments across the country to do with what they will.

That's why the trunk of this particular car was a veritable roving armory. It had been the Chief's idea to stock one car up with all the gear the department had successfully procured through 1033. State-of-the-art body armor, assault weapons, and assorted other gear designed to assist in the war in Iraq, now put to use in a town in which the coyotes outnumbered the citizens by a considerable margin.

God Bless America.

19

Her turn was coming up. Celia looked down at the dashboard to see the speedometer tick up to 93. She cursed, hitting the brakes in order to make the left turn that would take her off the beaten path, to the no man's (or woman's) land of Highway 706.

She flicked on her blinker, despite the fact there were no vehicles within what seemed like miles, and turned left, her tires kicking up dust as they passed onto the rarely traveled highway. After about a mile, she passed the winding road that would have taken her up to The Rocks and all of its trailer courts and honorable denizens. A mile after that, the road winding down and into the desert, she passed a rocky bluff that disguised an ATV path leading from The Rocks down to the highway. This was frequented by Rocks thrill seekers trying their hand at death defiance or looking to stealthily duck parole or move drug product by avoiding the main road.

She continued onward. She had a vague recollection of a callbox out this way, but it was so rare that the squad would ever be called out here that she was having trouble picturing it.

Back before the lakes, the economy, and the people had dried up, decades before, as a matter of fact, Highway 706 had been the premier way to get in and out of Ravencourt. Laid out east to west right through the heart of Nevada's most unforgiving desert country, travelers hoping to make a straight shot through to California and skip the glitz and glamour of Vegas and the shits and stammer of Reno could take 706. Of course, you'd first have to take Highway 50, pilot that on through to Highway 6, then veer off the beaten path to

take the two-lane winding hardtop of 706 instead of the more for-
giving, albeit slightly lengthier, stretch of 6, with its line of hotels,
rest areas, and fast food establishments. It was 6 that served most
of Ravencourt now, but 706 still lingered, like a 104-year old aunt
who keeps sucking on the coffers of her only surviving family members because they're the only ones around and she refuses to die.

706 refused to die. Younger truckers looking to save themselves
an hour or two would take it, their balls getting them further than
their brains ever would. Older truckers recognized that road im-
provement funds hadn't been used for 706 since Bush 1 refused to
eat broccoli and the people who still got that joke were middle-aged.
The road was more pothole than highway now, and even if you made
it through without breaking down and requiring help from the half
dozen or so local police entities scattered around decaying towns
just like Ravencourt, your shocks would be so fucked up and your
back to match that you wouldn't risk the route again.

The carcass had dropped off the road; all that was left was the
spine, jutting out from the desert just enough to allow two cars to
pass in opposing directions if they didn't mind sharing a bunk.
Static replaced the country song that was playing on the radio, and
Celia turned it off. Out of habit, she reached for her iPod, only to
grasp at air in the cup holder.

Oh fuck.

Yes, she still used an iPod rather than load her music onto a
phone. Yes, she took shit for it. No, she didn't care.

You do care but you do it anyway.

Celia typically took it along with her on every trip so that she
didn't listen to the old-school country that drifted in from the antenna of the only station in town. She preferred the Mormon rock
that seemed to have become Nevada's stock in trade over the past
few years (your Killers, your Imagine Dragons, your Neon Trees).

But because the Chief had called her up early and she had to get
ready fast, she had left it in its dock in her kitchen.

Silence it is then.

Celia saw a shadow in the distance. It looked to be a car stuck on
the road. She squinted through her sunglasses to confirm. It was a
car, but its appearance was incongruous, as she was still four or five
miles out from the callbox.

Hearing her approach, someone stepped out from behind the
car's hood, brandishing something in his hand that looked like a

weapon. Celia squinted against the sun's glare, still bright even through her shades.

What is that? A gun? What the hell's going on?

She lowered her speed and uncinched her holster strap. There was something that seemed off about this. What were the odds that someone would break down on this road at the exact same time she was investigating? Cops are never out here.

She drew closer. As she pulled up, she saw that the vehicle was a black Mini Cooper with Nevada license plates. She also saw that the man was holding a flashlight, not some kind of weapon. She had a moment to ponder that she only knew one person who drove that kind of car when...

"Brian?" she said to herself.

What the hell is he doing all the way out here? If he intended to skip town back to UNLV he'd be headed in the other direction.

Unless he has a girl.

Yes, unless he has a girl and was just passing through.

Passing in. And out.

Celia blocked that thought and pulled behind Brian's smoking vehicle. As she stepped out of the Challenger, Brian motioned back toward the hood, yet to notice that it was Celia who was approaching.

"Boy am I glad to see you, Officer," he said. "Here I was driving down the road and the damn thing just..."

He stopped his sentence short as he saw Celia standing in front of him in her cop attire, shades blocking her eyes, a scowl on her face. She crossed her arms in front of her chest and stared right through Brian, who momentarily looked stunned. He blinked a couple times, stammered and said:

"Wow, have I not seen you in your uniform before? That is, that is..."

"A surprise?"

"I was going to say hot. But yeah, a surprise, a pleasant surprise."

"It's hot out here, huh?" asked Celia.

"It is."

Celia walked across to the other side of the car, staring in the windows and coming toward the hood, opposite the side of the vehicle closest to the road, where Brian was standing.

"Shame to be out here all alone, isn't it? Good thing a cop showed up."

"You have no idea," he said. "Think you can fix it? Or call for a tow?"

Celia nodded.

"Oh thank God. You're amazing."

As he was coming around the car's hood to hug her, she opened the door and reached toward the cup holder. Celia grabbed the little orange bottle sitting there, then turned and held it up in front of her.

"I assume you have a prescription for this?" she asked.

"Oh, shit."

"You're under arrest."

"I can explain that," he said.

"Really?" She took a couple steps forward and he instinctively backed away. "You can explain how you took a bottle of illegal prescription drugs from a police investigation?"

"I told you, my back's been fucked up lately," he stammered.

"It's going to get worse," she said.

"I mean, you had those bottles just sitting there. Would you really miss one?"

"Hands behind your back."

Rather than complying, he stood there. He even smirked.

"You're not going to arrest me."

"You're not as charming as you think."

"Let's not call it charm, then. Let's call it you explaining to your department why you have bottles of pills, bags of meth, and why you've carried on an unofficial investigation behind their backs."

She glared at him, squinting against the sun even through her tinted glasses. She couldn't see his eyes behind his own sunglasses but she imagined them to be playful, which enraged her.

"Can I have my pills back now?" he asked.

"Fuck you."

She pocketed the bottle and pushed past him, back toward the Challenger.

Gravel crunched behind her as he raced to catch up. She felt a hand wrap around her wrist but she jerked away, spinning on her heels and grabbing him by his shirt.

"Do not touch me," she said. She turned, moving around the Challenger's front toward the driver's side.

"Celia, will you just give me a chance..." He hadn't followed her this time, just stood where he was.

Celia ignored him, opening her door and inserting the key into the ignition. She wouldn't wipe her eyes, not now, not while he was watching. Thank God for sunglasses.

The vehicle revved to life as Celia turned the key. Brian stood in front of the car to block her progress. She put the vehicle into reverse and pulled backwards. He followed her, dust kicking past him as he struggled to keep his hands on the hood while the Challenger spun to face the other way.

Brian hurriedly got back in front of the headlights.

"Will you just wait a second and let me explain? Are you really going to leave me out here in the middle of the desert?"

Celia got on the bullhorn equipped on the vehicle.

"Please step away from the vehicle. You are interfering with the egress of police property and I will run you the fuck over."

He smiled at that, and Celia could have punched the gas right then and run him down it pissed her off so much.

Instead, she took a breath, willing the tears away, and got back on the megaphone.

"Brian, will you please just move?"

She knew he could hear her voice catch in her throat as she said the word *move* and hated herself for that catch.

"Will you give me 30 seconds, please?"

Celia hesitated, and it was all the time Brian needed to walk around to her window. Instead of hitting the accelerator and pulling away from Brian's life for good, she found herself throwing the vehicle into park and rolling down her window. She didn't say anything, just stared forward.

"I came to see you yesterday because I wanted to be sure," he said. "I've been seeing this girl, Erin, she lives up north."

"Of course you are. Good for you."

She started to roll up the window but he put his wrist through the opening.

"We had broken it off but then she called me out of the blue. And all I could think about when she called me wasn't how I wanted to see her, but how excited I was that I'd have to pass through Ravencourt."

"Nobody passes through Ravencourt."

"Okay, so I was excited that I'd be able to go two and a half hours out of my way to pass through Ravencourt."

Celia could feel herself *wanting* to believe him, but the voice pestered.

He's lying.

"You're so full of shit. If I hadn't passed by this morning, I'd have never seen you again."

"I left your place this morning because I wanted to be honest with both of you. You and her. Everything we did just confirmed that I wanted to be with you and that I've felt that way for a long time. But I couldn't commit myself to that while I had someone else waiting for me. I wouldn't feel right."

"You could have told me," she said.

"Well, I kinda did. I left a note."

"Bullshit you did!" she said, finally taking the time to move her glasses up and wipe her eyes. "What kind of note?"

"Basically telling you what I just told you. I take it you didn't get it."

"Where'd you put it?"

"In your kitchen. By the iPod. You said you never leave without taking it with you."

Well, shit.

She supposed he could be lying about that. But that'd be a pretty bold play considering he couldn't know that she forgot to take the iPod with her because the Chief had called her in to patrol.

"You couldn't set it in the bathroom?"

He grinned now, and Celia wanted to both punch him in the lips and take them between her own.

"I thought about it, but bathrooms are gross. Fecal matter and whatnot."

Celia laughed. It was without actual joy.

"Can I kiss you?" he asked, already moving his head forward.

Celia pulled away. "Whoa, buddy, I may not be ready to leave you stranded in 114 degree weather, but you're severely overplaying your hand if you think I'm gonna kiss you before I get back to my house and see that note. Plus, you stole drugs."

"Fair enough. In the meantime, can I have a ride?"

20

Celia looked under the hood even though, in truth, she had no idea what she was looking for or what anything was. Her father and the force had taught her all about weaponry and takedown strategies and dispute resolution, but auto mechanics eluded her.

"You have no idea what you're looking at, do you?" Brian asked.

"I don't, but when you're a cop you always have to look under the hood for a couple seconds so that it looks like you're checking on something."

"Good point," Brian said as Celia took a step back and he shut the hood.

"Did you really quit college?" asked Celia.

"I'm thinking about it. Let's say I've just taken some days off."

"You're such a fucking liar. What are you doing out here any-way?"

"Well, I got sort of turned around and figured if I just went west I'd meet back up with the 6."

"Nope," she said.

"Then my car just clacked a couple times…"

"Clacked?"

"Seems as good a word as any. And I pulled it over and that was it. Thank God I had a bottle of water. I think I might have fried if you'd been much longer."

Celia scratched her head. Something seemed off.

"Were you the one that called on the callbox?"

"I haven't moved from this spot. Cellphone won't get any bars out here. I'm just glad you patrol this way. I tried to flag down someone about an hour ago, but they moved past. Looked like a group. Boy, you have no idea how glad I am you stopped by."

"You're lucky," she said. "We're never out this way. Someone called the department on a callbox about four miles that way. I can give you a ride back into town but I've gotta go see what's going on first. I'd call for backup but I won't be able to pick up anything out this way either, even on the radio."

"Not even worth a try?" he asked.

Celia rolled her eyes behind her sunglasses. She pulled out her walkie and keyed in the channel that would connect her to the station.

"This is Officer Miller, requesting assistance," she said, taking her finger off the button to listen.

There was no response, but there wasn't exactly silence either. Bursts of static came through, but behind the static there was something else. Music.

"Try rotating the..."

Celia put a finger to her lips, listening to the sound come through. It was...

"Is that piano?" Brian asked.

Celia nodded. "We must be picking up something from a radio tower around here. Some quack that lives in the hills maybe. I don't know."

"What about your cellphone?" Brian offered.

Celia shook her head. "No bars. When they call it The Big Empty, they mean it."

"Well, what then?"

"Hop in the car," she said. "We'll drive up and see what the story is out by that callbox, then I'll take you into town to call a tow truck. And you can call and tell your girl you'll be late."

"She's not my girl," Brian said. "You are."

Celia hoped the red wouldn't stand out on her cheeks in the bright sun or that the corners of her mouth didn't turn up too much as she fought to conceal her smile.

"I'm nobody's girl," she said. "Now get in the car. If you're lucky I won't even make you sit in the cage."

<h1 style="text-align:center">21</h1>

Brian sat next to her as the Challenger cruised onward toward the callbox. She resisted the urge to say anything, waiting for him to pipe up, but he just stared out at the endless desert all around.

The car made a turn around a group of rocks and over a slight hill. That's when Celia caught her first glimpse of it.

The callbox was a mile or two further yet, positioned about 100 yards before a cluster of large rocks that sat on the crest of a hill. It was barely more than a dot at this point. As the road continued, it moved west past the rocks and then curved downward out of sight into some valley. The scene was set so that Celia could view the little blue dot that was the callbox, followed by the rocks further on, and then the jagged edge of the horizon, heat shimmering off the concrete. The sun was reaching its apex.

There was also a car positioned forty or so feet away from the callbox, not in the road but in the middle of the desert. At this distance it was just a shape.

"Was that the car that passed you earlier?" Celia asked.

"I can't tell from this far. What's it doing in the sand?"

Celia shook her head. What made the vehicle's position especially odd was that it faced sideways, perpendicular to the road with its headlights pointed nearly head on with the callbox, rather than straight ahead in the direction of the road like it would have if someone would have piloted it off the highway.

Something is wrong. Turn around.

That was unusual. That voice of wariness typically only chimed in when Celia had to steel herself against some slight. Told her she wasn't good enough, that the colleague asking her to file their paperwork was right, that she wasn't their equal, she never would be, would never be accepted. It tried to get her to confront all those things she feared about herself.

So why was it now telling her that she should leave this ugly desert vista behind?

"They're probably inside the car, huh?" said Brian. "A/C running, trying to get out of the heat."

He's scared too. But he doesn't know why. You have your excuse. Take him back into Ravencourt. This is against protocol. You don't bring citizens in need along to an ambush.

Ambush. The word sounded strange, given that she was only dealing with a single car that called for help in the desert.

Celia bit her lip then stopped herself. She reached into her cup holder and took a sip of cold coffee, the last dregs from the cup. Her mouth suddenly felt dry.

22

She pulled up next to the callbox and left the engine running. From here, she could see the vehicle. Some ratty-looking thing from the '80s, a car like an old dog that refused to die despite repeated abuses by a master it was still loyal to. She couldn't see anyone inside the cabin, whose roof obscured the sun and any look inside she might otherwise get.

Celia pulled down her sunglasses and squinted past Brian. All around the vehicle was blinding brightness, yet inside was utter black. Celia could make out the faint shape of the steering wheel, but whether there were people inside or not she couldn't say. The vehicle seemed to repel light, steadfastly refusing to expose its contents.

She would have to all but walk right up to the car before she'd be able to see if anyone was inside.

Celia drummed her fingers on the steering wheel. Brian pressed his hands in an oval to the glass and then stuck his face in between them to get a better look.

"I can't tell if there's people in there or not," he said.

Celia didn't respond. Instead, she picked up her radio and spoke into it.

"This is Officer Miller. Station, please respond."

There was nothing, not even the eerie piano music from before.

"Well?" Brian asked, despite the fact he could hear just as well as she could.

"Check your cellphone," Celia said as she pulled out her own iPhone. She slid her finger across the screen. No bars. She dialed the station number anyway just to check. Just as she assumed, there was nothing.

Brian had the phone placed up against his ear, then lowered it, tapping at the screen. He shook his head no.

It's a simple breakdown, Celia thought. *They probably saw an armadillo or something on the road and skidded out, then the piece of shit wouldn't start up again.*

Then why is no one getting out of the car?

Maybe the heat got to 'em. Shut the fuck up Celia.

Celia sucked the insides of her cheeks.

Well, I've gotta go out there sometime.

"Wait here," Celia said.

"I'll go with you," Brian said, already opening the door.

"Do you have a badge?" Celia asked.

"No, but…"

"Then sit in the car and enjoy the A/C while I go sweat my balls off and see what's up. And don't touch anything."

She opened the door and walked around the side of the Challenger, a few feet away from the callbox.

The phone itself hung off of the hook, the cord completely motionless with the lack of wind. Celia walked forward and put the black receiver to her ear, checking for syringes like they were instructed to do (police training still seemed to be stuck in an '80s world where cops had to worry about AIDS-junkies putting needles in the receivers for the fun of giving a lawman an STD). Alas, there were no needles.

There wasn't a dial tone either, but that could be because the phone times out when it's been off the hook for upwards of a minute. Celia placed her finger down on the hook and then took it off, not expecting there to be any kind of noise.

But there was. A dial tone. If Celia wanted, she could simply hit the big white 911 button and be connected to the station.

And then what? They'd laugh behind your back or, worse, to your face, about how you called for backup to investigate a stalled car?

I don't need them. I am not some helpless girl. I am a goddamn cop, with real authority, capable of assisting stranded motorists in their hour of need and deserving of the respect of anyone who crosses my path.

It's just a dead car in a dead desert. Nothing to get worked up about.

And yet that feeling gnawed at her. Something about the situation was off in some small but indescribable way.

Back in the car, Brian attempted to find a music station, but to no avail. The closest he came were the staticky bursts of a preacher telling sinners to repent before the Lord almighty lest he unleash His wrath.

Celia had placed the pill bottle on the center dash. Brian glanced over to make sure she was preoccupied, then flipped the top and popped a pill into his mouth. He put the cap back on and made sure to place the bottle exactly where it had been before, then turned back to the radio.

If he would have been looking up instead of engaged with the radio or taking a pill, he would have seen a shadowy figure peek out from behind the rocky outcropping that lay 100 yards away. It slid away as quickly as it came.

Brian looked up and saw no one but Celia. He continued to negotiate with the radio.

23

Celia hung up the phone, stubborn in her refusal to call for backup despite the remonstrations of the voice inside her. Instead she pivoted her feet and stepped from the pavement to the sand.

Her boots immediately kicked dust into the air. Instead of scattering because of the wind, it came back down almost where it lay. Celia coughed and pushed onward, down the slight incline that led to the car.

As she got closer, she was able to make out that the car was a four-door sedan. A Mercury Topaz. Black.

She also saw that the vehicle sagged to one side. Its right front tire had burst, and now Celia was able to note pieces of rubber lying closer to the vehicle.

But if it had blown a flat, the rubber would have been in the road.

Celia kicked one of the pieces of rubber, causing it to rustle up more dust. She bent down. The rubber didn't have the uneven pattern of a tire that had completely blown out. It instead looked like someone had taken a knife to it the same way they would carve up a piece of red meat.

Celia wiped her brow and stood back up, brushing off her legs. From this distance, it was clear that no one was inside the vehicle.

Unless they're lying down.

Celia quieted the voice and approached the window, which was rolled completely up. At this temperature outside, it would have to be close to 130 or 140 inside. No one would be hiding in wait. A quick sweep of the vehicle confirmed this.

What she did find in the car was a wide array of drug paraphernalia.

Bongs, pipes, energy drink bottles filled with spent tobacco leavings. Empty baggies littered the back seat. Celia even took note of a couple used condoms.

What the fuck is going on here?

Celia tried the door, but it was locked. She placed her forehead against the glass to see further inside. Just more of the same.

The car shook as a loud BANG echoed from the trunk.

Celia jumped backwards, almost losing her balance as she tripped on a piece of rubber tire beneath her. But she caught herself and now looked toward the trunk. Another BANG, like something inside was trying to force its way out.

And now Celia heard a whimpering, animal-like. Whatever was in there was in pain.

Her instincts now taking over, Celia peeled around to the trunk and tried it. Like the car, it was locked.

"I'll be there in just a minute. Hold on!" she yelled, silently praying to God that it wasn't a kid inside.

As she moved toward the driver's side door, she stole a glance back at Brian. He had opened the door to the police car and was staring toward her, one hand shielding his eyes from the sun.

She didn't have time for him now. She pulled her police baton out and swung it into the window. The glass shattered and rained down on the scraps of paraphernalia inside. Celia unlocked the door and then popped it open.

She was assaulted by the smell of fresh, sunbaked shit when she leaned her head in the door. The temperature inside coupled with the smell made it nearly impossible to breathe. Coughing, she swatted at the air around her and pressed on.

She looked for the lever to pop the trunk open near the steering wheel, didn't see it there, and then directed her gaze lower.

Well, there's our culprit for the smell.

A pile of shit lay near the seat. It seemed to shimmer in the heat of the vehicle. Celia coughed and was about to look elsewhere when she saw a part of a lever sticking out from beneath the decaying scat.

It was the lever of the trunk.

Celia stood up and caught her breath outside the car. If there was shit on the trunk lever…

It means someone left it for you. They knew exactly how you would react.

Celia felt cold then despite the heat. What had appeared to be a random set of circumstances suddenly felt anything but. The person who had placed the call had known that a cop would come out here, investigate, and need to gain access to the trunk. They had spread shit around the lever anticipating this.

This is purposeful.

But was it purposeful to her or just a cruel joke being played by some kids out of school for the summer who had nothing better to do? DNA tests would reveal whose shit it was, whose condoms those were, whose hair was in the bags of meth, so this wouldn't have been carried out by someone of sterling intelligence. A group of lowlifes from The Rocks, or maybe just some assholes passing through.

A flash of light as if from a mirror reflecting the sun caused her to look up and toward the outcropping that lay further down the road, then as quickly as that it was gone.

Is someone watching me?

Celia continued to look up, thinking that maybe the light source would reveal itself again, but no luck. Just rocks. And desert. Lots and lots of desert.

The whimpering picked up its pace now, getting louder and more frantic.

"Oh, fuck," Celia said, going back into the stench-ridden car and reaching for the lever. Her hand hesitated; she wasn't one to be overly concerned about the prettiness of her nails but for fuck's sake.

She stood back up and stuck her foot inside, scraping the shit off of the trunk lever as best she could, wiping it on the floor mat. She tried to pop the trunk with the toe of her boot, but to no avail. Cursing under her breath, Celia stuck two fingers beneath the lever, trying not to think of what was squishing in her hand, and pulled forward.

The trunk gave with a *POP* and the whimpering stopped. Celia rushed to the back of the car and then pushed the trunk all the way up.

A coyote lay inside, so gaunt that Celia couldn't believe it was still alive. It was panting and whimpering intermittently, looking up at her with black eyes. Celia was confronted now with a different smell, that of blood and matted fur.

Both of the coyote's hind legs had been broken and now dangled loose beneath it. The fur around that area was nearly chewed off

     PERSISTENCE

and blood had formed from the coyote gnawing on itself in a feeble attempt to staunch the pain.

Celia reached for the animal and it nipped at her, surprisingly fast for its condition. She pulled her hand away just in time.

Who would do this to an animal?

Tears filled her eyes. She had always been able to handle any number of violent incidents against people, as fucked up as they tended to be. But when people messed with animals it really, really pissed her off. She got a vision of taking whatever redneck was responsible and breaking <u>his</u> legs and stuffing <u>him</u> in the back of a trunk.

The coyote continued to pant and now yowled at the sky. Celia reached forward again but it just bit at her. It was torn between its need for assistance and its animal instinct to expect none.

You can't save it.

Celia unholstered her weapon. There was nothing that could be done. Her and Brian working together wouldn't be able to maneuver the wounded coyote out of the car and toward her squad car. The pain would be too intense for the creature.

Celia flicked the safety off of her pistol. By all accounts it should have been dead already, given the loss of blood and the heat inside the trunk.

Never underestimate a cornered animal that wants nothing more than to live.

Celia suddenly had a flash of a memory, of her father taking her fishing when she was six years old. One of her dad's friends had caught a catfish while her father was off going to the restroom. He had reeled it in and then slapped it on the dock. He took a bowie knife and pressed as hard as he could against the fish's skull while it flapped.

But the skull wouldn't give. A catfish's upper portion is made almost entirely of bone and was damn near impossible to get through. You're supposed to go through the bottom.

But this guy didn't know that, and Celia watched as the skull had finally cracked. The fish had flailed more frantically then, and all Celia could do was stare, not crying, not saying anything really, just watching as the guy took his knife back and forth across the fish's skull, trying to cut off its head. When that failed, he turned the fish over and gutted it, pulling its guts out one by one, and still the fish continued to struggle. It had lost its every organ and yet it still moved, either out of muscle memory or a final attempt to get away.

Celia's father had walked up then, with a machete, and jammed the knife deep into the fish's gullet, driving the blade into where Celia imagined its brain would be.

"Thanks, Darryl," said the family friend. "Jesus, that thing was giving me a helluva time."

Celia's father had slapped the man in the face then. He gasped and reached his hand up toward a cheek now burgeoning with red.

"Don't finish what you can't start," said Celia's father. He took Celia roughly by the hand to lead her back to their truck.

The memory faded and Celia was left looking at the coyote, its eyes staring up at her and its tongue lolling out of its mouth.

"You were brave," she said.

Then, before she could talk herself into changing her mind, she pointed the pistol at its head and pulled the trigger.

The noise of the shot reverberated throughout the desert, but it didn't echo. There was nothing for it to echo against, and just like that it was silent again. The coyote's panting and whimpering seized.

Celia holstered her weapon and her eyes passed over the interior of the trunk's lid for the first time. She had been so consumed with the dying animal that she failed to notice a message scrawled in what looked like blood.

Maybe they were expecting her to gasp. If so, they didn't know her nearly as well as they thought. Instead, she scowled and slammed the trunk shut.

Still, as she walked back toward what must have surely been a befuddled Brian waiting expectantly in her squad car, her breathing shorter than she would have liked, she couldn't get the message out of her mind or stop from wondering about its significance.

The message, in blood, had read in full:

Its Fate Is Nothing Compared To Yours, Celia.

24

Brian watched the incident play out from his perch inside the squad car. He saw Celia look over the vehicle, rushing from the front door to the trunk and then back, smashing out the front window before leaning inside.

He considered running out to Celia to help at this point, but had to stop himself. He may have felt slightly emasculated, but there was little he could do in such a situation that she wasn't better trained to do herself. He also knew that he was on thin ice with Celia as it was, and so he decided that it might be best to stay put.

Instead, he cranked the A/C another notch, thankful for the cold air. Celia may have been from Nevada but Brian was not. He was a New England boy through and through and had never much cared for the heat. He kicked up the air again, to its full potential, and then leaned back, closing his eyes.

A gun shot caused his eyelids to jerk back open and his head to turn in Celia's direction. He was unable to see her and so assumed that she was behind the trunk.

Just as he was getting ready to pull the handle of the door and go see what was going on, the trunk of the wrecked car slammed shut and Celia came back around, walking toward Brian.

He untensed his body as Celia came closer and closer to the car.

25

Its Fate Is Nothing Compared To Yours, Celia.

Celia had had enough of this shit. Whoever had brought her out here knew who she was and was trying to scare her.

You are scared, the voice inside her said.

She wasn't about to let them get any kind of satisfaction. She wasn't the dumb broad in some horror movie that runs upstairs instead of out of the house and into the street. She was a cop for chrissake.

You're just a little girl.

Then let them think that. Let them think what they want. They had tortured an animal like it was nothing.

They'll do the same to you. You and Brian. They'll force him to watch.

Celia shut the voice out, drawing closer to the callbox. Brian rolled down the window and peeked his head outside, shielding his eyes from the sun.

"What's going on?"

"Don't worry about it. Roll up the window and wait inside."

"I thought I heard a gunshot."

"You did, but it's nothing."

"Celia, what the fuck is going on?"

"Brian, I swear to God, get inside of that car."

He leaned back in then, but he didn't roll up his window. Celia headed toward the callbox.

She would call backup. Fuck them if they laughed at her, told her she was letting herself get spooked by a couple of rednecks who got her name off of a duty roster. They would tell her to call animal control, not the police, it's not a cop's job to pick up roadkill, even if it is in a trunk instead of the road itself.

You're a joke to them. Everything is. Like life's a Warner Brothers cartoon and you're Wile E. Coyote, chasing respectability but always getting screwed in the end. Meep meep.

Maybe that's what this was. The coyote in the trunk had rented an Acme anvil and crushed its own legs.

Meep meep.

The thought of the coyote being nothing more than a cartoon had the effect of cheering her up, of getting her to see past the horror of it all. Although she wasn't smiling as she reached the callbox, she wasn't deathly afraid either.

She intended to dial the station and have them send another squad car, maybe two, to help her clean up the mess. She expected a dial tone. What she got instead was silence.

She pushed down on the hook a couple times. Nothing.

No. Not nothing.

Not quite. Static. And then, the closer she listened, she picked up light piano music like what they had heard on the police radio before.

Celia pressed the hook a few more times. Still nothing. Then:

"Hello, Officer Miller."

She didn't recoil, didn't tense up. Only looked around at the desert, trying but failing to spot the source of whoever was on the line.

"Are you there, Officer Miller?" asked the voice, tinny and distorted as if passed through a filter.

Celia still said nothing. She looked back at Brian, who was squinting at her, trying to piece together what was going on.

"I'm going to assume that you can hear me and you're trying not to let the quiver in your voice show," said the person on the other line. "If you don't respond to what I have to say, I'll put a bullet in your boyfriend's head."

"You're bluffing," said Celia.

"Do you believe in God?" The person on the other end of the line sounded pleased to hear her voice.

"Goodbye, asshole," said Celia.

"Do you believe in God, Celia?"

Although fully intending to put the phone back down in its cradle, get into her squad car, and peel away toward Ravencourt, Celia also had a twisted desire to hear this person out, to figure out what they were doing.

"Yes," she said.

"We are your God now," said the voice. "You should have left it alone."

The static and the light piano music cut out. There was pure silence on the other end. No dial tone, no anything.

Celia turned back to the Challenger and her breath caught in her throat at what she saw.

Someone was standing across the road, in the middle of the open desert. He had appeared as if out of nowhere, there being seemingly no place for cover within hundreds of yards. He wore all black, except for his face. That was where an alien mask perched over his face. The mask was white and tear-dropped shape, like the standard version of a "grey." Its eyes were also teardrops, its mouth a straight line brooking no expression.

Celia unholstered her weapon and pointed it at the man, who simply stood motionless. Out of the corner of her eye she saw Brian turn toward where she was pointing the gun, but the rest of her focus was concentrated on the masked man.

"Raise your arms!" Celia shouted.

The man with the alien mask just stood there. As a merciful wind that had been missing just minutes earlier kicked up sand, he cocked his head to one side, as if to study Celia.

Shoot him.

But she couldn't. He was unarmed. Unnerving, but unarmed. She'd be kicked off the force.

She heard movement from behind her. And that was when shit really started to go downhill.

26

Celia's thinking went like this: the rev of an engine alerted her to the fact that there had to be a car behind her. Brian's wide-eyed expression and yelling of "Ce—" confirmed that suspicion. With no time to dodge to the left or right, and no real idea as to what approach the vehicle was taking, Celia jumped.

Her movement took her onto the roof of the Challenger, the gun dropping from her hand and rolling down the windshield to land on the wiper blades. Her breasts pushed against the roof, and Celia had one moment to pull herself further up, taking the pressure off her abdomen and swinging her legs level with the window. She felt one toe strike soft flesh, Brian letting out a yelp.

It was just in time. It seemed like her feet had barely cleared the door handle when the Challenger buckled from the weight of being struck by another car. Celia didn't see this car, but she felt its impact. The Challenger jerked to the left, pushed further into the road, its wheels coming slightly off the ground. She heard the pop of an airbag, surely the side curtain, which would have hit Brian with an impact hard enough to create a concussion.

Celia scrambled to grab a hold of something, anything, but there was no purchase on the roof. She caught a glimpse of the man in the alien mask, still looking on, expressionless, but her mind barely registered this fact as her hands, thick with sweat, slid off the roof, leaving smears of desert sand behind.

The car was struck again, not as powerfully this time, the second vehicle not having enough space to get going. Still, the force was enough to cause Celia to roll off the roof and down the windshield, landing on her back with a *THUD* on the hood of the Challenger.

Splayed out, her knees dangling from the car's hood, Celia raised her chin and looked toward the callbox.

The black Mercury, the one with the dead coyote in the trunk, had inexplicably appeared and was now reversing, past the callbox, until it stopped. Its fender was bent from the run-in with the sturdier Challenger.

Another man in a hoodie wrapped around an alien mask was behind the wheel. The lack of expression was unnerving as the driver switched into drive and plowed forward.

Where the hell did he come from?

The car revved past the callbox, and Celia became aware that the driver wasn't aiming for the doors as before, but for her legs, which hung past the wheel well on the passenger side.

Celia lifted her legs up just as the Mercury plowed into the Challenger again. She kept herself from moving by keeping one hand wrapped in a vise grip around the windshield wiper. When the vehicle was struck, she felt the Challenger fall down to the right as the tire gave out from the full weight of the opposing vehicle. The Challenger itself may have been built like a tank, but wheels were wheels. Puncture-resistant or not, they couldn't take multiple shots from a speeding car.

There was pounding on the windshield. Celia looked inside to see Brian yelling. His voice seemed far away. It was his pointing that registered. The tip of his finger was tapping against the glass, right where the pistol had landed when it had fallen out of her hand.

Celia let go of the windshield wiper blade and grabbed the gun. The Mercury had reversed course again, moving past the callbox, *that goddamn callbox that started this mess.* The car left tracks in the desert as it went.

Celia sat up now, feeling but ignoring a throbbing pain in her elbow as she raised the pistol in the stance her father had taught her long before she entered the academy. There had been multiple instances when a trip to the arcade with a boy who had a crush on her in middle school would cause the boy's crush to falter the moment she left him in the dust in a light-gun game.

The Mercury stopped, its tires spinning out dust, its engine revving as the driver switched gears. The tires struggled to find purchase but then caught in the dry earth, sending the vehicle bucking forward, right toward Celia.

She took a breath and aimed at the area in the center of the alien mask. Although expressionless, she imagined the eyes of the man behind the mask were going wide at the sudden thought of his imminent demise.

The man ducked and the car continued forward. Celia squeezed off a shot, which immediately shattered the windshield of the opposing car. The vehicle veered slightly off kilter, heading toward the front corner of the Challenger.

Sit back up and look at me you mother fucker.

But he didn't. Instead, the vehicle plowed ahead, crashing into the corner of the Challenger. From her vantage, Celia could see Brian's head ricochet backwards as the front passenger airbag popped open.

Two concussions for the price of one.

Shards of glass from the aggressing Mercury's shattered windshield now scattered across the hood, cutting up her legs, and then Celia was sliding backwards off the driver's side of her own vehicle. Suddenly there was no car beneath her and she was falling. Her back struck the concrete and she grunted in pain.

Celia waited for the rev of the engine to indicate that it was backing up yet again, but there was no such noise. In fact, an eerie silence had descended, the other vehicle having broken down, the only sound the ringing in Celia's ears and the red-hot pain at the base of her spine.

She sat up, pistol still clutched in one hand, and used the hood of her car to hoist herself to her feet.

The man in the alien mask was trying to get his door open, but it was pinned shut by the corner of the Challenger. He saw Celia as she raised her gun, gaining satisfaction out of an imagined look of panic she saw on his face as she squeezed the trigger…

She was tackled forward from behind, her shot going wide of his face. Still, she heard a yell, and out of the corner of her eye caught the masked man clutching at his shoulder.

Celia had her face pressed against the hood of the hot car, her skin being mashed against the shards of glass that were still deposited there.

This is what a perp must feel like. At least the glass in my face distracts me from the searing back pain.

Someone was behind her, pushing and pushing her face into the car. Celia struggled but to no avail. Their hands moved downward, toward her neck, and now they were choking her, flecks of glass that had gotten caught up in the burlap of the gloves now digging into her neck.

Don't wear gloves if you want to choke someone, asshole.

It was true. The man couldn't gather the force necessary to cut off her breath. So while she was indeed pinned against the car, the threat of her life being snuffed out by the man's ineffective hands was small.

The gun was still in Celia's right hand, but she couldn't aim it effectively with her arm pinned awkwardly beneath her.

Instead, she pushed it forward, across the hood, where Brian waited. He had crawled out of the window when Celia had been tackled. Now, he lifted the gun and pointed it at the man who had Celia pinned.

Celia would have laughed if she weren't being choked to death. Brian held the gun the way one would hold a venomous python with an STD: at a distance and with thoughts of washing his hands when the incident was over.

But what he lacked in enthusiasm he made up for in action. No sooner had he raised the pistol then a muzzle flash erupted from the chamber, its sound cutting through the air like a knife. The first shot did nothing, but Brian was ready with two additional shots.

The third finally struck home. Celia felt pressure removed from her abdomen as the man behind her fell away. Celia got to her feet, looking back and down to see the man who was behind her clutching his stomach.

Jesus that shot had to be a couple of inches above my head.

Celia kicked the man in the neighborhood of where the bullet had struck. Then she kicked him again. And again. And again and again and again, her foot striking out up and down the man's body, Celia gaining particular satisfaction from the *crunch* she felt when the toe of her boot punched through the cheap plastic of the man's alien mask and made contact with the bridge of his nose.

Brian was yelling her name, but it was as if from far away. Celia's head pounded, her every desire focused on the toe of her right foot, going in and out, in and out, no thought given to anything else.

A gunshot rang out behind her. Survival instinct kicked in once again. Celia reeled around.

Brian had the pistol pointed in the same ineffective manner. It was he who had fired the shot, up in the air. He looked at her now, his frightened eyes unbecoming of a man holding a gun.

"What?!" she yelled, more forcefully than she intended but just forceful enough given the shit she had just been through.

"Look," he said.

Celia turned around and her heart sank.

Five men were walking toward the road from the western side of the desert. Each was clothed in black and wearing a nondescript alien mask. Some carried knives, others pistols, one a shotgun.

The man in the lead must have stood six foot five, or perhaps Celia simply imagined it that way. Or maybe it was the chainsaw that looked like a child's plaything when cupped in his meaty hands.

He revved the chainsaw, its blade coming to life and interrupting the unsettling silence. He cut through a cactus that stood in his path and moved on, his foot finally reaching the cement and bringing him within 10 yards of Celia.

She screamed to Brian at the top of her lungs:

"Get in the car!"

27

Celia slammed the door and locked it behind her. Brian did the same on the other side, rolling up his window. Through everything, Celia forgot that the keys had remained in the car with Brian this entire time.

She lunged for them now, starting the engine as a loud metal on metal whirring and screeching sound reached her ears. Miraculously, even after the repeated buckling incurred from the other vehicle crashing into it, the car started right up.

Celia looked up to identify the metal on metal sound and, to her horror, the masked man with the chainsaw was moving the blades across the rubber of the front driver's side tire. Although she couldn't see it, she could smell it, the smell of burnt rubber drifting in through the vehicle's vents. The car buckled on that side as the tire gave out.

She threw the vehicle into drive and hit the gas. It bucked forward, making an unpleasant screeching sound as the hubcap of the tire spun against the concrete.

The Challenger didn't move.

"Celia," said Brian from beside her.

"I know, Brian!" she yelled, throwing the car in reverse, not expecting much and cursing the heavens when her suspicions were confirmed. The car wouldn't move, no matter how much she pleaded with it. A car without tires is just a Brooklyn apartment wrapped around an engine.

Celia put the car in park.

"What are you doing?" asked Brian.

     Persistence

"They can't get in," she said.

"What do you mean they can't get in? They've got a chainsaw. And guns."

"The glass is bulletproof. It can withstand anything."

"I don't want to put that to the test."

The masked man raised the chainsaw in his arms. He looked around at the other masked men as if for approval. They had surrounded the vehicle on all sides, cradling their weaponry and watching things transpire.

An alien-masked man at the front of the car's hood looked directly at Celia. He carried no weapons. Instead, his fists were clenched down at his sides. They were covered in gloves along with everyone else's.

This man nodded his head.

You. You're the ringleader. I cut off the head and the body dies.

Whereas the rest of the masked men wore black jeans, his were blue, as if he failed to read a company-wide email about the dress code.

SUBJECT: Company Trust-Building Retreat.
Attention All:

Hey Gang, can't wait to see you at the big desert retreat! Dress is business casual, black jeans are encouraged, bring comfortable shoes, and last of all, don't forget to bring your nondescript alien mask for when we all murder the cop.

Celia snorted at her own macabre joke as the man with the chainsaw jumped on the hood. He stood up to his full height, and Celia felt the entire car sink beneath his weight. He lifted the chainsaw to the top of his head, looked around at the rest of those gathered, and then brought the tool down on the glass.

The noise reminded Celia of when she had been mowing the lawn one summer, she must have been about 12, and the mower had gotten away from her and crashed into a garden gnome. The blades had cracked against the gnome's head, *crack crack crack,* the sound deafening.

This was like that, but more rapid fire. The glass got scuffed up at the point of contact, but it didn't bend or break. The man moved the chainsaw from side to side across the windshield. Still nothing.

Frustrated, he lifted the chainsaw again and brought it down, this time as hard as he could. There was a crunch but still no give. The entire vehicle vibrated but wouldn't cave.

Now, the man dropped the chainsaw and pointed a pistol at the glass.

"Celia…"

"It won't give, Brian. Let them waste their ammo."

He squeezed the trigger, the muzzle flash barely registering in the bright light of day. The bullets cracked against the glass, and while these registered more than the chainsaw, the glass held solid. A jagged cloud pattern formed in the center of the windshield where the bullets struck.

The man dropped his pistol to the hood and picked up the chainsaw anew. He pulled its ripcord to get it going again and brought it down on the area where he shot the glass. The sound was a bit different, thicker somehow, but the blades failed to penetrate the windshield.

He raised the chainsaw again and Celia slammed on the horn, which caused the main with the chainsaw to jump in alarm at the unexpected sound. Through the glass, she heard the sound of muffled laughter.

The aliens are giving him shit for jumping like a girl.

The man was about to bring the chainsaw down when the masked man at the head of the car raised his hand and his voice. Celia couldn't tell what he said, but the man with the chainsaw stepped down off the car and approached him.

"What are they talking about?" asked Brian.

"The state of American exceptionalism abroad. Who gives a fuck?" Celia said, not meaning to sound so bitchy but also kinda meaning to sound so bitchy.

The man with the chainsaw turned now, back to Celia. The other man, the one in the blue jeans, yelled something at two of the other masked men. They came around toward the driver's side of the car and picked up their compatriot, the one who had been shot in the belly by Brian and kicked repeatedly by Celia.

They draped his arms around their necks and hoisted him on top of the car, laying his body on the hood and his head on the windshield. The man was facedown, letting Celia and Brian look into his blank alien's eyes.

His stomach pressed and depressed against the hood as he let labored breaths in and out. He clutched at the bullet wound with one hand. That hand, though, as well as the other, were now being pulled toward the corners of the windshield as his fellow masked men grabbed him. They held each hand toward a corner.

A shadow filled up the sky. It was the man with the chainsaw, hovering over the one splayed on the windshield.

"No," said Brian.

The man revved the chainsaw. It came to life in his hands. The masked man who stared at them struggled now, trying to get his arms out of the grasp of the other men.

His struggles were useless. The chainsaw came down on the glass on the left side of the man's face. Celia didn't watch. Instead, she kept her eyes fixed on the other man, the leader, who stood immobile at the head of the Challenger. As the blade of the chainsaw moved to the side, cutting through sinew and arteries and finally bone, she never took her eyes off the one with the blue jeans. Even as Brian gasped and covered his eyes and the chainsaw finally pulled away from the man's body and the head slid toward the side with a sickening squeegee sound, she didn't look away.

Instead, she popped on the wiper blades so that they cut a path through the blood. The blade on the right picked up the severed head and sent it scurrying off the right-hand side of the car. Through the smear of blood, Celia leaned forward, never letting her eyes leave those of their leader.

One of the others picked the head back up and pushed the body off the hood of the car. He then took off his gloves, dipped his thumb in the bottom of the dead man's neck, and painted an upside-down cross on the front of his own mask.

His face-painting complete, the man now sat his dead pal's still-masked head up on the hood, facing directly into the windshield at Celia and Brian, like the world's most macabre hood ornament.

"What's wrong with these people?" asked Brian. "Who just turns on their own people like that? They're like animals. Savages."

He looked over at Celia, who continued to stare ahead, unblinking.

Scream. Yell. Shout. This is easily the most horrible thing you've ever seen. Cry to the heavens, let yourself fall into Brian's arms. He would let you.

But she didn't feel like doing that. Not now. Instead she felt angry. Very angry.

"Celia, what's wrong with you?"

Am I shell shocked? Is this what shell shock feels like?

"How can you just sit there feeling nothing? Look what they did!"

Now she snapped her head around, and Brian pulled away, toward the glass.

"I don't feel nothing. I feel joy," Celia said, the words feeling like a lie but sounding how they needed to sound for her to keep her sanity.

"Joy?"

"They came out here to kill a girl," she said. "But they fucked with the wrong woman."

28

"Did you try just throwing it into one of these gears?" asked Brian. "And maybe reversing back and forth a little bit?"

"It won't work. All we'll do is wear out the battery. Without the tires we're screwed."

"Maybe that other car. It ran, right? We could set up a distraction, run to it."

"We're surrounded by half a dozen people with guns pointed at us, Brian. A distraction isn't going to cut it."

"Let me think, let me think." He eyed the key in the ignition. "Maybe let me try, see if I can get us moving."

Celia's annoyance grew. Right now, all she needed Brian to do was be quiet and let <u>her</u> think. Clearly he was just trying to help, but all he succeeded in doing was testing her patience. His attempt to help was really just another way not to trust her judgment, the judgment of a cop. Instead, he wanted to try things that she herself knew would be pointless.

And that was what really irritated her, she supposed. In his quest for a solution to an unsolvable problem, Brian would still suggest that he try it, even if Celia tried and it didn't work. She would turn the key, rock the car back and forth on worthless tires, stop, and then Brian would rub his chin, and make the same goddamn suggestion that they switch seats so that he could try. After trying and failing, but doing so in a way that showed his muscles strain as he really worked the clutch into the various gears, he would then rub his chin some more, and say something like, "I just don't know."

And then Celia would shoot him in the head. Not really. But the thought occurred.

"Celia?"

"I'm thinking. And no, you're not trying."

Brian sat back, defeated, and stared at the alien mask-wearing men surrounding the vehicle.

"What do they want?" asked Brian.

"It's not <u>what</u> do they want. It's <u>why</u> do they want," Celia replied.

The voice from the callbox reverberated in her head:

"You should have left it alone."

Had they found out about her investigation somehow? She had told no one yet except for Brian. She had been on the verge of telling Haddock yesterday but was interrupted…

"Haddock."

"Huh?" asked Brian.

"Haddock," she repeated, following the train of thought. "He was carrying on an investigation into these guys. But now it seems convenient. A random State Police detective, swooping in out of nowhere despite Ravencourt PD keeping all but a couple scant mentions of the Illegals' crimes out of the press.

"You think his appearance wasn't really all that random?"

"I don't know what to think right now. Maybe it wasn't. Maybe it was damage control."

"Could he know what you've been up to? All that stuff in your kitchen?"

"Maybe. Maybe it's someone else. Or maybe I just cut someone off in traffic and their payback has gotten out of hand. There are too many unknowns."

"And," said Brian, "does it really matter when we're stranded in a car with no means of escape?"

The masked men had taken a few steps back after finishing off their friend, their hands never leaving their triggers. A few of them — Blue Jeans, Crossface, and The Giant (as Celia had quickly come to think of them) — had gathered in a meeting of sorts while the others, having pushed the broken Mercury away from Celia's vehicle and past the callbox into the desert, looked on a few feet from the vehicle. After some discussion, and after the man Celia shot in the shoulder had gotten bandaged up, they all surrounded the car. All except for Blue Jeans, who had broken off from the group to walk to and then crest the bluff up ahead, for what purpose Celia couldn't nor didn't want to fathom.

"They want me," said Celia.

There was no doubt, in her mind at least, that it was indeed her that they were trying to get to. The message on the trunk's interior left no doubt about that, nor did the voice on the phone. Brian was a surprise, as was the Challenger. If he hadn't been going to ride out to break things off with his girlfriend, a bottle of Oxy in his pocket…

Pretty convenient, isn't it?

Celia's skin felt clammy in an instant. She looked over at Brian, who still eyed the key, working through his mind if he was going to suggest letting him try the ignition again.

He just happened to be out in the desert? When you get a call inviting you out to the callbox in the middle of nowhere, on a road that no one travels?

That was when Celia noticed that the gun was still clutched in Brian's right hand. Since the moment she had watched a man get his head cut off, she hadn't had time to give much thought to her gun…

But it was Brian who had shot the man in the first place. If he hadn't done that, the masked man would have killed Celia. If he wanted her dead, he wouldn't have shot the man…

The same man whose head they just chopped off. Maybe someone who was expendable. Someone else they wanted killed. Brian started the job and the aliens had finished it.

"How many bullets are in the chamber?" asked Celia.

Brian looked down at the gun as if he forgot it was there. He raised it up, holding it against the back of his palm like he was showcasing a watch, scrutinizing the weapon for some kind of switch.

"I don't know how to…"

But Celia was already grabbing the gun out of his hand. The ring around the trigger caught his thumb, slashing it as Celia pulled the weapon away. As Brian tried to stanch the blood flow, Celia was already backed against her window, pointing the gun directly at Brian's head.

The men in the masks approached the vehicle.

"Call them off," said Celia.

"Celia, what the hell…"

"Call off your men or I'll blow your brains out."

"You think I had something to do with this?"

Brian's eyes were wide with genuine shock.

Not genuine, she thought. *He's been lying this entire time.*

"What were you doing out here, Brian?"

"I already told you."

"Do you know how few people come out this way on a given day? Hell, in a given week? What are the chances?"

Now Celia's hand was shaking. She had slept with this man not hours before, had entertained *(more than entertained; hoped for)* the idea of going on a few dates and starting some sort of life with him. And in the end he had betrayed her.

They all betray you.

Her finger squeezed the trigger lightly. Brian saw the movement and panic entered his eyes.

"Celia, please don't do this."

"You lied to me. This is why you came to me last night? To punish me? For what, for wanting something more?"

And yet you must be sure.

Brian eyed the gun, unable even to speak. Celia took a deep breath, forcing herself to calm down.

"What were you doing out here?"

"My car broke down."

"Because you got lost."

"Yes."

"Because you were breaking it off with your girlfriend?"

"Yes."

"Do you know how unbelievable that sounds?"

"Okay, maybe I wasn't going to break it off with her exactly. But I thought about it."

"Tell me the truth."

"Fine" he yelled, slamming the dashboard with his palm. "I was in the area and just wanted to hook up. Is that what you need to hear? Jesus, Celia. I didn't quit college, I'm not breaking it off with the girl I'm seeing, I don't feel all that bad about pocketing your OxyContin, and this is the part I really hope you understand, *I didn't pay an armed militia to murder you in the desert.* Do you know how insane that sounds?"

It did sound insane. What motive did he have? Her finger wavered on the trigger.

"We had fun last night," Brian said. "Can't that be enough? How can I prove to you that me being out here stranded is genuine?"

Celia bit her lip, then stopped herself, hating when she bit her lip. She looked at the men outside the vehicles, who were looking on with interest.

But their guns aren't raised.

No, they weren't. They were fixed on what was transpiring in front of them, but one thing not one of them had done was lift their weapons.

If he were with them, they would have moved quickly. They would have fired based on instinct, even if they knew they couldn't get through the car's defenses.

Was it a coincidence? Did he just happen to be on this road when this happened?

She couldn't be sure. Maybe she'd never be sure.

You'll have to live with him. For now.

"Celia, please tell me what you're thinking."

She was thinking that they were paying more attention to watching the soap opera play out in the car than they were to their own shuffling feet and lack of awareness. She was thinking that their weapons were loose in their hands, not ready to be cocked. She was thinking that by looking past Brian, just to the right of his head, she could see one of the mask-wearing men, the one with the fresh shoulder bandages, bent over, craning his neck downward to see what was going on inside, the butt of his rifle nearly hitting the concrete as he peeked in the car.

"If you want to prove to me that you were just in the wrong place at the very, very wrong time, you can keep looking at me, not reacting."

"Okay," said Brian.

"And without looking back or moving your head at all, not one inch, and while moving your arm very slowly, you can reach behind you and press the power window switch down."

He did as she asked, his hand crawling toward the window switch.

"And Brian. Do not move your head. At all."

To the masked man behind Brian's head, it appeared as if Celia was pointing the gun directly at Brian, when in fact she pointed it roughly two inches to the right of his left ear.

Brian's fingers found the power window switch, hesitated, and then he pressed down.

The window rolled down smoothly, and as Celia suspected, the man in the alien mask didn't react right away. It wasn't until the window was down a good three inches and Celia had pivoted her gun away from Brian's head and toward the dead center of the oval-shaped alien face that the man made a movement. His hands scrambled for his rifle as Celia squeezed the trigger.

The first bullet pierced the white plastic of the mask, shots of red squirting out like a popped pimple. The second bullet sank into the black eye hole, the damage to the man's eyes concealed behind torn black velvet. The third caught the man in the soft part of his chin as he fell backwards.

There wasn't a fourth shot. Celia did as she was trained, enough to get the job done, not enough to waste valuable ammunition.

"Roll it up!"

Brian did as he was told, the power window instantly moving back into its frame, sealing them off from the rest of the masked men. Three of those men were now running toward their downed comrade as two others fired their weapons impotently against the side of the squad car.

Celia lowered her pistol, the scent of gunpowder filling her nostrils as it emanated throughout the cabin of the car. The alien in the blue jeans had appeared back over the bluff, running toward the group that had gathered around the man who now lay motionless, half his body on the shoulder of the road, the other half in the desert sand, which was becoming pronouncedly darker as his blood pooled out.

When he got closer, Blue Jeans leaned over the one who had been shot, his body blocking the view of the downed man. From Celia's vantage point, she couldn't see the wounded man's face as they pulled his mask away.

Blue Jeans shot up instantly, turning toward the Challenger, covering his mouth with the back of his hand. His expressionless eyes bored into Celia, his body language giving away the anger he now felt.

He yelled something at the others, who put the mask back on the dead man.

Blue Jeans unslung his own weapon, a shotgun, and fired it directly at the window. Brian flinched, but the glass didn't give. Celia just stared at the man, who fired off five shots before finally giving up.

She brought up her right hand, extended her pointer finger, and lifted her thumb toward the roof of the car to make a finger gun gesture. She clicked her thumb down on the imaginary trigger and then blew the imaginary smoke off the tip of her finger.

   PERSISTENCE

Blue Jeans stared at her, his left fist curling into a ball.

"That should get him good and pissed off," said Celia.

"Oh," said Brian. "Fantastic."

29

It did get him good and pissed off. First, Blue Jeans grabbed the chainsaw from his pal and used it to no avail on the windows. Then he tried to pry the hood open, using the blade to dig into the crevice between the hood and the side of the car. When that also failed to bear fruit, he grabbed his other buddy's shotgun and fired directly at Celia's driver's side window. The glass was now pockmarked to the point where it looked like an opaque glass pizza, but still it refused to budge.

Celia shut off the car as Blue Jeans paced back and forth, trying but failing to come up with some way to get in the vehicle.

"Do you believe me now?" asked Brian.

"I don't know. But I'm leaning toward not killing you."

"That's not funny."

Celia unloaded the clip from her gun and weighed it in her palm. To confirm that it was spent, she looked at it quickly and then discarded it by Brian's feet.

"Look in the glove compartment," she told him. "See if there's any ammunition."

Brian opened the glovebox to find a half pack of Life Savers, insurance papers, vehicle registration, and a copy of a *Busty Bimbos* magazine. Based on the proportions of the woman on the cover, the editors of *Busty Bimbos* certainly held to the journalistic maxim to never bury the lead.

"I see a couple of guns but no ammo," said Brian, pulling the magazine out and quickly thumbing through its contents.

"That's sexist. She could be trying to get her GED. Are you really going to look through that right now?"

"Celia, why do you have a dirty magazine? The internet is a thing that exists now, you know."

"Not out here it doesn't. And it's not my magazine. It's Jason's."

"Who's Jason?"

"You met him last night."

"Oh, that's right. The charmer who about broke my arm."

"He certainly has his moments," said Celia.

"Do those moments include dressing up like an alien to get back at the woman who scorned him?"

Celia's eyes snapped toward Brian.

Was there something to that?

But then she thought back. Back to the string of killings. She realized that it couldn't possibly be true. And when she thought about the murders, it framed everything in a whole new way.

"It wasn't Jason," she said.

"How can you know?"

"Because Jason's a cop. And because this isn't the first time this has happened. You saw my kitchen."

"Do you think these are the same guys?" asked Brian. "The ones the State Police have been after?"

"I don't even know if the same guys <u>were</u> the same guys."

"What do you mean?"

Celia looked around, confirming that the men stationed around had not moved, were not trying anything. Blue Jeans had wandered off somewhere, likely to formulate a plan as to what to do to gain access to the vehicle.

"It doesn't make sense. It never made sense. If this were a gang we were talking about, or even a like-minded group of serial killers, there would be some sort of pattern. That's what has me stopped in my tracks. Let's say you get your jollies off eating the eyeballs of college coeds..."

"Graphic," said Brian.

"Once you kill one person," said Celia, "you don't deviate. You have your type. It's the same with all criminals. Even gangs, organized crime, there's some pattern. Something you can point to that leads from Point A to Point B.

"But this is different. It starts off with a robbery of a liquor store. Small change, maybe a few hundred dollars. Then it progresses to an execution-style murder of a man with no rap sheet left with three lowlifes whose records read like the novelization of an episode of *Cops*. Capping it all off is a heist requiring careful planning, weeks of casing, and balls like grapefruits. *Ocean's 11* these guys weren't, but knowing what to hit and when to hit it still took patience and foresight. And intelligence. Add to that random unsolved crimes throughout the area and the property purchases up at The Rocks and none of it adds up."

"What are you thinking?" asked Brian.

"Not much until now," said Celia. "You can't act on an urban legend. Plus it wasn't my case. I'm not a detective. And Ravencourt isn't exactly the kind of department known for putting together a task force. Cases are filed singularly, coming across the Chief's desk if there's any mention of a man in an alien mask.

"But there has to be some connection. It's like we're missing a piece. Like I'm missing a piece."

"You have to be close to something, right? That incident you talked about at The Rocks. Something to do with that?"

"That's the million-dollar question, isn't it? What am I close to? What's the one piece of the puzzle that brought us into their sights?"

Brian sighed. "You're thinking if you find that, you may figure out who they are."

Celia nodded.

"The bust-up by The Rocks. A microwave full of drugs and cash. Two rednecks sprung from jail far easier than they should have."

"And the other investigation," said Brian. "Haddock, right? The State Police just happen to have someone stationed in Ravencourt, his investigation running concurrent with your own?"

"Maybe that's it," she said. "Maybe he's not involved. Maybe it's the opposite."

"I don't understand," he said.

"Let's say the noose is tightening, they're getting nervous. They went quiet for a while but the casino job took things too far. The masks, the very things that concealed their identities, now have them at the center of a state investigation. And if I can connect the meth to it, the meth that traveled across state lines, and I go to Chief Burton or someone even higher up with my suspicions, suddenly you're talking Feds. Real cops with real resources. The types of resources that can look at the big picture and ferret out the things a small-town police force would miss."

"What kind of operation are they?" asked Brian. "Cartel, something like that?"

Celia shook her head. "Cartel crime is overblown. People think the cartel is responsible for every crime between here and bumfuck Nebraska but don't stop to think that the last thing a drug-running enterprise wants is to get the attention of a highly motivated, multi-billion-dollar anticrime force like the DEA.

"No, this is different. A local operation, maybe. Neo-Nazi upstarts from up in the hills branching into the drug trade to gain more income. Or an offshoot of some East Coast mob looking to expand, something like that."

"Or maybe they're just garden variety psychos," said Brian.

"That's shockingly plausible," said Celia. "Ravencourt and the surrounding counties have had, what, six missing persons in the past year? Not a lot, but also not exactly a small amount by the standards of a town this size.

"Whatever it is, they've been perfecting their art for a long time now. They're good at what they do. As far as I know, they have never failed when they set out to do something. And what they want to do now is hang my head from the antenna like a foam pair of Mickey Ears."

They stopped talking for a few minutes then, Celia examining the clues from every angle in her head and Brian no doubt becoming increasingly uncomfortable next to her. Finally, when he couldn't take it anymore, he broke the silence.

"What's with the masks anyway?" asked Brian. "Are ski masks not good enough anymore?"

Now Celia smiled. "Don't you know how close we are to Area 51?"

"Huh?"

"The government declassified the area not long ago. Finally admitted to the existence of Area 51, not too many desert miles south of our proud little town. Of course, they didn't admit the aliens, just the aircraft testing. For years Ravencourt has had a little alien cottage industry. There's even a bar in the proper side of town decked out with all manner of greens and grays. Aliens in sombreros, aliens in mariachi outfits, aliens dressed like Elvis."

"Dressed like Elvis?"

"Yuh huh. You can't swing a dead cat without hitting some kind of alien paraphernalia in the town. Tourists who really need an education as to what a vacation consists of have been dropping in since the '80s trying to sneak a peek at a ship in the sky. Sometimes they get lucky. Usually they see nothing. Ravencourt may not be Roswell, but its alien population at least pegs it as a distant cousin. So these bastards clearly have a sense of humor."

"I fail to see it," said Brian.

"Live in the desert for a few more years," said Celia, turning off the vehicle and pulling the key out of the ignition. "Everything will start to seem funny."

"Why'd you stop the car?"

"I've got about an eighth of a tank of gas. We need to conserve as much of the power for air conditioning as we can."

"What about right now? It must be 114 degrees outside."

"Let's cross that bridge once we see what he wants," said Celia.

"What who wants?"

Celia pointed out the windshield, where Blue Jeans was walking toward the car.

"Our buddy here."

30

It wasn't supposed to be like this, thought the man that Celia had come to not-so-affectionately call Blue Jeans. *We got cute. We should have just killed her.*

But that was the past, and now she was trapped in there, with some Ivy League nigger who barely knew how to brandish a pistol. And yet he was still alive, as was she, two of his own men were dead, and they were no closer to getting into the car.

She wasn't supposed to be in <u>that</u> car. The police department had a half dozen vehicles, five of them from many moons and winnowed-down budgets ago, but she had to go and drive the tank.

They could theoretically get in there. But that would take time. And ammunition. And drives back in to town and back to get the ammunition and the necessary weaponry.

When he came over the hill and saw the car positioned 100 yards out, his vision turned red, anger getting the best of him.

Why did she have to be in that fucking car?

But it was impotent anger. He squeezed his hands into fists and repeated. And repeated again. He never had been able to get over his anger issues, nor in fact had he really tried. If someone were to tell him he should control his anger he would just get angry and the scene wouldn't be pretty.

You cunt. You fucking cunt.

Oh, how he wanted to scream it in her face. To let it drip off his tongue, to savor the word as he choked the life out of her.

She would not escape. Her vehicle was going nowhere. He had considered prying open the hood, getting at the engine, making sure they had no power so that they would fry in the heat. But one of his men had gotten a look inside, had seen the reading on the gas gauge, and assured him they would have no more than a couple of hours.

A couple hours was nothing. They would give up once that ran out. They had no food, no water that he was aware of. He and his men could wait a couple of hours if that's what it took. Time was on their side. They could wait it out as long as was necessary.

But he didn't want to wait it out. The thought of having to sit in the desert waiting for some cunt to die did not appeal to him in the least.

No, he would expedite the process.

Just like a woman, he thought, a smirk spreading across his sweaty face (he had gotten used to the suffocating nature of the alien mask by this point). *You try to move them along, try to get them going, but they're always late. Always dragging their feet, always putting on whore's makeup. You want them to cum, they take four times as long, and by then your dick's as limp as a noodle.*

And here we are, I'm telling you to die, you have to hem and haw about it, drag your feet, test my patience. Just like a fucking woman. Just like a cunt.

He never took his eyes off Celia as he walked up to the callbox. It had brought her out here. With some slight reconfigurations, it could bring others out here too.

She was a cop. Aside from being a woman, it would be her one weakness. Her desire to protect and serve (particularly the former, as the bitch never seemed willing to serve anybody) would compel her to act foolishly. Like a woman, she would let emotions cloud her judgment, cloud her own self-preservation even.

You fucking cunt, he thought as he picked up the phone. *Look what you made me do. Look what you fucking made me do.*

He would kill. And kill. And kill and kill again and again and a-fucking-gain if it meant he got to personally bash her brains in.

And with that last confident thought, the thought of knowing this would end with him sending her out of this world, bringing a respite from the anger, the man Celia had taken to calling Blue Jeans ordered a pizza.

31

They saw the dust cloud long before they saw the car. Where before there was only clear blue sky, there was now a tan fog in the air. The vehicle kicked it up as it weaved its way along the pavement.

Celia noticed it first. Her senses were as sharp as ever, despite the oppressive heat. Brian had tried, repeatedly, to get her to turn the air conditioning back on, but she refused. It wasn't half past noon, and she didn't want the car dying while the sun was still high in the sky. This time of the year, it wouldn't even begin its descent until 6:00 p. m. If they could hold out until then, they could hold out the entire night.

"Look alive," Celia said when she saw the dust kicked up in her rearview mirror.

Brian, hunched down in his seat, the three buttons on his polo shirt unbuttoned, sweat gathered on his brow, sat up and looked back. He had asked for something to drink five minutes ago, but there was nothing.

"More of them?" Brian asked, his throat dry, smacking his lips as if trying to suck the moisture out.

"I don't know."

Celia turned in her seat to peer through the slatted cage separating the front of the car from the back. In the background she could now make out a vehicle slowly coming closer, like a ship trailing a wake of dust rather than churned-up water.

She switched her focus to the foreground, to the back seat of the car. Behind that seat, in the trunk, were supplies that would give them a fighting chance. A rifle. Pistols. Ammunition. Body armor.

And unless one of the other men on the force had drank it, a warm but fully stocked gallon of water.

But right now the trunk may as well have been as far away as Vegas. They weren't getting into that trunk now. The moment she stepped foot outside of the car they would shoot her, and that would be the end of it.

The car drew closer. Celia could see now that it was another beat-up junker, (Ravencourt was just lousy with them) maybe from the early 2000s, not as ratty as the vehicle containing the coyote but not a winner either. It had the gray mundanity of an American make, maybe a Chevy.

As the car drove to within a half a mile or so, the alien men retreated at the behest of Blue Jeans. Rather than maintaining their places around Celia and Brian, they now ducked down behind her Challenger, behind the Topaz with the bodily fluids and the dead animal, and behind the little inclines of sand that trailed off on either side of the road.

Only Blue Jeans stood by, waving his arms toward the vehicle.

"What the hell's going on?" asked Brian.

As the car drew within a couple hundred meters, Celia saw a triangular shape on top of it. Like the kind of thing you would see on a...

"Is that a pizza delivery guy?"

The car kept coming, toward Blue Jeans, unaware of the various masked men that lay in wait just out of sight.

"If this were backup," said Celia, "they wouldn't hide. They would usher him in like a plane on the runway."

"What's that mean?"

"He's driving into a trap."

She turned her attention from the window to the controls on the dashboard. She flicked a switch and the lights fixed to the top of the Challenger came on. She moved her fingers over to the next switch, the one that controlled the noisemaker, and let out a *BOOP boop BOOP BOOP* that traveled across the empty desert, which was turning out to be not so empty after all.

The incoming car stopped, the driver no doubt surprised to see the familiar reds and blues of the police. The Challenger didn't look like a typical cop car, not from behind, but once you hit the lights there was no question.

Celia hit the noisemaker again and tried to get the pizza delivery

    PERSISTENCE

guy's attention, pressing her face up against the glass and hitting it with her palms. From there, the car but fifty feet away, she could make out the pimply face of a scrawny teen, a Schneider's Pizza cap pulled over his head to cover wild tufts of red hair, his face twisted into an expression of bewilderment.

With his attention focused on the cop car and the bizarre man in the blue jeans and the alien mask, the kid failed to notice another man in an alien mask, the Giant, circling around behind him. He had jogged a wide semicircle around the road to evade the delivery guy's sights, but now he had positioned himself in a manner that allowed him to hunch down and come at the beater car from an angle.

Though the kid in the car couldn't see him, Celia did, and she pounded harder against the glass. Now Brian joined in, although the kid couldn't possibly see him from his vantage point. The teen rolled forward slightly, trying to see what the person inside the vehicle was doing.

"Goddamn kid, just run, reverse, take off and never come back."

But he didn't. The gawky teen had probably been offered a hundred-dollar tip to bring a pizza out to the middle of nowhere, by the old callbox, and he figured, *shit, for 100 bucks I'll drive all the way to Reno. Probably just some hippies having their own personal Wicker Man festival in the desert and got the munchies.*

A hundred bucks was hard to pass up for a kid living in a town like Ravencourt. And so his vehicle moved inexorably forward, coasting on its own power rather than any gas input, going slow enough that the giant masked man was able to get right up to the kid's window.

Frantic, now, Celia turned in her seat. She lunged for the speaker that controlled the megaphone outside the car and pressed the button that activated the sound.

"Get the fuck out of here. Drive. DRIVE!"

The kid's eyes widened as he caught a flash of the man in the mask in his rearview mirror, but by then it was too late. The butt of a rifle came through the kid's window, spackling his skin with tiny shards of broken glass, and then the delivery boy was being pulled out of the car by the lapels of his Schneider's Pizza t-shirt. His Schneider's Pizza hat fell off his head and to the concrete, barely beating his body to the same place. The 16- or 17-year old kid rolled and then was immediately picked up by one meaty arm.

The lumbering giant had the boy on his feet and, though he struggled, the kid's fists were ineffective. The Giant didn't even react. The only move that elicited a reaction was when the teen thrust one bony arm upward and caught the chin of the mask, pushing it up on the man's face and allowing Celia to see a bare patch of tanned skin. When that happened, the man grabbed the boy by the hair and turned him around, lifting his boot and kicking the boy in his bony ass, sending him skidding across the concrete and toward Blue Jeans.

Blue Jeans didn't watch the boy, though. He looked at Celia, and Celia stopped her futile protests on the driver's side window. Instead, she looked back at the man in the mask with a look that she hoped suggested hate and loathing and I'm-gonna-kill-you-you-son-of-a-bitch scorn.

But what she really felt was fear. Fear for herself, for her own helplessness. Fear for the boy. Fear for what was about to happen next.

Rather than stay put, the boy got to his feet, his face turning red and his tears soaking up breath. He took off running, toward the desert, but two men in alien masks stood up like materialized phantoms. He pushed onward nevertheless, only to be caught by the two men. Though not as large as the man who had pulled the boy from his car, they still had the kid beat by a good couple of inches and pounds upon pounds of muscle.

They grabbed the boy's arms, lifted him off the ground, and then dumped him back on the concrete. Pinned in on three sides now, the boy ran to the cop car, figuring it was his last bastion of hope.

The masked men in Celia's vision, including the Giant, drew their weapons, ready to shoot. Though she didn't turn around, she assumed that those on Brian's side of the vehicle were also ready to shoot.

If she unlocked the door to let the boy in, they would open fire. He would die, and so would she.

The boy tried the back door first. When he found that it was locked, his throat gave a little hitch and he came around to Celia's door. It too was locked.

"Please," he yelled, his voice muffled as it carried through the bulletproof glass. "Let me in. You're a cop!"

Celia now saw a name tag on the boy's shirt: Lester. It hung down from the teen's scrawny frame as he pounded on the glass.

                    PERSISTENCE

It was the name tag that did it. Tears filled Celia's vision and then began to fall.

"I'm sorry, Lester" she said into the megaphone through tears that were very un-cop like but that she couldn't bottle up if she had the Hoover Dam in her tear ducts. She placed her hand against the glass. "I'm so sorry. Please forgive me."

"Celia, let him in." It was Brian, calling as if from far away.

Celia tried to respond, but her voice caught in her throat. She lowered her head, raised it, and tried again.

"I can't," she said through tears.

"He'll die," said Brian.

"So will we."

Blue Jeans now walked up behind the teen, who had ceased pounding on the window and now just stared at Celia through the glass. Sensing Blue Jeans's presence, the kid whipped around.

Blue Jeans showed the teen a knife. A large one, the kind you use to gut deer, or coyotes, with. It glinted in the light of the desert.

"We have to do something," said Brian.

"We can't."

"We can't just watch this."

Blue Jeans now looked from Celia, to the teen, to the knife. She sensed a smirk behind the mask.

That's when the teen spit in the man's mask. Celia suddenly felt a kinship with the teen, who had suddenly shown more bravery than most would be able to find in that situation. She wanted to open the door, to let him try his luck and dive in, but the Giant was standing with his gun at an angle that would allow him to immediately open fire on Celia if she opened the door.

So instead she sat there, vowing to kill everyone who now surrounded the car.

Blue Jeans wiped his mask with one hand, then looked at the teen. He looked back at Celia and cocked his head, as if to tell her she had one last chance to open the door.

Celia looked back, wiping tears from her face.

"I'm sorry," she whispered into the speaker. "I'm sorry."

Then she heard the passenger door fly open and the scuttling of feet as Brian leaned out of the car.

"Over here, get in, now!"

The teen turned to run, but Blue Jeans grabbed him by the shoulder and pushed him down, forcing the teen to slam awkwardly against the side of the cop car. Brian stood up and threw something at Blue Jeans, and as it fluttered down, Celia saw that it was the Busty Bimbos porno magazine that had been in the glove box.

Brian had a slight advantage over Celia in that they were focused on the other side of the car, but that had bought him two seconds at best. That time had expired, and the men on Brian's side of the car opened fire. Brian ducked his head back down, below the level of the window, grunting as he sat back inside. Bullets pinged along the dashboard.

"Shut the door, shut the door!" Celia repeated even as she now leaned over Brian to pull the door closed. One of the men in the alien masks was running toward the car full tilt while the others opened fire. Her hand grabbed around the handle and she pulled with all her might. She smelled gunpowder as a bullet zinged past her head and another landed with a salute next to her thumb.

Somehow, she got the door closed and, just before the charging man in the mask made it to the exterior handle, she pushed down on the lock and sealed them inside once more.

The perp struggled with the handle, growing frustrated and us-ing the butt of his shotgun to batter the windshield. Enraged now, he flipped the gun around and let out two bursts at point blank range; all they did was spackle the windshield, and the man cursed as he took a few steps back.

Brian clutched at his upper arm and hunched down in his seat. Celia noticed blood oozing out from between his fingers, coloring his dark skin an even darker shade of maroon.

"Move your hand," Celia said, trying to get a look at the level of damage they were dealing with.

Brian didn't comply, and in fact seemed to squeeze the skin tighter, sending a fresh spurt of blood out between his fingers. It was now wicking down his arm and toward his elbow.

"Brian, move your goddamn hand."

Looking down at the wound and moaning, Brian moved his hand away.

It honestly wasn't that bad, but you wouldn't have known that from the look on Brian's face. At first, Celia thought that he might faint, but the woozy look left his eyes shortly after it arrived, re-placed with a grimace as Celia reached her hands in to pull apart the patch of light blue cotton getting in the way. She rolled up his sleeve, revealing the wound in its totality.

            PERSISTENCE

"Is it bad?"

"You'll live," she said, lightly moving his flesh around with her thumbs to get a better look at the bullet. It had struck muscle before striking bone, and now it remained there, embedded and more or less intact, a gnarled shape the size of a dime.

There was pounding on the window. Celia turned, and then immediately wished she hadn't.

Blue Jeans had the poor kid from the pizza delivery car pressed against the Challenger, his face smushed against the glass. He held up his knife, locked his tear drop alien eyes with her, and then slid the knife across the teen's throat. The blood spurted outward, coating the window like the world's most macabre car wash, gushing down and out of sight.

The boy's body stayed upright, Blue Jeans and the Giant holding him in place. Celia averted her gaze, but even out of the corner of her eyes she saw his body first struggle, then give over to mere twitches. After ten seconds, even those stopped, and the boy's lifeless body was dropped to the hot pavement.

Celia glared at the two men, but Brian's heavy breathing brought her back to the more pressing situation.

"They killed him," he said.

Celia nodded. "Yes. And they'll pay for it later. I promise."

"What are we going to do?"

"Right now, we're going to get this bullet out of you."

"How?"

Celia's eyes shifted to the back of the vehicle, toward the trunk, where a first aid kit, a rifle, and ammunition for both that and her pistol awaited.

"I'm working on it."

32

Celia's possessions were splayed out in the middle seat between her and Brian. They weren't much to look at: a badge, a bottle of pepper spray, a taser, a police baton, a depleted pistol, and the bottle of OxyContin. Celia had relented to Brian's continued request and given him one of the pills from inside the bottle. Her keys she had stuck back in the ignition; she now had to keep Brian cool or else the wound could turn more serious.

"We need a first aid kit," she said.

"Good thing I keep one in my back pocket at all times," said Brian.

"There's one in the trunk."

"Great," said Brian. "Give a quick pull on the lever by your feet over there and I'm sure they'll let you leisurely stroll to the back and come back here to help me out."

Celia wasn't looking at Brian now; her eyes were cast toward the horizon, her mind spinning.

"There's also body armor," she said. "A rifle too. If I could just get back there."

"Celia, how can you get outside when opening the car door pretty much ensures your death?"

"Maybe I can find a way back there from inside. Go through the cage that separates the perps from the cops, which is, of course, designed not to be taken apart from either side. If I had bullets maybe, or even some matches, I could MacGyver something together from a matchhead and gunpowder, create a tiny explosion that lets me pry open the metal slats.

"Of course, even if I somehow get through that cage, I would still have to contend with the foam cushion and metal backing of the actual seats that separate the interior of the vehicle from the trunk. Which would actually be more difficult than getting through the cage. FUCK!"

Celia gritted her teeth. The tools laid out at her disposal were not tools at all. They would do her no good in the situation.

"I'm sorry I got shot, Celia."

"It's okay," she said. "It happens to the best of us."

"Have you ever been shot?"

She shook her head. "By a beanbag gun. And a taser. But those don't count. They make all of us go through it before we're allowed to actually use them."

"That's a stupid policy."

"I agree. But hey, cheer up, you've gotten shot more times than an actual cop. You'll have a gnarly scar, it'll give you a perfect ice breaker. Honestly, I'm getting a little turned on right now just thinking about it."

"Oh, shit. The damage must be pretty bad if you're trying to make me feel better about how I left things."

"Getting shot makes us even."

"I'm a spoiled rich kid already sporting half an addiction to white collar prescription drugs. You deserve better than what I could ever give you."

"Now you have an excuse to use even stronger stuff."

"You read my mind, Celia Miller."

Celia smiled. In truth, she was trying to make herself feel better about the situation as well. There was *nothing* that was good about what was happening except that Brian's wound could have been more serious. Or the vehicle could have been an unarmored Crown Vic.

"I should have just died, Brian. Surrendered myself. The kid would still be alive."

"They did this, not you. His blood isn't on your hands."

Celia looked at him, deep in thought. "Maybe it should be."

Celia swiveled her head to look at where the blood was quickly drying on her driver's side window. The men in the alien masks had retreated, were in fact gathered up ahead about 20 feet, talking amongst themselves. Two of them, the Giant and some other goon, were left to guard the vehicle while the others plotted their next course of action.

Celia looked at the blood, and then looked down at her relatively unscathed frame. Bangs and bruises, a laceration here and there, but nothing too bad.

How far are you willing to go? Would you be willing to get blood on your hands? What would you do to survive?

A plan was formulating in Celia's head. She thought it might work. *Might.* It was a long shot, but it would allow her to get to the trunk, to grab the first aid kit, the body armor, the rifle. It would allow her to even the odds.

"I tried to save him," said Brian, his thoughts on matters far different from what Celia was thinking of.

"I know you did. There was nothing that could have been done."

"I'm sorry I endangered us. Endangered you."

"Don't be. It was noble."

Celia smiled at Brian. He smiled back, but it was clear it came with some effort, having just witnessed an innocent kid's throat being sliced and being rewarded for his bravery with a bullet stuck in his own arm.

"I have to try something," said Celia. "And I have to try it now, while their focus is elsewhere."

"What are you gonna do?"

Celia looked at the window now covered in the teen's blood.

"Something stupid. But I need you to do something for me."

"Anything."

Celia locked eyes with Brian.

"In a few seconds I'm going to open the door and get out. And I need you to lock it behind me when I do."

33

It was now or never. Celia had laid out the admittedly batshit plan to Brian who, to his credit, did not interrupt or tell her it was too dangerous or that she was going to get herself killed. Celia's own voice was telling her that stuff anyway, and she was thankful that Brian had simply listened without interjection.

But you <u>are</u> going to get yourself killed. He may not speak up because he knows it will do no good, but we both know the truth. You need to know the odds. There are more of them than there are of you. They have better weapons, better positions. You can't keep catching them off-guard; eventually they'll stop underestimating you.

After Celia told Brian her plan, Brian waited a couple of seconds before saying anything. When he did speak, the words caught her by surprise.

"They underestimated you, didn't they?"

Celia couldn't help but smile, not because it was about the sweetest thing that he could have said right at the moment (although it was), but because he had no idea how close he had gotten to the Celia recording that constantly played in her own head.

"We better hope so," she said.

"<u>I</u> underestimated you," said Brian.

To this Celia said nothing, simply turned to verify that the men in the masks were still gathered in a semicircle save for the two who waited on either side of the car with their guns at the ready. Their current grouped position wouldn't last for long.

Celia was about to make her move when Brian's hand touched her arm. His fingers trailed blood stains on her sleeve.

"If this doesn't work, thank you for keeping us alive this long."

"Brian…"

"We both know if they get to you I might as well unlock the door. I can't survive like you. I can't do this."

Celia took his hand into hers and pressed it against her cheek, closing her eyes and leaning into the skin. His flesh was warm, and he smelled earthy and sweaty and really pretty gross, but his hand also felt like it belonged there. She squeezed his hand as hard as she could.

"Neither of us is going to die today."

She had never felt less confident of anything in her life. Regardless, she dropped Brian's hand, spun around as quickly as she could, and opened the driver's side door.

34

The man Celia called Blue Jeans was still unhappy, but the rage he had previously felt had subsided somewhat when he drew his knife across the throat of the unlucky pizza delivery boy. He had felt a slight twinge of guilt at that, but laid most of the blame on the bitch in the car.

He had really thought she would unlock the doors, give herself up to save the kid's life. She was colder than he thought. Who would have thought it would have been the nigger that had laid it on the line? He wasn't a cop like Celia. It wasn't his duty to save the kid, it was hers. That she would let someone else fight her battles for her, another man going off to die while she stayed in the air-conditioned car, spoke volumes about the bravery of men and the heartlessness of women.

But now she was stuck and the nigger had a bullet wound, so they could consider that a victory.

"What are you thinking?" asked one of his men, the voice intruding upon his thoughts.

"I'm thinking she's out of bullets."

"Even if she is," said one of them from the right, "it's still gonna be a pain in the shits to get in that car. A chainsaw wouldn't go through that fucking thing."

"What about the gas tank?" It was the one who had painted the bloody upside-down cross on his mask, the same one who had insisted upon bringing the chainsaw. He had always struck Blue Jeans as being too smart for his upbringing and a little too eager for the jobs they pulled off. When they had met to discuss this particular job, he had grinned, a little too widely, had a few too many ideas.

Every group of trailer trash had such a person. Someone who thought he dreamed big but whose dreams amounted to cooking meth in a way that wouldn't blow up the entire lab or who thought of using ten-year-olds dressed like Girl Scouts to deliver cookies but replace all the cookies with cardboard and get away before the buyers had the chance to catch up and get their money back. Someone who failed algebra and basic biology but had studied certain subjects enough to know the precise places to cut to make a coyote suffer.

He had been one of those gentlemen. And Blue Jeans trusted him. Their history ensured that the man had earned his trust. And he certainly had his uses. Still, he worried Blue Jeans sometimes. As their operation grew, he did things that put them at risk of higher visibility. And they couldn't afford an official investigation right now.

As for the unofficial investigation? That was being handled today. When Blue Jeans had broken into Celia's apartment, he wasn't sure what to expect. What he certainly didn't count on was a series of files and notes that rivaled that of the most dogged, obsessive detective you see in the movies. He was surprised there weren't pieces of string connecting random mug shots and places on a map.

She was close. Maybe closer than she even realized.

That could not abide. Blue Jeans had called a meeting quickly. A plan was thrown together. He and Cross Face had come up with it. Draw her out to the middle of nowhere and put an end to it.

Blue Jeans cursed at his own stupidity. It had been he who insisted on fucking with her first. On making her feel miserable and hopeless before they ended the entire endeavor, pinning it on one of the lowlifes from The Rocks whose car they had stolen and shoved a dying coyote into.

That ship had sailed, and now they had another incident that could be pinned to the growing infamy of the Illegals, all because he had to make her suffer.

They could still get out of this, but that meant getting into the car and ending Celia's life as quickly as possible. Doing so would let them put everything behind them for good.

Cross Face had gone along with Blue Jeans's idea because it matched his own proclivities so well. He wasn't the type to look down upon excessive violence. In fact, he was always coming up with ideas that didn't necessarily align with the plan but that didn't really contradict it either. Like how quickly and eagerly and without hesitation he had cut their comrade's head off…

And now the man looked at Blue Jeans from behind an alien mask identical to his own, save for the splashes of blood in the shape of an upside down cross.

"What <u>about</u> the gas tank?" Blue Jeans said back to the man.

"Well, a chainsaw's not 'sposed to cut through glass, let alone bulletproof glass. Shit. But you give it enough pressure I'll bet you could cut through the plate on that gas tank. Can't be as reinforced as the rest of the car, even if it does have a lock on it."

"Gas tank's on the driver's side. All she'd have to do is open the door a crack to get a shot at us."

"You just told us you thought she was out of bullets."

He thought about it. It could work. If they pried that open, they could take some of the gasoline they had, pour it in on a rag, then stuff the rag into the tank.

Watch her burn? That could be fun. He would have liked to get his hands on her, but he supposed seeing her flesh darken and melt from her body would be the next best thing.

"Alright," he said. "Let's try i…."

His last word was cut off as he saw Celia open the door to the car and reach for the body of the pizza boy at her feet. Blue Jeans ran forward at once, unholstering his gun and readying it to fire.

35

The door swung open and Celia wasted no time leaning down and grabbing hold of the teen's body, lying face down in a pool of his own blood. Celia grabbed him underneath the armpits and lifted.

She was vaguely aware of shouts coming from the direction of the group of masked men, and then shots were whizzing past her. On that side, though, she had the benefit of the reinforced door and bulletproof window blocking their view of her.

That didn't save her on this side, though, as the Giant was already raising a shotgun toward her, taking two large steps forward as he did. Celia lifted with all her might and got the dead teen up in front of her just as the trigger was pulled.

Celia was prepared for some force, but *holy shit.* The shots struck the teen in the back, slamming his body awkwardly atop Celia as she crouched with one leg in the vehicle and one leg out, his forehead propped up by the roof of the car.

She felt pressure on her back, for a split second thought they had already gotten behind her, then realized it was Brian helping her push the body.

She used his strength to push the body forward, holding it steady even as another shotgun blast struck the teen. The Giant was descending on Celia, walking forward even as he fired at her. This time, a few of the pellets tore into her right index and middle finger. She cried out, but the adrenaline that surged through her body gave her the strength she needed.

Celia was now pushing the teen forward at the Giant, who was getting ready to fire another round. The boy's body struck the shotgun and caused it to fall out of the Giant's hand. He crashed against the Giant's body, and it felt like she was pushing him up against a wall.

But Celia had momentum on her side. Her feet were pedaling on the ground beneath her. There was a moment where she almost slipped on the gravel, but she caught herself in time. Gritting her teeth, Celia got her legs underneath her and then pushed forward with all the strength she had.

It worked. The Giant stumbled backward due to the combined weight of the kid and Celia. She let go and the immense man was forced back a couple steps as he fumbled with the dead weight of the pizza boy.

Celia couldn't celebrate her victory for long. Not only was the other group getting closer (Celia wasn't sure exactly how far, and she didn't dare take the time to look), but the man on the passenger side of the vehicle was now pointing his pistol forward, over the hood of the trunk, at Celia.

She ducked down and the shot went high above her head. Celia said a silent prayer that it struck the Giant, but that was not to be. He had finally gotten a good grip on the corpse of the teen and now tossed it aside like a rag doll.

Celia peeled around the car as the trunk flew open. Brian had done as he was told, shutting the door once she got clear and popping the trunk with the release lever on the inside. In so doing, the trunk's hatch had also knocked the hand of the man with the pistol up in the air.

She was almost out of time. The Giant was no more than ten feet away, and the others were no more than 30 and closing fast.

She reached toward the trunk and a hand grabbed her around the arm. It was the man with the pistol. Keeping her wrist in his grip with one hand, he whipped the pistol in a wide arc toward her face with the other.

Celia was quicker. With her free hand, she had pulled the baton kept at her waist out of its holster and swung it around. It cracked against the cheap plastic of the alien mask, and Celia was pleased to see the plastic give and feel the familiar clang of metal on bone.

The man's grip on her wrist instantly slackened. He dropped the pistol to the cement as he himself crumpled.

As she whipped her head back toward the trunk, Celia saw the Giant reaching for her. Out of the corners of her eyes, she saw the others coming around the sides of the car and drawing on her.

She was surrounded. There was no way she'd be able to reach the rifle in the trunk in time and make it back around to the car door.

But she wasn't going to the car door. As the Giant's fingers clasped around her shoulder, Celia jumped *into* the trunk, using one hand to pull it down behind her. The Giant lost his hold, Celia landed, and blinding white light was replaced by utter darkness.

36

Celia's tailbone struck something solid beneath her, and tears filled her eyes as the pain radiated outward. Dots of light swam in front of her eyes. She heard yelling from the outside, frenzied screams of pain coming through the hood, but was unable to concentrate on the sound because of her own white-hot agony.

It felt like someone had pressed a molten piece of metal against her lower spine. She bit her lip, trying to contain the pain, but to no avail. The scream left her lips, tears filling her eyes, her contorted position not helping matters. She pounded on the hood that was inches from her face, trying to will the pain away.

She wiped her eyes and forced herself to focus on the situation.

You're in a trunk. The first aid kit is to your left. Along with the road flares. The rifle is beneath you. Get to it.

The pain subsided a bit, and Celia forced herself to think more about the situation, her immediate situation, not the muted shouting and arguing coming from the desert that lie outside the trunk.

You need to turn over. Try to find a release panel that will let you push the back seat forward and get into the cabin.

The heat was stifling. Celia felt sweat already accumulating underneath her armpits and across her brow. Her shirt had come untucked, and beneath it, it seemed as though she could feel the bruise spreading across her tailbone.

Celia turned to her left so that she was facing the back seat, and as she did, her right hand brushed against something wet, hard, and fleshy next to the trunk latch. Her entire body jumped, and Celia's first thought was of the coyote (the comparison between her and it at this particular juncture did not fail to escape her). Gathering her courage, Celia now moved her hand around, trying to grasp the wet jumbo shrimp-like piece of meat in her hands. In doing, she realized there were not one but two good chunks.

She grabbed one, and though it made her queasy to squeeze whatever it was between her fingers, she forced herself to bring it toward her face. Her knuckle scraped against the interior of the trunk as she did so and the meat nearly slipped out of her grasp. She caught it between her thumb and forefinger, which now wrapped around a portion that felt like smooth marble.

With her other hand, Celia pulled her cellphone from her pocket and used it to illuminate her surroundings. Her vision was immediately filled by the bluish sight of a severed thumb, little tendrils of flesh dangling toward her.

Celia immediately startled, tossing the thumb down toward her feet, losing it somewhere out of sight of the glow of her cellphone. The phone's light caught another finger down by her hip.

So that's what that guy was screaming about.

When Celia had jumped in, the tall man, the Giant, had his hand firmly clasped on her shoulder, and when she slammed the trunk shut behind her, the trunk had come right down on his thumb and pointer finger.

Celia smiled at this.

Gunshots interrupted her pride in herself. Bullets were striking the top of the trunk, making loud popping noises and vibrations that shook Celia's body.

Panicked now, and with the cellphone still clutched in her hand, Celia turned and looked for a release switch that would allow her to access the back of the squad car. She pivoted the phone toward the side closest to her head and then scanned down toward her feet, her knees bent painfully over the carrying case that contained the first aid kit.

Nothing. There was no release hatch, just the backs of the seats.

It had been a long shot. Most vehicles don't come with releases to the cabin, just to the outside. But a release to the outside wouldn't do her any good in her current predicament.

Celia began to kick at the back of the seat with her leg. She did this repeatedly, the seat barely moving each time. It did get *some* movement, which was a good sign, but given Celia's awkward position, she couldn't pull her foot back enough to get a sufficient amount of power to push the seat forward.

The whirr of a chainsaw erupted from outside, and when the wielder brought the appliance down upon the trunk of the car, her teeth began to rattle. Celia imagined that sparks were being sent out everywhere in the bright daylight.

The trunk isn't as reinforced as the rest of the car.

Celia imagined the rending of steel and kicked harder than she had before. The seat moved, but again, not enough to reveal a sliver of daylight or give her any real hope that her efforts would pay dividends.

As the chainsaw dug into the metal above her prone body, Celia turned over further and grasped at the large black case that contained the squad car's government-surplus rifle.

She wiggled her hand beneath her, the top of her wrist placed beneath her breast. She fumbled with the latch on the side of the case, pushing her body up with her other hand. The back of her head struck the hatch, and she felt the saw blades rattling across the trunk, digging deeper into the metal. The blackness that was her field of vision shook as if in an earthquake, and Celia saw swimming lights.

Her fingers wrestled with the latch, and she was able to pop it loose.

Great, now you just have to find some way to get the case open despite your entire weight pushing down on it.

Celia rolled again, this time so that she was facing the tail end of the vehicle. A good half of the case was still positioned beneath her, as was her right hand, which was now pinned uncomfortably. Celia reached her left hand toward the case, grasping its outer edge, and pulled. The case at first didn't want to give, but Celia gave a heave and it moved out from beneath her body, which sank into the felt lining of the trunk.

The chainsaw stopped and Celia hesitated in her movement to open the case. She heard voices and then quiet. Then the chainsaw came on again, only this time it wasn't directed toward the trunk.

Celia heard the tinkling of glass, and then suddenly a light popped into the trunk.

They had taken a chainsaw to the tail light.

She could see the chainsaw moving back and forth, tearing out chunks like a predator that had finally found a good piece of meat to sink its teeth into. Celia looked on in horror as the gap widened, letting in more and more light and letting her see blue sky and sand and men in alien masks.

There wouldn't be time to get the gun ready, not in quarters this tight. Rather than try, Celia instead shimmied her body, moving the box of road flares that now lay close to her legs into a more reachable position. She pushed her knees together, around the box, and pulled it toward her face, untangling her right arm from beneath her as she did so.

She pulled the box open as the operator of the chainsaw stopped. She wrapped her hand around a flare, and once she had it in her grip, she struck it against the top of the trunk.

An alien eye appeared in the hole where the taillight had been, and without hesitating, Celia took the lit flare and jabbed it directly into the mask. The heat from the flare sunk right into the black eyehole, causing the man to reel backward and out of sight.

As the man had pulled away, though, Celia lost her grip on the flare and it dropped into the trunk, its smoke immediately filling the enclosed space. Celia began to cough, tears filling her eyes, and she tried once again to grasp the case that held the rifle.

Just as she opened it, she made out the muzzle of a pistol pointing in through the tail light. Celia shoved the rifle case forward, positioning it between her and the pistol, and her efforts were just in time. Bullets slammed into the case, causing its lining to buckle toward her.

With smoke and bullets filling the trunk, Celia wasted no more time. She wrapped her arms around the rifle and pulled.

Thank you, Department of Defense Army Surplus Program.

She fumbled the rifle out of the case with one hand, and after quickly loading it with the available ammunition secured to the inside by a metal clasp, Celia brought one leg up and pressed it against the metal case. Her muscles screamed from the effort, a cramp shooting through her calf. Celia sucked in breath, giving herself room to push her neck against the back of the seat, her legs now splayed in a contracted V pointed toward the trunk's opening.

Bullets continued to pound into the case, and she felt a dull pain like being struck with a beanbag gun push into her foot. Then, eclipsing that dullness was a bright, white hot pain, her flesh feeling as if it had been ripped apart.

She was out of time; the case had finally buckled, the bullet careening through and hitting her foot.

Celia cocked the rifle and pointed it into the corner of the back seat. She pivoted her neck, trying to get as much space between her ears and the muzzle of the rifle as possible. She slammed her eyelids shut and gritted her teeth, unlatching the safety by memory and pulling the trigger three times in rapid succession.

If the pain in her foot was heavy petting, then the sound in her ears was a giant screaming orgasm. The sonic boom that erupted within her brain carried her away into a realm and a type of pain she had never experienced before, a type of raw sunburnt bleeding that roared inside her head and couldn't escape, rattling around and bouncing off the walls of her mind. Not only was she unable to hear, but she also found herself unable to see, the muzzle flash encompassing her vision, a nuclear explosion going off in her head.

With tears filling her eyes and unable to see or hear, afraid to touch her ears because she was sure that blood would come away, Celia dropped the rifle and groped blindly at where she thought she had shot.

Her hand moved across solid seat, and her heart fell. All of that pain had been for nothing. She was stuck in the trunk of a car, unable to get into the seat...

Her hand shot into open space and relief washed over Celia. It wouldn't be enough to fit her body through, but that was never the point; the shots had dislodged the seat itself from its bearings.

Celia pushed and felt the seat give beneath her weight, though not completely. It still rattled against some hidden track in the middle of the perp seat, but Celia hadn't gotten this far to let such a little thing stop her. She propped her feet against the trunk, using her legs as leverage and placing her back against the seat itself.

She felt more than she heard additional gunshots, the roar of chainsaw on metal, but it all seemed to come from somewhere far away, like a waterfall that you hear well before you see it. Celia was able to focus on nothing but pushing.

She strained with all her might against the seat, feeling it give, but it still held fast. The insistent whirr of the chainsaw got louder now, forcing Celia to realize that she maybe had some strength left in her after all. She screamed a scream she herself didn't hear and pushed.

The seat gave, popping forward against whatever restraints the police car overlay people had put in to prevent a perp from negotiating the seat away from the back. Darkness turned to light, although all Celia was able to see were just the fuzziest of shapes.

She crawled forward, into the back seat of the Challenger, still going off of feel rather than sight and sound. The low moaning of the chainsaw stopped and Celia imagined that the men in the alien masks were looking aghast inside the cabin of the vehicle.

Instead of catching her breath, Celia reached back into the trunk. When her hands returned from that darkness, they were holding the rifle and a box of road flares. When she reached back in and came out a second time, she had in her hand a piece of body armor and the first aid kit that had prompted this little misadventure in the first place.

Celia rolled these into the foot well of the vehicle and then rolled herself into that same space. She pushed the seat back into place, not surprised that it wouldn't fall back into its regular position.

The shapes of the men in the masks surrounding the vehicle came into view. She noted that there was one less muddled shape than there had been when she crawled into the trunk. She assumed that one was still bemoaning the loss of his fingers.

Celia raised her own hands and pointed the middle finger of each toward either side of the vehicle. Then she laughed hysterically, the sound never reaching her ears, one of which had begun to leak blood.

37

Brian had tried to speak with her, but gave up when Celia pointed at her own ears and shouted louder than she intended, "I CAN'T HEAR YOU!!!!!"

Once she had arrived in the back seat, she still had a problem; she needed to get past the metal grating that separated the perps in the back from the cop in the front. That turned out to be not nearly as problematic as her foray into the trunk. She had plenty of ammo, and the rifle, while still likely loud to Brian's ears, sounded to her like a distant engine backfiring when she shot it into the grating. A few well-placed shots toward the left-hand side and downward (so that the interior of the glass wouldn't be hit) and the grating gave way on the driver's side. Brian helped her pull it away.

"TALK ABOUT YOUR IRON CURTAINS!" Celia shouted as she pushed her way back into the driver's seat, landing with her head near the pedals and having to pivot her body back up into a seated position.

"Are you okay?" Brian asked from the opposite end of a tunnel. He reached his hand toward her ear, but as soon as a finger touched the lobe, a bright rivulet of pain pushed its way back into her brain and she batted his hand away, grimacing and holding her skull in one hand.

"I'm sorry," he said.

She shook her head from side to side, meaning to say it's okay but ending up not saying anything at all. The pain subsided again, but her hearing remained desperately out of reach, like a dream where you try to run or punch but the movements just won't come.

She willed her auditory abilities into existence but to no avail.

Celia reached back and hauled the first aid kit through the opening and into the front seat. She unlocked the clasps, a pang of fear shooting through her gut that there would be nothing inside, but there was. Bandages, rubbing alcohol, gauze, tweezers, scissors, gloves, bottled water, and compresses, all stacked inside and ready to be used.

Because this was a police-issue kit, there were some items that would not be in the standard Red Cross pack. Two blister packages of Tylenol were contained inside, along with a half dozen hydrocodone for more intense pain. There were also two scalpels, two hollow items roughly the size of a pencil that could be used to provide an open airway to someone whose throat was blocked, and benzocaine that could be applied directly to the site of a wound to numb the area.

Celia ignored the Tylenol and instead rolled two hydrocodone into her palm. She held her palm out and Brian took the hint. He took the pills out of her hand and tossed them in his mouth. He uncapped the water with his good hand and swallowed.

"What are you going to do?" he asked, and, to Celia's relief, his voice came through clearer than it had before. Not to her relief, she could see the Giant pacing back and forth behind Brian's head. He would lift his gun every once in a while toward the car, but then he would drop it and pace again, upset at his own impotence of being unable to access the vehicle. The thought of having lost two fingers seemed to have become secondary to the thought of murdering the bitch who took them.

"They're going to come at us hard now," said Celia. "Once they're done panicking and the anger subsides, they'll regroup. And they'll think harder than they've thought before. They already broke the tail light leading to the trunk. I won't catch them by surprise anymore. They will come after us with a ferocity."

"Let them," said Brian. "I've seen what Celia Miller is capable of. You have guns now, and body armor. I like our odds."

Behind the car, Blue Jeans and another of his cronies tended to the man who had taken a flare to the eye. His mask was peeled off, but Celia couldn't see the face that lay behind it.

And just behind her stood one more man, the one with the upside down cross of blood. He didn't move, just looked at her as she prepared what was needed to access the bullet in Brian's shoulder.

     PERSISTENCE

Despite the oppressive heat from the trunk, which was just now beginning to wash away thanks to the air conditioning of the cab's interior, a chill went up Celia's spine. There was something different about this one, even though he hadn't immediately struck her as particularly impressive or noteworthy. He was small yet lanky, his clothes hanging off of him compared to the others.

It was the stillness that drew attention. Whereas the others were in various active states, this man remained perfectly still, watching, *analyzing.* It was disconcerting. Almost as disconcerting as the cross he had splashed in blood on his mask.

She turned back to the first aid kit and pulled out the benzocaine.

"Thank you," she said. "And I'm sorry."

Before Brian could even ask what she was sorry for, she applied the benzocaine to the bullet wound on his arm, all gristly flesh and congealed blood. He winced but didn't yell.

Now she moved other items aside and pulled out the tweezers, heavy duty ones designed for just such a task. She wrapped her fingers around a scalpel and then set them both on the seat. She took the bottle of rubbing alcohol and doused some on her hands and then on the tools.

"What now?" asked Brian, his eyes like a glazed donut. The drugs were doing their work quickly.

"I need to dig the bullet out of your arm," she said, catching her voice at the start, realizing the loudness of it, and then bringing things down a decibel or two. "To do that, I need to cut away some dead flesh and then…you know what, don't worry about how it's gonna happen."

"Will it hurt?"

"Like a motherfucker," she said. His eyes, which had widened when she had said "cut away some dead flesh" drooped. He nodded.

Celia went to work. The scalpel touched the flesh near the bullet and then sliced inward in one solid movement. Brian yelped but bit down on his lip when Celia leveled him with a glare, her own ears still ringing from the rifle blast in the trunk.

She cut at the skin until she felt the metal of the scalpel make contact with the hunk of bullet. In doing, the blade pushed the bullet against the bone, and Brian howled again, unable to help himself this time. Now that Celia had an idea of where the bullet was exactly, she hacked at the muscle in the immediate area.

Finally believing herself to have a clear path at the slug, she sat the scalpel back in the first aid kit and then lifted the tweezers. She sunk them into Brian's arm and attempted to bring the tweezers' two points in line on opposite ends of the bullet. She missed on the first pass, feeling the end of the tweezer scrape against bone. Brian beat his fist against the dashboard and squinted his eyes shut, willing the pain away.

On her second try, she was able to get each end of the tweezers around the bullet.

"Ready?" she asked.

"For the love of God, just do…"

Celia yanked the bullet out in one swift motion, Brian giving a grunt of pain as the bullet slid out of its cradle within his arm. She held the bullet up to the light.

"Look at the little guy," she said. "Do you want to keep it as a souvenir?"

Brian waved her off with his good arm; blood had begun to ooze fresh from the wound in his not-so-good arm. Celia tossed the bullet over her shoulder, catching a flash of movement from the men outside as she did so, but decided she didn't have time to worry about their bullshit right now.

"Are we done?" asked Brian.

Celia chuckled without humor. "Don't look."

Brian looked, and Celia splashed alcohol onto his arm. He cried out and Celia cleaned the wound as quickly as she could. All told, it wasn't as bad as it could have been. When that was done, she quickly applied a bandage and then taped it down.

"Now you're done," she said. "Not bad triage. Not EMT good, but those guys can't shoot like I do."

"Great," he said. "If you don't mind, I think I'm going to shut my eyes now."

"Actually, you're not," she said, leaning back against the driver's side window and lifting her foot. "I need you to pull off my shoe."

Brian looked at the sole of her foot and his eyes widened. "Jesus, Celia, they shot you too?"

"I need to know how bad it is," she said. "Pull."

With his good arm, Brian reached forward and grabbed her boot between his fingers. She untied the laces for him and he pulled. A sharp pain shot through Celia's leg, but not near as bad as she feared. Brian was able to get the boot off.

Celia held her foot up for Brian to see.

"What's the damage?"

Brian turned the boot toward her, and Celia saw the bullet stuck there embedded in the leather.

"It didn't get you," he said.

Celia peeled off her sock and examined her foot, which bumped up against the steering wheel as she pulled it toward her face.

There was a hell of a bruise, and a small slash of blood about a centimeter long, but the bullet had otherwise not been able to breach her skin.

"Thank God for small favors," Celia thought, then looked around at the men in the alien masks. "Very small favors."

But that wasn't quite true either. She had been granted one very large favor since she got into this predicament: If she hadn't taken Jason's Homeland Security-granted, armor-plated, bullet-resistant honest-to-God assault car, and elected instead to drive away in the standard police issue Crown Vic, she would be dead. Brian, too.

She understood why Jason had such a hard-on for the car now. She even took a slight satisfaction knowing that he would never see it again in one piece. He was probably still nursing a hangover, waking up around this time and making himself a breakfast burrito and a cup of coffee, no idea that his car had been swiped by his bitch of an ex-girlfriend. She would love to be the one to tell him; hell, at this point she'd love to be the one to tell anyone anything.

"They're done toying with us now, said Celia. "We need to keep our thoughts focused. The playing field is far from level."

"No," said Brian, "but it's getting closer thanks to you."

When the ordeal had started (an hour ago? two hours? she turned her eyes to the clock on the middle console. 2:35. She tried to do the math, but realized she didn't know what time this had begun), the Illegals had been many. Now one had his head cut off by a chainsaw and Celia had shot another when his guard was down. And her latest misadventure had ended with one man losing a finger and a thumb and another with a flare shoved through his eye.

"The alien with the cross on his forehead," said Brian. "And the one with the Blue Jeans. They're the most dangerous ones, aren't they?

Celia nodded. "One is smart, the other is unpredictable. They'll do whatever it takes to kill me. To kill us."

"What about the others? Hired help? Shit, Celia, there's still a lot more of them than there are of us."

"I will whittle them down," she said. "I'm smarter than them. I'm better than them. They didn't know it before, but maybe they do now. It's time to start making them realize what a mistake they made."

"I don't doubt you, but how long can we last, really? Being stuck here in the desert like this?"

Time. That was the one truth she couldn't ignore. They could wait her out. They could wait until her battery went dead, until sleep took her, until she ran out of food, of water, of sanity. They could wait until she slipped up, made the one mistake that allowed them to force their entry into her car (because it was her car now; fuck Jason), and then they would kill her. They could work in shifts, she could not. They could go back into town, or whatever hellhole they crawled out of, to get more ammo. They could get food, water, could take their masks off and just *wait.*

"You're right," she said. "We can't wait. We don't have the luxury of time."

She needed to act. To force them to make mistakes. To get them so angry that they would trip up, would forget themselves, would enter into a situation where she could cause them more pain.

Celia ran her fingers down the rifle she had pulled from the trunk. She moved her eyes across the body armor she had set by the gas and brake pedals.

Brian must have noticed, because he piped up.

"What are you thinking?"

The rifle she couldn't use unless she was out of the vehicle. The armor for the same reason. She needed something that would allow her to get to them out there from her position in here.

Her eyes alighted on something that she had thus far overlooked.

"I'm thinking maybe they just need to hear the sound of a woman's voice."

38

You have got to be fucking kidding me, thought Blue Jeans.

She had been out of the car! Out of the fucking car. All they needed to do was grab her, shoot her, do anything other than act like complete fucking amateurs. The fight shouldn't have been this hard.

That fucking car. Goddamnit. If it wasn't for that she'd be dead. The bitch wasn't playing fair. She was holed up in her own personal panic room, not willing to engage them directly.

Bandages were now being wrapped around the hand of the man whom Celia had been referring to only as the Giant.

Goddamnit. He had lost his fucking fingers. His fingers! He had been close enough to touch her, *had* touched her for Chrissake. Had wrapped his hand around her shoulder.

Why did she jump in the trunk? Who thinks like that?! And to use the dead kid's body as a human shield so that she could do it…

She was enterprising. He would give her that. But goddamn she was pissing him off. Another one of his men had a flare stuck into his eye. He'd probably be half blind for the rest of his life.

"What are we going to do?" asked one of his men, the one who had his nose broken by Celia's baton before she made her mad dash into the trunk. The five remaining men were getting more and more banged up as the day progressed.

"I don't know," said Blue Jeans.

"You don't know?" asked the man with the upside down cross. He had been standing by the car, just staring in at Celia, apparently lost in thought, but was listening more intently to the conversation

Marc Costanzo   161

than he had let on. "What do you mean you don't know?"

"Just like I said."

"We're going to get in there and kill that bitch. And her boyfriend."

"That's the idea."

"Well, what are you waiting for?"

"I'm waiting for the armored car to turn into paper. What do you think, that I want to sit here with my thumb stuck up my ass?"

"I told you, we get at the gas tank. It can't be as protected."

"She has a rifle now."

"And we have a half dozen." He was in Blue Jeans's face now, and even through their masks, he could smell his rank breath, tobacco intermingled with some type of chili.

"Remember who's in charge," said Blue Jeans.

The man pulled up his mask and spit on the concrete, and for an instant, Blue Jeans was able to see a clean-shaven face with a scar running along the chin.

"You best remember the same," he said, as he pulled the mask back down over his face.

"Gentlemen," said a tinny voice from the speaker system of the Challenger, causing all of them, even the injured ones, to turn their heads. "I think we should have an honest conversation about our relationship."

39

They all craned their necks as she spoke into the speaker in her hand. Seeing their masks with the tear drop-shaped eyes all turning in unison would have made her laugh if it wasn't so terrifying. As she depressed the switch on the side of the mic, she hoped her voice didn't tremble as she spoke.

"I'm not going to cry," she said. "I'm not going to whimper. And I'm not going to beg for my life."

She had their full attention now, and it didn't sound like her voice trembled. She sounded like the badass that she prayed to God they believed she was.

"But what I will say is this: walk away. Retreat to the other side of the bluff. Let me and my friend take the pizza delivery car and drive back into town. I don't know who you are. Yet. Thanks to your cute little masks, you haven't even been spotted on my dashboard cam. You let me go back to town and I will file my police report, but that will be the end of this. You've had a good run of crime. It doesn't have to end today. Sure, I'll come for you eventually, and put you in a prison where you'll die a bunch of old men, but you'll get to see plenty of sunsets between now and then."

The man she thought of as Blue Jeans walked forward, separating from the rest of the group. Cross Face trailed behind him, scratching at his neck as if his mask was becoming itchy.

Good. Let them sweat it out.

Blue Jeans approached the window and placed his mask right up against the glass. She wished she could just roll down the window and shoot him right in the face, but he would see that coming now.

They wouldn't drop their guard anymore.

"What do we get?"

His voice was muffled but the words were clear. The voice was non-descript, maybe slightly deepened like he was trying to put on a tough guy Batman facade.

She raised the microphone back up to her lips.

"To live."

The man in the alien mask shook his head from side to side. She imagined that he was laughing. She needed to impress upon him the fact that she was not kidding.

"It's getting pretty hot out there, isn't it?" she asked. "It's an ice-box in here. Your men need medical attention. If you stick around much longer they're gonna need a morgue. You're playing this stupid. Your surprise attack didn't work. There's no point to this. You think I have something, maybe, or think I did something to you, but I assure you that I don't and I didn't. But if you persist, if you continue to push me, maybe I won't be able to kill all of you, maybe I'll only kill just a few, but I swear to God I'm not going out alone. Every drop of blood I have will hit this pavement before I give you the satisfaction of seeing the life go out of my eyes, and as that blood flows, I'll be sticking a knife in your gut.

"What do you say, Blue Jeans? You're clearly the brains of this operation. What kind of leader are you? One that leads his men into oblivion, or one that knows when to cut his losses?"

The other men shifted in their position down near the front of the car. Blue Jeans looked to them then back to Celia. Brian breathed in and out, slightly out of it since the painkillers hit his system.

Blue Jeans leaned forward, the forehead of the mask pressed against the glass. She could see the outline of a pair of eyes behind the eyes, and they watched her intensely.

"I'll tell you what," he said, "Give us the nigger and we'll let you walk."

Celia looked at Brian, who sat up in his seat. She got back on the mic and depressed the switch again, flicking her eyes back to Blue Jeans as she did.

"Go fuck yourself," she said.

Blue Jeans stood up to his fullest height and walked back toward his gathering of men. As he did, the man with the blood splayed between his eyes walked forward, toward the car. Blue Jeans tried to place a hand on his chest, but the other man swatted it away,

     PERSISTENCE

never breaking his stride.

He unbuckled his belt while he walked, letting the two ends fall to either side of him as he stepped up onto the hood of the car. As he gained his footing, he kicked his buddy's severed head out of the way and onto the ground by the front left wheel. Celia watched with disgust as he stood upright and dropped his pants to below his ass. He wasn't wearing underwear.

The man took his cock in his hands and unleashed a stream of piss onto the windshield, letting it spray from side to side. The urine cascaded down the windshield and dripped off the sides and onto the hot concrete.

She wanted nothing more than to pop open her door and shoot his dick clean off his body. But she supposed that was just the type of move he was trying to elicit.

If Celia wasn't sure before, she was now: this was the one she needed to watch out for. Blue Jeans may have been the leader, but things had begun to grow beyond his control. And for all the cruelty of the day, there was a meaning to his actions.

But this man. Normal human beings, even killers, don't whip their dicks out and piss on the hood of a police car. Whatever reason there was for their attempt on her life, this man wanted destruction, depravity. And while the others maybe only wanted to see Celia dead, this man would much prefer to see her pulled out of the car alive. For a little while at least.

When he was done, he pulled his pants back up and put his belt back together. Celia flicked on the windshield wipers, sending piss shooting off the side of the vehicle, and then got back on the microphone.

"I've seen bigger cocks on weather vanes."

The desert must have been getting to her. Because that line, though she intended it to sound badass, didn't sound cool at all.

40

"You want me to smoke her out?" asked the man who had just pissed all over what used to be a pretty nice car.

"No," said Blue Jeans, standing around his men in a semi-circle. He looked over his shoulder toward the bluff, where all of their cars and gear were stashed.

But the bitch didn't know that it was all stashed up there. She didn't know anything about her situation except the fact that she was fucked. Maybe she intended to scare them on the microphone, to rile them up, get them to do something stupid.

Instead, she had given him an idea. Simple in its execution, but the fact that this was supposed to be a quick and easy job that turned anything but had clouded his judgment.

There was another option, not a fun one, not a particularly exciting one. The men might not like it, it would require them to spend God knew how much time in the desert, but it wouldn't require any more bloodshed. Her blood, maybe, but not theirs. He was done letting his men get hurt because she thought she was clever.

"Well, what do you want then?" asked the one Celia called the Giant. He had part of his t-shirt, which had been torn away from his lower body, wrapped around the hand with the severed fingers.

"We watch," said Blue Jeans. "And we wait."

41

She had expected bullets. She had expected frustrations taken out in the form of pounding against the windshield, chainsawing against the windshield, more shooting against the windshield. She had expected RPGs and homemade explosives and all manner of physical violence in a bid to enter the vehicle.

What she hadn't expected was silence. For them to retreat. To move behind the bluff and let her and Brian sit and stew.

Well shit.

Hours had passed. Or at least what had seemed like hours. Every time she had looked at the clock, swearing to herself that it must have been at least two or three hours since the last time she had glanced down, only ten to 20 minutes had gone by.

She and Brian had attempted to pass the time by talking about any manner of things, but their conversations tended to trail off. It was hard to talk about Brian's thesis or Celia's cat when they were looking pending doom in the face. Brian also got less talkative as the drugs she had given him for the pain wore off. To his credit, he hadn't asked for more, although she could see him wincing out of the corner of her eye.

As four o'clock passed, Celia made the decision to cut the air conditioning. In her peripheral vision, she could already see Brian sit up about to protest.

"The battery won't hold out much longer," she said, "we need to conserve it in case of an emergency."

"I think this qualifies," said Brian.

Celia didn't respond. They waited in silence some more, Celia completely still, biting her lip, Brian drumming his fingers on the interior of the door.

"Do something," she said. "Anything. Shoot at me, try something, let me act."

This was worse than anything they had dished out so far, because of the not knowing. As she sat and sweat and felt her clothing stick to her body and willed herself to wait another ten minutes before taking a sip from their lone water bottle, she would find herself thinking dangerous thoughts, thoughts about opening the door.

And Brian wasn't helping.

"Maybe they left," he said. "They took your advice. Maybe we're sitting in the middle of an empty desert with a perfectly drivable car parked right behind us and we're not doing anything."

"Shut up, Brian."

But Celia was thinking the same thing. She had already, multiple times, caught her hand moving toward the door handle, had even been on the verge of rolling down the window once, anything for just a little bit of fresh air, and then she would stop herself. She would honk the horn a couple times, startling herself and startling Brian next to her.

But the thought was persistent. Another 15, maybe 20 minutes would pass and she'd find herself thinking the same, falling into a dangerous loop.

At these times, there were other thoughts that would pop up as well, and these disquieted her more than the idea that there might be a cadre of armed men waiting on the other side of the bluff.

"Why will no one help us?" asked Brian, and Celia heard his voice catch in his throat as he gave voice to words she herself had been thinking. "Someone, anyone, they have to know I'm out here. Someone has to know you're out here."

"I've been wondering the same thing," she confessed. "But it makes sense that no one is coming to our rescue. Chief Burton, he would have gone home after taking care of his paperwork. The officer working 911 and dispatch would have turned over since the morning. Jason won't be in to find this car missing until Monday. That's me. You? There's almost no chance someone would find you even if they were looking for you. A wrong turn brought you out here and it would take days before you're reported missing, and another few days after that until the search brings them to Ravencourt."

     PERSISTENCE

Ravencourt. The town Celia sought to leave but that pulled her back only to try to murder her. She protected it, patrolled its streets, and now soldiers from its army had come to kill her.

The town should have been as dead as this stretch of road. Its budget had been gutted when the economy took a nosedive, not that Ravencourt ever had much of an economy to begin with. Hardscrabble people eking out hardscrabble lives had been Ravencourt's stock in trade.

Ravencourt had no real industry, not since the oil ran dry five or so years ago. It didn't have farming to rely on, or a local college to churn out bright young minds. It had existed, much like the road they were currently positioned on, simply as a living space for hard desert people to put down stakes.

Yet still it continued on, even though its chief export had become people like Celia fleeing the town and its main import had become people like Celia realizing the big cities were filled with people like her who only belonged at home. Ravencourt had continued on because, by now, the residents had no place else to go. Why trade one place for another when the current desert shithole would suffice?

"My thoughts keep coming back to Ravencourt," said Celia. "Why is that?"

"Maybe because there's nothing else to think about and it's 190 degrees in here."

"Why does it survive?" she asked. Then followed it quickly with: "Who are these men?"

"Scumbags that want us dead."

"They're more than that," she said. "First they hit a convenience store. Then they burned down a church. Then they knocked off a casino in Las Vegas. They're dealing drugs across state lines. Now they want to murder a cop with no authority who just happened to get into a scuffle at The Rocks a month or so back.

"Their crimes are random," said Brian. "They have no pattern."

"There is a pattern. I'm just not seeing it. Why Ravencourt? *Why Ravencourt?*"

42

More time passed and still Celia failed to see an out. Desert stretched in every direction, gusts of sands the only movement Celia could take note of save for the occasional carrion bird flying overhead, casting its shadow below.

She guessed that the sun would go behind the bluff in about an hour. It couldn't come soon enough. The lone water bottle she and Brian had to share was nearly empty. Her clothes had stuck to her, and Celia had already taken to fanning herself with an almanac from the glove compartment. Her lips were cracked, the upper one starting to bleed. Brian leaned up against the window, his eyes closed in a bid to sleep and shut out the heat. By his constant fidgeting, Celia guessed he hadn't had much success.

"We need to do something," said Celia.

"What can we do?" asked Brian. "They could be out there. Watching. Waiting."

"So what if they are? We have to act at some point. It does us no good to sit here waiting to die."

"Look out there," he said. "The sun is nearly behind that bluff up ahead. We made it through the day."

"Tomorrow will be a different story," she said. "When it gets hot again, and it won't take long, whatever is left of the car's battery will only get us so far. If it dies, we follow. We can't sit in a hot box for that long without repercussions. We need to get out there and act."

"That's what they want," said Brian. "They want you to do something stupid. They could have a sniper rifle on you right now."

"You're scared."

     PERSISTENCE

"Goddamn right, Celia. And you're not?"

This is what they wanted. For the first time, your adrenaline has dropped and you don't know what to do. You don't see a solution that can get you out of this. There's just desert.

"I don't get scared."

Brian rolled his eyes. It made her want to punch him in the throat.

You're scared of everything, she thought. *You're scared to stand up for yourself in front of other officers because they'll think you're a cold bitch. You're scared to be passive because then they'll think they can walk all over you.*

So you shut yourself out, you let no one get close. Except Jason, who just wants to possess you. And the Chief, who still thinks of you as a harmless little girl. They all think of you as a harmless little girl.

You just showed them how wrong that is.

How long have you been out here now? Six hours? If Jason went missing, how long do you think it would take for the other officers to notice something was up? Or Hilcox? Or Wilson? They'd send the cavalry out within a couple hours if they didn't hear from them.

Nobody knows you're out here. They can't find something that they don't know is missing. You weren't even supposed to come in today. They'll notice on Monday.

Will they? That's the saddest part of all, isn't it? When they arrive back at the office for morning meeting, the biggest thing they'll feel is relief. Relief that the interloper in their midst is sick, probably with lady problems, one hell of a killer flow, she'll be in in a few days.

They don't miss you. They won't miss you. Nobody notices you now because nobody notices you ever. You think that your presence as the lone female officer, as the feminine voice in a sea of men, is some progressive thing.

It's NOTHING to them. You're an annoyance, the reason they have to drop their voices when they tell a dirty joke. You're not an affront to their status quo. They do not care.

If you go missing, their lives get easier.

You can picture it, can't you? Of course you can. Your body found dead in the desert, how it will all play out from there. They'll make a big show of it of course, swear to track down the bastards that hurt you.

"*I may not have liked the girl, and there were times when she could be cold as a cucumber, but goddamnit, it ain't right what they did to her. She was a cop, too."*

Not "one of ours." They'll never call you one of theirs. They'll drink to you, they'll rustle up local meth heads and weirdos, see what they know about the crime. They'll haul in a couple suspects for questioning.

Two weeks will go by and you'll be a footnote, a photo on a wall. Maybe they'll name this stretch of road after you: "The Celia Miller Memorial Thoroughfare." Then you'll fade into memory.

No one will even remember your place in this world.

Despite the heat, a chill went up Celia's spine, and she felt herself getting angry all over again. She may have hated the voice, but she also knew when it was right, and this pissed her off. She would not be a Memorial Road. She would not let all the shit she put up with on a daily basis be for nothing.

She would act. Maybe it was stupid, and maybe it would get her head blown off, but she'd rather go out trying to save her own life and take away theirs than die of heat exhaustion in her ex-boyfriend's four-wheeled compensation for a small- to medium-sized cock.

Celia put on her sunglasses and opened the door of the police car, waiting for a gunshot. When none came, she pushed opened the door a little further.

Brian stirred, turned, and attempted to grab Celia's arm.

"What are you doing? Get back in here."

Rather than follow his directions, because she had decided she would follow no one's directions anymore, she pushed the door open a little further. She picked up the rifle from where it was propped and slowly angled one foot out the door until it hit the concrete.

Still nothing. No movement, no gunshots, anything.

Celia pulled her body out of the vehicle and brought the rifle up to her chin, propping it up in the area where the car's door met the vehicle body. She looked down the barrel at the bluff but saw nothing. No movement at all.

"Come on, you sons of bitches."

Then she saw it. A glint of sunlight reflecting off of some piece of metal high up on the bluff.

Without thinking, relying on pure instinct, Celia angled the rifle toward that glint of metal and fired off a shot. The report echoed across the desert, followed shortly thereafter by a tuft of dirt sprayed up in the air by the bullet in the distance.

Celia fired another shot, then another and another. She wasn't worried about ammo; she had plenty in the trunk, which was now easily accessible. She fired and fired and fired until the clip was empty, and then ducked back into the vehicle, closing the door behind her.

"What was that all about?" asked Brian.

"Just keeping them on their toes."

Brian looked out across the desert, which concealed five men intent on killing them. He turned his attention to the area inside the cabin, wiping sweat off his brow as he pointed at the computer positioned where the center console would be on a normal vehicle.

"Can you get the internet on that thing? I feel like I should update my Facebook status to 'It's complicated.'"

"No internet," said Celia. "Not out here. We use it to keep track of warrants and addresses and stolen vehicles."

"But you need an internet connection to get it to work."

"Actually no. When we pull into the station, the computers connect to the router and update wirelessly with the latest information. But the system itself is all internal. That way we can check on outstanding warrants and persons of interest out in the field without having to worry about establishing a connection."

"Too bad we don't know who any of these bastards are."

Celia looked over at him. It was true, they didn't know who these guys were, which put them at a disadvantage. You can't negotiate or combat someone you couldn't even fathom.

"I think I can figure out who they are. Some of them at least."

"How?" asked Brian. "And does it even matter? Then you're a desperate cop inside of a police car fighting someone whose name you know instead of a stranger? What leverage does that give you?"

"It keeps my mind off my pending demise. And it could help me figure out the next step."

"Where would you even begin?"

Suddenly, Celia knew exactly where to start looking.

43

She spun in her seat and crawled backward into the trunk of the vehicle where she had made her play for supplies and weapons. She took a flashlight with her, using it to light up the boot of the car. What she was looking for was small, and just groping around in the dark likely wouldn't produce it.

After 30 seconds or so of searching, Celia found what she was looking for. She wrapped her fingers around it, forcing herself not to get nauseous as she did so. She was a cop, she should be used to grotesqueries. This wasn't even as bad as what you would find at some crime scenes.

Yeah, but at least you have evidence bags at crime scenes.

Celia shimmied out of the trunk with the flashlight in one hand and her prize in the other. She crawled through the opening in the barrier between seats. Brian's eyes went wide when she set the object on the center console.

"Hitching a ride somewhere?"

"Not quite," said Celia. "Every squad car, including this newfangled Challenger we now call home, comes equipped with a computer console that allows officers to carry out police work in the field when coming back to the station isn't timely or feasible. This particular computer includes a warrant tracker, pending court cases, and information on ongoing cases, all kept relevant via a daily software update performed when the vehicles came within range of the station."

"Why would that be necessary in such a small town?"

"Because Ravencourt and the outlying land is a lot of ground to cover for such a small force, it's more productive to take care of certain booking procedures while out in the field. That means marking down the suspect's name and relevant information. It also…"

She held up the thumb.

"…means applying their thumb to a portable scanner that logs their fingerprints into the system and checks to see if they had a history of felonies or misdemeanors."

Brian couldn't take his eyes off the bloody, disembodied thumb that was now sitting on the dashboard. He looked at it like it was an animal that was going to pounce. The thumb was rather hefty, even for a man as big as the one it had been cut from.

Celia, though, couldn't worry about this. She started the car and booted up the onboard computer, getting the thumb scanner into place.

"That asshole left something behind when he tried to grab me," Celia said. "Now we're going to use it to figure out who he is."

With the computer on, she accessed the fingerprint database and grabbed the thumb off the dashboard. She pressed it in a slight rolling motion across the drive, making sure to get the entire thing on there so that the scanner would pick up each individual groove of the man's skin.

The outline of the thumb appeared on the screen and Celia's eyes lit up.

"Holy shit, it worked," Brian said.

"You bet your ass. Gives new meaning to the term thumb drive, huh?"

Brian rolled his eyes.

Celia scrolled down and clicked the "Search" button with the mouse. She tried not to hold her breath as the computer did its scan of all those names that were in Ravencourt and surrounding counties' criminal database.

After what seemed like an eternity, the computer finished its search, displaying the message:

"0 of 0 search results found. New search?"

Celia's heart dropped. So this guy, whoever he was, didn't even have any priors. That meant he was either really good or really well protected.

"Well, I guess that's the end of that," said Brian.

Celia looked at the hood of the car, where a dark stain of blood still remained from when the head of one her assailants had been placed there like a mounted trophy. An idea formed.

She tossed the thumb somewhere down by her feet and closed out of the fingerprint database. Instead, she looked for another application.

"What are you doing now?" asked Brian.

"Trying something other than waiting here to die."

Celia found another icon used by the police in situations in the field: POI. Persons Of Interest.

"You hiding any more thumbs I'm not aware of?"

"This is a collection of all the assorted scumbags that have been through the system in Ravencourt and nearby counties. Every name on it has an associated photograph of the perp."

"Except we haven't seen any faces of the men who trying to kill us."

"I think I have a way to identify one of them."

Celia handed Brian the rifle. He took it, a puzzled look on his face as he wrapped his fingers around the hilt of the gun.

"When I open this door," she said, "I need you to point this rifle up at the top of that bluff and start shooting. If you see a reflection of any kind, like the sun coming off of a mirror, turn the barrel toward that and keep pulling the trigger. I'm only going to be outside the car for a few seconds, but I'll be exposed, and I need cover fire."

"What are you going to do?" asked Brian.

"It's time to get ahead."

44

Celia took the body armor that she had removed from the trunk and slid it over her shoulders, strapping the ends to one another. It wouldn't offer her any head protection, but she would have to hope that they didn't have good enough weaponry or a good enough shot to line up her skull in their sights.

She wrapped her hand around the door and nodded at Brian, who nodded back gravely.

She opened the door and he followed suit. Out of the corner of her eye, Celia saw how he tried clumsily to mimic the position she had taken, with the rifle propped up in the crux of the door. He pulled the trigger, and the first recoil nearly made him fall backwards onto his ass. He was able to right himself in the door frame and get his leg beneath him in a way that didn't betray his footing, and at that point, he was able to start firing with more confidence, though he still winced with each shot.

Celia propped the door fully open and then leaned out, resting on her haunches as she hurriedly moved around the protection of the door. She moved her head around, not seeing what she was looking for, before her eyes alit upon a lumpy object on the ground near the front tire, partially hidden by the shadow cast by the vehicle.

It was an alien mask, still attached to the severed head. Blood had stopped flowing and now just crusted at the nape of the man's non-existent neck, a darkish-brown mass with bits of matted hair sticking out from beneath the cowl.

She moved quickly once she had it in her sights, half running half crawling, her feet kicking up road grime. It was only four steps but it felt like an eternity outside the protection of the car.

She wrapped her hand around the backside of the alien mask and began to turn around when a bullet smacked up against the armor-plated side of the car. The sudden whistle caused her to fall back onto her ass, the head falling out of her grasp and actually rolling beneath the vehicle.

Celia cursed silently and then crawled on her hands and knees, reaching beneath the vehicle, trying to get her hand on something. She had two fingers pinched on a piece of cloth and pulled, but the head eluded her grasp and actually rolled a couple inches further away.

A bullet smacked into the pavement next to her shoulder, and Celia now lay flat on her belly, using the car's tire to block her own head from harm. Another bullet hit the pavement, then another, and then Celia felt a sharp pain in her side, a bullet striking the bullet proof vest she had adorned for this latest misadventure.

Groping deeper into the car, Celia moved her hands forward as far as she could, reaching for the head, turning her own in such a way as to press her cheek against the concrete.

She overestimated the distance, her hand moving forward into the man's head, the inside of his neck now engulfing her fist. She gagged as her hand dug into tendrils of flesh and then wrapped around a severed piece of spinal column, still attached to the head.

She bit into her sleeve and forced herself to grab hold. She could feel the pieces of bone cutting into her own fingers, as if she were grasping a jagged, broken beer bottle.

Trying not to think about the macabre nature of her action, Celia pulled the man's head toward her with the top of his spine, only to find that the top of the alien mask had gotten stuck on a piece of the undercarriage. As she shouted the word *fuck*, Celia twisted the piece of spine and the head followed, rolling over and allowing Celia the necessary space to bring the severed head toward her.

Not wasting any time, she got back to her feet and quickly got around to the other side of the door. Brian darted in a split second before she did. Celia shut the door behind her with one hand as she tossed the head onto Brian's seat with the other. He almost sat on it as he scooted over to his own seat. His left cheek pushed the head over and onto the floor, where it rattled around between their feet, the plastic of the alien mask making a wet rustling sound.

Celia breathed hard, giving her adrenaline the chance to wash away naturally. Her pulse pounded in her ears, and sweat clouded her vision. She pressed her fingers into her eye sockets to wipe away the moisture and grime.

"Are you okay?" asked Brian from beside her.

She nodded her head, and moved her palm down her body to feel her side, where a bullet had struck the body armor. She winced as her fingers landed where the bullet had struck but was relieved to feel the irregularly shaped slug protruding from the vest. It hadn't gotten through. The pain she felt was the beginning of a wicked bruise.

"I'm truly starting to think you're out of your mind," said Brian.

Celia unstrapped the bulletproof vest, pushing it toward the window and away from her. It felt good to draw in breath unencumbered.

"I told you," she said, "that we were going to get a head."

45

"Is that him?"

"No."

"What about him?"

"No."

"You sure? He has kind of a Lurch from the Addams Family thing going on."

"He's white, Brian. We don't all look alike."

For the past few minutes, they had been scrolling through the mug shot database, trying to put a name to a face. The head sat between them, staring up vacantly at the ceiling. The alien mask had been pulled off and now lay at Brian's feet.

Their admittedly quick search had yet to turn up results. It was surprisingly difficult to match a dead face up to a mugshot of someone who had still been alive at the time of the photo. The man's face was lumpy, chubby, sunken in, but Celia didn't know if that could be attributed to his natural features or the fact that his head had been cut from his body. His mouth gaped open and his green eyes did the same. He had a goateed stubble around his mouth and a pair of small hoops in his ears.

Celia didn't recognize him at first blush, but that didn't mean that he wasn't in the computer's database. Usually all you had to do was plug in a name for information on that person's record, but in this particular instance, she didn't have a name. All she could do was get into the database as a whole and filter by county results. Ravencourt wasn't a big place, and if this guy had a record, as Celia hoped he would, he would be in here.

Thus far they'd had no luck, their only success being that Brian was quickly becoming acquainted with Ravencourt's poor man's attempt at a criminal underworld.

"Jesus, Celia, how many criminals live in this town?" asked Brian after another dozen or so faces that didn't match their guy went by.

"You're basically either a cop or a criminal. Two chief industries."

"Wait, go back," said Brian.

Celia had been half paying attention as she was scrolling through, the heat getting to her even as the sun continued its long descent behind the bluffs. She hit the back arrow once and a face popped up on the screen.

It was him. The face was a little more lively, to be sure, but there was no mistaking the heavy brow, the goatee, the tight lips, and generally the type of mug that only a mother who hadn't died years ago from a crack overdose could love.

"Dirnt Havelock," said Celia.

"The guy's name is Dirnt?"

"Sure. Second only to Edward over at the Rocks."

Dirnt Havelock. His "Rockland Circle" address confirmed that he was a resident of the storied community known as the Rocks, just a couple short miles away from here. This man's address would have been just a few trailers down from the trailer Celia had been pinned down in last month.

5' 10", 175 pounds.

A litany of arrests, but nothing that stood out.

"Holy shit, I know this guy," said Celia.

It was the name that clicked it into place. She stared at the severed head and thought back to the first time she had heard the name.

"It was while I was in a near-shootout with a guy named Hoyt. When I was stuck inside, Hoyt had called out to another man, and the name stuck because it wasn't exactly common. Dirnt. Havelock, apparently."

She stared at the face. "This doesn't make sense."

Brian raised an eyebrow without saying a word. Maybe he was getting as tired of being the one to ask Celia what she was talking about as she was of explaining herself.

"Look at this. One arrest and conviction for possession of methamphetamine, a DUI, and a domestic disturbance. The Rocks trailer trash trifecta, but fairly low-grade. Certainly nothing to suggest that he would be involved in the murder of a cop or any of the other bizarre yet high-end stuff the Illegals have been up to in the past few months."

"Maybe he's graduating to bigger and better plots."

"No, not this kind of guy. He's not the brains. He's expendable. It's probably why they cut off his head without a moment's hesitation. The hired hand, the one they could afford to lose but needed just to have an extra body and gun for intimidation."

"So this gives us nothing?" asked Brian.

"Not exactly. If Dirnt and Hoyt ran in the same circles, it makes sense that he would be out there too, one of the men stalking us. And other lowlifes they hang out with might be too."

Celia moved the cursor up to a tab reading "Known Associates." A list of four names popped up. She clicked the first two to find men with similar rap sheets, low level crimes that didn't stand out, names she knew in passing. The third was indeed a man named Hoyt Murkison. These men may very well be encircling her vehicle, but she couldn't be sure and it wouldn't help her if they were.

But there was the fourth name, a name she didn't recognize: Cyrus Everhaart.

She clicked on his name.

The man was strangely handsome, big blue eyes and the kind of devil-may-care smirk that women purported to hate but that Celia could attest held a certain odd appeal. He was clean-shaven, even had a few dimples, but his mullet suggested he was far out of touch with the latest fashions of anywhere but a trailer park like The Rocks.

She looked at the screen for a good long while, not saying anything. She could feel Brian watching from beside her.

"That's him," she said. "He's out there."

"How do you know?"

"The scar."

Beneath the man's chin was a scar that ran across the skin. Small enough to somehow make him more handsome in a rugged sort of way, big enough to be noticeable. And identical to what Celia had seen when Cross Face's mask had been pulled up for the briefest of moments on the hood of the car.

"It's a reach," said Brian.

"It's not," said Celia. "It's him. Cyrus Everhaart. He's the one we have to worry about."

"Everhaart?" asked Brian. "Last night you mentioned the name of a holding company…"

"Haart of the Sea. With two 'a's. They've been buying up every Rocks property they can over the past six months."

"He's the one with the upside down cross."

Celia nodded. "I've got you motherfucker."

His rap sheet didn't read like the others. Rather than a smattering of small crimes, there was only one big one that stood out at the top of the list:

"Assaulting an officer of the law," said Celia.

Other than that, it seemed like Mr. Everhaart had stayed on the right side of the law, which was more worrisome than if he had a criminal record a mile long. If this really were the man who was stalking her from outside, who had whipped his dick out and taken a piss on the car, it meant he was running some sort of criminal enterprise so successfully that he hadn't drawn the attention of any police entities. You don't just decide to sign up for a cop-killing crew on a whim.

"What is this about?" asked Brian. "Revenge for what you found up at the trailer park, The Rocks was it? To stop you from finding the truth? To get clear of the Feds?"

"It still begs the question," said Celia. "Why buy up all that land? Worthless land in a worthless town. What's the point?"

Brian shrugged.

"You're really no help."

46

"Now we know who a couple of these assholes are," said Brian. "But how does knowing who our executioners are help us?"

"You have a very defeatist attitude," said Celia. "Do me a favor and open the glove compartment."

Brian did as he was told without argument.

"Is there a pen and paper or something in there?"

Brian shuffled through the random jumble until he came up with a pen and small sheaf of lined paper. As he did this, Celia unwound the chain she kept around her neck. It still held the bullet that her father had given her years ago.

With a sigh, a silent prayer to God, and an apology to her father, she twisted apart the end with a grunt and then placed the two parts of the bullet on the dashboard.

"What are you doing?" Brian asked as he handed Celia the paper and pen.

She started writing on the piece of paper.

"I still plan on getting out of this alive," said Celia. "But if that's not possible, I'm not going to let these assholes get away with the things they've done. It wasn't just me and you. The Illegals have been twisting my town into a gnarled shadow of its former self for months now. The identity of one could lead to the identities of others. And I'm not going to let that die with me."

Celia held the piece of paper up to Brian. Its message, scrawled in a small but distinctly loopy text, read thus:

"Cyrus Everhaart and a gang of seven men, including Dirnt Havelock and Hoyt Murkison, killed me."

Brian looked from the note to Celia. "You think you can get it past them if we die? Won't they pour over this entire car?"

"They're not going to find it in the car," said Celia.

She carefully tore the strip of text away from the rest of the paper, then used the pen to roll that strip up into as small of an object as possible. When that was done, she grasped the minuscule strip of paper between her thumb and forefinger and deposited it inside the bullet she hollowed out. It unrolled to match the interior circumference of the bullet casing. With that complete, she took the cap and twisted it back onto the top of the bullet. She reached into the first aid kit, pulled out a small band-aid, and then used that to secure the cap back in place.

She looked back at Brian and then lifted the bullet like it was a shot of tequila.

"Cheers," she said, and then popped the bullet into her mouth. She picked the water bottle out of the cup holder and then took a big gulp of water, tilting her head back and swallowing as she did.

When the bullet was down the hatch, Celia took another sip of water.

"If they find me dead," said Celia, "which I imagine they would because these assholes will want to keep my body around to send a message, they're going to run an autopsy to determine how I was killed."

"Celia, don't say that."

"I'm being realistic about this, Brian. One of the standard procedures for an autopsy is to examine the contents of the digestive system. Any coroner worth her salt would recognize a bullet wrapped in a band-aid and wonder about how it got there. If the world never hears from us again, Cyrus Everhaart is still going to jail."

Brian smiled. "I had no idea you were this resourceful."

"Neither did they. Neither did I. And I have another idea."

Celia picked up the microphone connected to the loudspeaker.

"I think we should fuck with these guys some more and see if we can't get them to make another mistake."

47

The metallic twang to Celia's voice as it came out of the loudspeaker carried across the darkening desert.

"Cyrus Everhaart, this is your life," said Celia.

At the mention of his name, the man with the alien mask splashed with blood in the shape of a cross jerked his head up from the sights of a gun that had been pointed down at the cop car.

"29 years old. Born at Ravencourt County General. Despite current residence at The Rocks, only one conviction: assaulting an officer. Tell me, Cyrus, are you that good of a criminal that you haven't been caught for anything else or are you so piss poor that you're not worth the time of the Ravencourt PD?"

"How the hell does she know who I am?" asked Cyrus.

He looked at the one Celia called Blue Jeans, who had yet to take off his mask. Cyrus had taken off his shirt but kept his own mask on as well. Hoyt kept a gun trained down on Celia.

"Educated guess, maybe," said Blue Jeans.

"Bullshit. There's no way she should've been able to figure out who we are. This is more fucked by the minute."

"Every cop car has a computer that can pull up a database of persons who have been booked at the station, along with all known associates of such. Your name probably popped when she picked up Dirnt's head. Probably why she went to get it in the first place."

"That bitch," Cyrus said.

"I told you she was smart."

"You didn't tell me she'd be driving a goddamn tank. What are we going to do?"

"It's fine. Who cares if she knows who you are? She can't tell anyone if she's dead."

Cyrus fumed behind the eyes of his mask. "You seem pretty confident for a man who can still afford to hide behind a mask."

"She's stranded and outnumbered. All roads lead to us. She isn't getting out of here."

"Then you take your mask off and march up to her car. Let her know who *you* are, chickenshit. Believe in the courage of your convictions, soldier."

Blue Jeans said nothing, instead opting to turn back to his binoculars to watch Celia. He had had one of his men crawl slowly up to the north, circling around to the passenger side of Celia's car. The man was positioned lying down in the sand, out of view of Celia. He had sent two others, Hoyt and the one Celia called the Giant, in a pickup to the south so that they could get behind Celia if somehow she figured out a way to get going on the road from which she came. The truck left a dust cloud as it took its wide path around the vehicle, but so what if she saw? She couldn't do anything about it.

"Forget this mess," said Cyrus, content in the knowledge that he had won the argument. "I'm tired of waiting around."

He stood up, hoisting a gun to each shoulder and moving as if to walk back down the bluff toward the stalled cop car.

"You're not going anywhere," said Blue Jeans.

"Try to stop me," said Cyrus. "Let's not forget that you need me more than I need you."

Blue Jeans was about to protest, but then said nothing. What Cyrus had said was true. He sat back down. Let him waste his feet. He would watch from his perch and plot the moves from above.

48

There was movement from the bluff. Celia and Brian watched as an alien mask materialized from the shimmering heat of the diminishing sunset. The head was followed by a naked torso and a pair of black pants. Cyrus had a shotgun slung on one shoulder and a rifle slung on the other.

"I think you riled him up, Celia," said Brian. "I just wish I knew if that was a good thing or a bad thing."

"I might be able to catch him off-guard."

"Anything you want me to do?"

She shook her head. "Just follow my lead. If I can think of something that can get one of us out of here alive, I'll go for it."

"He's alone. We might be able to surprise him, even the odds a little bit more."

"He's not alone," said Celia.

"What do you mean?"

Celia gestured toward the callbox. "One of the men in the masks circled around behind the drift there. I saw the top of his head peek out when I got on the megaphone and he jumped about a foot."

"Shit," said Brian.

"I think they circled around behind us, too," said Celia. "About an hour ago, a cloud of dust kicked up off to the south and kept on moving around to the east of us. That could mean one of two things: they went back to town to get supplies to root us out, or they positioned themselves strategically so that we couldn't get away. And they clearly have the firepower up on the ridge to shoot at us. All of this to say, they still have the upper-hand in terms of numbers. So don't try anything unless I tell you to."

"You're getting very bossy," Brian said. "I would complain if I weren't still alive."

"The day is still young," said Celia.

Cyrus drew closer to the cop car. He still had his mask on but for some reason had decided that couture fashion in a desert dust-up was shirtless and tats all the way. Without having any kind of top on, Cyrus stood out as remarkably scrawny but also taut, every drawn piece of leathery skin wrapped around ox-like muscles. His tattoos weren't what Celia would have immediately thought of as obvious. Instead of the requisite tits, skulls, and swastikas, Cyrus opted to have a "My Little Pony" character over his left pectoral, Buzz Aldrin on his shoulder, and an erect cock ejaculating into his belly button. Scrawled along the cock were the words "Keep It Classy."

Yeah. He kinda failed in that whole "keepin' classy" regard.

Cyrus brandished the rifle at the car as he approached, trailing one hand along the hood as he wound his way to Celia's window. He rapped on it with a knuckle.

"Pleased to finally meet you, Officer Cunt."

Celia keyed in the button for the megaphone.

"What do you want?"

"Now, when you say 'you,' do you mean me?" asked Cyrus. "Or is it more of a collective you, meaning we?"

"Both," said Celia.

Cyrus hopped onto the hood of the vehicle and then sat down with his legs folded in front of him, the shotgun next to him and the rifle draped across his knees.

"<u>We</u> want you dead."

"What do <u>you</u> want?"

"I just wanna talk," he said.

"I'm listening."

"It's a shame this had to happen. I feel like you and I would have gotten along famously if we had met under better circumstances."

"I don't think we run in quite the same circles," said Celia.

"You'd be surprised. Right now I feel like all we're doing is going in circles. I'm getting bored."

"Let me go and we can end this now. I'll forget this ever happened."

"Maybe we could have done that a half hour ago," Cyrus said.

"But you had to be too smart. Figure out who I am. Now we have to kill you. Can't your friend talk? What's wrong with him?"

"I have the microphone," said Celia. "You'll talk to me and only me."

"Easy. Sheesh, I'm just trying to have a conversation here. No need to get all uppity just because you went to some big city college. Shit, I've been to Vegas too, learned to play cards, that's the only kind of education you need in this kind of burg."

"I'll ask you again," said Celia. "What do you want?"

"I don't know," he said, looking up at the sky, the alien mask tilting with his face as if he was waiting to be beamed back up to the mothership. "I s'pose I got pretty upset when you said my name, so I got storming down here with my guns ready to shoot. But that's about a quarter mile walk in the heat and by the time I get by your car, I'm hot and tired and the anger's gone from me.

"Do you ever do that, Officer Miller? I do that, sometimes, it doesn't take much to set me off, I'm trying to work on it, but then I get upset and carry on like a crazy person, and ten minutes later I can't rightly remember why it was I was mad in the first place.

"Take this situation. You say my name, and I worry 'cause this here was supposed to be anonymous. You weren't supposed to know any of us, not Cyrus Everhaart, not Dirnt, certainly not…oh, see, I almost slipped up again. Thought I was going to go giving you another secret identity there.

"But then on the walk down here, I'm getting ready to take off my mask, seeing as how you know who I am and all, and I get to thinking. My mama always told me not to think, that it would get me in trouble with my daddy, but I ended up killing both of them, so it don't much matter now.

"That's a lie, Celia, I didn't kill either of them. The cancer took one and a bullet did take t'other, I'll let you figure out which took which.

"There I go rambling again. So I'm thinking as I'm walking, why take your mask off? Who really cares if she knows the name Cyrus Everhaart? So long as you can't see me on that there dashboard cam of hers, I'm still good as gold. The girl's gonna be dead, and it ain't like her brain is gonna retain that information. It's like having those, whaddaya call them, hard drives but without a computer. There might be some information on there, but unless you've got a computer to plug it into it's just a paperweight.

 PERSISTENCE

"I think I'd like to use you as a paperweight, Officer Miller. Some part of you. Can you help me decide which? So many good ones to choose. The eyes, the heart, all the good sexy bits of course."

"Fuck you," said Brian.

"It speaks!" said Cyrus. "I think he's taken my waggling tongue as an affront to your womanhood."

"You talk a lot for someone who thinks he controls the situation," said Celia. "You think you're scaring me, but all you're doing is making me more confident. I've scared you. Sure, when you rattled your saber before, shot off some bullets, yelled and carried on, you sure looked scary. But I think that's your normal demeanor. You feel in control when you can dominate the situation. But this, this is your nerves speaking. And I like it."

Cyrus was silent for a moment or two, and then chuckled.

"Shit, maybe you're right. Hell, I know you're right. You did get under my skin, mayhap in a way no other woman's ever done, on account of my usually not giving two quiddly fucks about what a pair of tits thinks. I would have liked to buy you a beer before this. I'm still holding out hope that maybe I'll get a kiss out of you by the time this is said and done. What do you think? You and I just run away together? I think you could make an honest man out of me."

"I'll make an honest woman out of you if you let me at you with a knife."

"Shit, I do like you! Maybe I love you. I just wish you weren't so damn smart."

He looked down at the car's hood, and then directly at Celia, the alien eyes seeming to stare through her.

"You know that's what this is all about, right?" Cyrus said, hunching forward conspiratorially. "It's 'cause you're too smart. You were bound to figure out something you weren't supposed to. Something happened and you started to piece it together, and somebody, they couldn't let you piece it together, 'cause it would mean very bad things for them. My pal up there, he doesn't want me to tell you, doesn't want you to know the truth, but what do I care?

"Do you want to know, Celia? You must. I mean, this has gotta be killing you, a veritable armed militia encircling you, trying to get at you, to harm you, to maim you, to kill you. And for what? That's the million-dollar question, isn't it?

"I wish I could tell you. But you'll have to die not knowing. And that's the worst part of all, i'nt it? You will never find out why it was you had to die."

Celia stared at him, through him. Then she got back on the microphone.

"Did you actually want something? Or are you just going to stand there talking like a bitch all day?"

Cyrus laughed.

"I do love you," he said. "But that won't stop me from cutting your tits off."

He drew the pistol from behind his back quickly, the laugh instantly evaporating, Celia reeling back from the windshield even though the bullets weren't capable of traveling through the glass. Instead, they smacked into it, turning the see-through glass opaque. *Whap whap whap.*

He stepped down from the hood and came around to the driver's side window, the pistol back in his waistband and the rifle now in his arms. Cyrus sent bullets cascading into the glass, and though the bullets failed to penetrate, what they did do was cloud things over, each bullet leaving about three inches of cloud, blotting out the clear view that Celia had been relying on for the past hours.

"What's he doing?" asked Brian.

"He's blinding us."

Cyrus walked around the car, peppering it with bullets. Each one that struck diminished their sight that much more, from the driver's side to the back and then over to the passenger's side. He even took time to shoot out the tires on the pizza delivery kid's crummy car. When he was done, it was still technically possible to see out, but to get a view of the entire landscape, Celia had to press her face right up against the glass. Otherwise, she would see a patch of sky here, a clouded piece of dirt there, Cyrus's unimposing yet intimidating shape there.

"I may not have your heart," said Cyrus as the whine of bullets died down, "but I can take your eyes. Good luck, Celia Miller. I hope you get a couple more of us before I kill you. You've put up a helluva fight so far; I'd hate to see that stop now."

"Fuck you," said Brian, pounding his hand on the glass of the front windshield and then extending his middle finger.

"You shut up," said Cyrus. "You've yet to impress me."

The sun finally descended behind the bluff. Cyrus watched it go, shading his eyes and letting the last few rays wash over him as if he was showering in them.

"I best be getting back up to the big boss man," he said. "I stay down here much longer he's gonna get jealous something fierce. He thought this would be over quick, you know? I don't think he planned on it taking so long. You've got him flustered."

"Who is he?" asked Celia.

"Some asshole, taking orders from some other asshole. What does it matter?"

Cyrus took a step toward the bluff, then stopped and looked at the car in the dying light.

"I hear you all in the police force call us the Illegals. Is that true?" he asked.

"It is."

Cyrus nodded. "You figure out why it is we did what we did, you'll know who we are."

He walked away, slower than the gait at which he came down the mountain, shuffling up the incline that would lead toward whatever encampment they had behind the bluff.

49

Answers (and sleep) remained elusive as day gave way to night. As the sun went all the way down, the oppressive heat went with it. Celia let Brian rest his eyes for a while, but even with her thoughts to herself, no matter how often she turned her current predicament and Cyrus's own words over in her mind, the more frustrated she became.

"A convenience store," said Celia. "A church. A casino. What do they have in common?"

"They all start with the letter C," said Brian. He widened his eyes in mock horror. "Dear God, Celia, are you behind this?!"

She punched him in the arm.

"And those are only the reported sightings of the Illegals that the police are willing to directly attribute to the group. The force has been ready to jump on every parking ticket and attribute it to the men in the alien masks. What makes things so difficult is the lack of anything concrete; no witnesses to testify, no evidence to implicate anyone, no motive to account for the crimes."

"So every robbery," said Brian, "every kidnapping, every unsolved murder without a prime suspect in a six county radius, well, it must be the Illegals."

Celia nodded. "Exactly. And amid everything, I pissed them off somehow. The incident at The Rocks. Or the investigation. Or maybe Haddock's own investigation."

"But how? What got them so worked up?"

Celia thought back, thought hard.

"The only incident of note was my trip to The Rocks last month, when I blasted my way out of that trailer. But even at that, no one had been arrested, no one sent to jail, my only success was getting a hold of a bag of meth and a fistful of cash stuffed into a micro-wave."

"Maybe that's what this is about," said Brian. "The meth."

Throw a dart at the United States in the wake of the financial crash and you'd be bound to hit a town where methamphetamine was the drug of choice. It was cheap, it was widely available, and when no respected industries existed, no factory jobs, no farms, no tech giants, meth would eventually swoop in as a viable alternative.

"Ravencourt has its share of methheads," she said. "Cooks on the outskirts of town who think they're Heisenberg incarnate. The Rocks is a particular hot spot. But it has nothing in the way of or-ganization. In fact, in the past year or so, the trade had died down considerably. Methheads still exist, it doesn't matter how many labs you shut down, the customers will find a way to get their fix. But large-scale shutdowns are increasingly uncommon. Instead, us cops are stuck raiding small scale users in their trailers, sending them from The Rocks to the prison they came from."

"At which point their properties are snatched up by Haart of the Sea?" asked Brian.

Her eyes flicked toward him.

"Son of a bitch," she said.

"What?"

"The Rocks. It's mostly parolees, right? And most of them are recidivists. They're in and out of jail so many times they never have the opportunity to put down stakes."

"Okay…"

"So we go up there to check on them, make sure they're abiding by the terms of their parole, and if they don't, we're required to send them back. And their properties, every piece of them, from the trailer to the dirt yard to the patch of lot it all sits on, gets sold to the next ex-convict.

"Except that's not what's been happening lately. Instead, this Haart of the Sea, owned and operated by Mr. Everhaart up there, has been buying up the properties for pennies on the dollar.

"So Cyrus and his men, they supply The Rocks with meth and god knows what else. They take users trying to get their lives right and tempt them with the one thing that landed them in prison in the first place. Then we come in, confiscate their property and put it up at auction. Where Everhaart's shell company can swoop in and buy it for almost nothing."

"So what does that mean?" Brian didn't seem all that interested and, to be quite honest, Celia was mostly thinking out loud to herself to make sure it all stood up to scrutiny.

"It's not about the drugs. Not at all. The drugs make the money. But they also make it possible to get what they're really after: the land. It's a means to an end. They don't want the drug trade. They want the land that's right underneath the trade's feet."

An idea struck her.

"That's why they needed to pull off the casino job," she said. "That's why they risked the attention."

"Mm hmm," said Brian. He was staring out the window.

"Let's say Haart of the Sea wants to build something at The Rocks. They're never going to get all the properties at auction. Believe it or not, some of the people up there haven't broken the law. They're actually trying to turn their lives around. You would need to pay them off to leave the land, if not all of them, then enough that you could declare eminent domain and move them elsewhere against their will. And dozens of trailers like that, it wouldn't be cheap."

"You would need a job big enough to make the final investment," said Brian.

"That's it," she said. "The pattern I was missing."

They were silent then, Celia turning it over in her mind, testing her theory's boundaries. It fit, but there was still something missing…

"So if they want the land," asked Brian. "What do they want it for?"

Celia deflated.

"Can you not let me have one win? I'm sitting here spinning gold and all you do is ask me the one thing I'm not sure of. How about, 'great detective work, Celia'?

"Great detective work, Celia."

She rolled her eyes.

50

Celia really wished that the assholes would do something instead of just sit back and wait.

Now that darkness had fallen, they could be hiding anywhere. And it was making her paranoid.

She looked out the rear windshield and saw the lights of Ravencourt far in the distance. Closer by stood the glow of The Rocks, only about a mile and a half away atop a bluff, but impossibly far off in her current position.

She pressed her face to one of the clear portions of the windshield, looking up at the stars, thinking that this might be her last chance ever to see them. This far from town, they stood out clear alongside the moon, which had begun its slow traversal of the night sky.

Celia sighed and turned her attention back to her immediate surroundings, hoping to spot one of her tormentors. Considering that they were wearing all black, they could be hiding right outside and she wouldn't know it, not even as the moon made the area brighter and brighter.

Wait a second. The moon couldn't do that.

The desert around the squad car <u>was</u> getting brighter, like a ghost gaining substance in front of her eyes.

Celia whipped around and there, drawing toward her position like some sort of miracle, was a semi-truck, its brights on, illuminating the entire desert around it. If the driver couldn't see her yet, he certainly would soon.

Within a matter of seconds, Celia had the rifle cocked and the bullet-proof vest secured around her frame. She shook Brian by the shoulder and he startled awake at once.

"What is it?" he asked, bewildered.

"There's a truck coming," Celia said, unlocking her door.

"What are you doing?"

"Getting us out of here. Cover me."

Celia set a pistol on Brian's lap before he could protest. She opened the door, lit a flare, and then ran into the road and toward the incoming tractor trailer as fast as she could.

51

From his perch up on the bluff, Blue Jeans saw the truck coming long before Celia did. In fact, he had known it was incoming thanks to a communication from the men he had stationed in a truck down the road and out of Celia's sight. The semi had passed them before they could move, and so Blue Jeans had told them to trail it until it reached Celia's position and then to end whoever was driving it.

He also had a man positioned on the side of the road in the area of the callbox. This individual he told to stay put, to bide his time until Celia or the trucker made a move.

He couldn't get Cyrus positioned down there in time to head off the truck, but he was running as fast as he could from their current perch as Blue Jeans surveyed the entire scene from his night vision scope. At first, when Cyrus had personally requested to be the one to put a bullet in Celia's skull, Blue Jeans was uneasy. Now, he simply didn't have the energy to argue. He was tired of sitting here, tired of waiting, and just wanted it done. He no longer cared if it was him to do the deed as he had originally intended.

Celia leaped out of the vehicle and tossed a flare off to the side, temporarily causing Blue Jeans to wince at the sudden brightness. Not caring, he put the scope down and radioed down to his men.

"Take her out. NOW!"

52

Celia heard the squawk of radio chatter from her right and immediately started shooting at where she thought the noise had come from. She jogged backward toward the truck as quickly as she could while strafing her fire toward the dirt.

She saw a muzzle flash as whoever was positioned by the callbox opened fire, and as she turned her own gun toward that flash, she was relieved to see a muzzle flash emanating from her own squad car. Brian had seen the shooter and had homed in on him.

Trusting him to cover her because she didn't have a choice, Celia stopped shooting and now ran straight at the truck. The environment around her became brighter and brighter as the truck closed in, and not wanting to have this whole game end with her splattered along the concrete by a speeding big rig, she lit another flare.

She waved her arms in the air, making herself into a tempting target, hoping that Brian could keep the men occupied long enough to let her get far away.

New gunshots from up ahead of the Challenger joined the fray, and Celia realized she couldn't allow herself to be this visible any longer. Cursing, she flung the flare forward, toward the truck that was now no more than 100 yards away, and ran sideways, off the road and into the darkness, where she wouldn't be caught by the high beams.

The gunshots continued for a second or two before they died down. Celia hunkered down on her haunches about 20 yards from the roadway, trying to contain her breathing so she couldn't be overheard. After the intense bout of activity, this lack of motion was troubling.

As she pulled in breath, Celia tried to force her eyes to adjust to the darkness around her. The wind made the hair on her arms stand up, the gooseflesh seeming alien given that even a couple short hours ago she was being tormented by oppressive heat.

The wind kicked up again and suddenly Celia felt more defenseless than she'd been all day. She had no armor plating around her, no bulletproof glass, just the night sky, a bullet-proof vest and the temporary light-blindness from the truck's headlights and the muzzle flash. She wouldn't have long before they figured out her position.

The pounding of feet on pavement drew closer, and the truck slowed to a stop on an even keel with the flare. Not wanting to waste any more time, Celia made her move.

She ran as fast as she could directly at the passenger door of the big rig, the rifle slung over her shoulder. She jumped up onto the platform directly above the wheel and tried the door, but much to her chagrin, it was locked.

Her badge was out in an instant, held up to the window, displayed in front of the eyes of a 40ish trucker with a scraggle that could never grow into the Duck Dynasty beard the tired-eyed driver hoped it would.

"Open the goddamn door, this is an emergency!"

His eyes widened and he knocked over his liter of Mountain Dew from the cup holder as he fumbled for the door latch. Gunshots erupted anew, sparks snaking across the hood of the truck. This caused the trucker to duck down, the door still locked.

"Open the door now!"

The man looked up and met Celia's pleading eyes, which must have looked wild given her current state. The man reached for the door and hesitated as more bullets hit the hood. He looked back at his ignition and then right at Celia. She watched the thought form in his head even before he had even maybe decided it himself.

Oh no, dude, you are not trying to save yourself.

The trucker put the truck into gear from his stooped position as Celia unholstered her pistol. She blew out the passenger window, making sure to angle the bullet in a way that wouldn't put the man at risk. Glass sprayed inside, causing the late-night impromptu savior to cover his head and take his hand off the stick.

Celia reached in and unlatched the passenger door just as the windshield cracked and then shattered inward as well, showering the trucker with glass. She pulled the door open and then dove inside, pulling the door shut behind her as she did.

"Listen lady, I ain't done nothing, maybe just had a drink or two, nothing that would warrant an execution."

"I don't care. Just drive this piece of shit as fast as you can. Now!"

Not risking putting his head up, the trucker once again put the truck into gear, this time with more success. His foot hit the gas and they were up and running, each of them with their heads down and out of sight as bullets caromed off the interior of the cabin. Without the windshield, wind blew into the car and caused Celia's hair to fly everywhere.

"I can't see, lady."

"It doesn't matter," Celia said. "Just keep straight."

The driver peeked out and then quickly brought his head back down. As he did so, Celia noticed him pulling the wheel slightly to the left, likely so that he wouldn't strike her own squad car or the poor pizza delivery guy's ride.

The gunshots dissipated. Celia assumed they had made it past the position of the man on the side of the Challenger. The trucker exhaled deeply.

"Goddamn, girl, what did you get me into?"

"I'll tell you later, just keep driving on this road."

"I still can't see."

"Just a little longer. What were you doing out here anyway?"

"Running behind schedule. Name's Norm. This old road's the only way I was ever gonna make it on time and even that was pushing it. Sure didn't expect to be picking up no lady cop while getting shot at."

"Today hasn't gone the way either of us were probably thinking, Norm."

"I've gotta see the road, this is just dangerous."

Norm repositioned his body to lift his head. Celia dug her nails into his arm.

"You can't. Keep your head down."

"Lady, I gotta be able to see the road or we're gonna be killed by a wreck rather than bullets."

He sat up to his full height. Celia tried to pull him down but to no avail.

"You can't drive like that, they'll see you."

"They're all behind us."

"Get down!"

"It's alright, sweetheart, they ain't—"

Whatever they ain't, Celia would never know, because the top of Norm's head was peeled away by a bullet from a high-powered rifle. Blood splattered against the interior of the cabin and into the truck's sleep space. Norm's head rolled back and then slapped forward, his chin resting on his chest, his eyeball hanging in the scraggle of beard that would grow no more.

Celia screamed, not in fear or terror but in pure unbridled rage. She was sick of people getting caught in the crossfire for doing nothing more than driving down the wrong road. And she was tired of having other peoples' blood very literally on her hands.

Since the semi was driving up an incline, it coasted to a stop. Celia, still stooping behind the dashboard out of sight, reached up and unlatched the lock on the driver's side. She pushed open the door and then unceremoniously shoved Norm's not inconsiderable girth out into the desert, saying a silent sorry as his body slapped against the pavement.

While she did this, she heard additional gunshots and felt the semi slump beneath her. They had shot out the tires. She wasn't going forward anytime soon. They'd be able to catch up with her instantly.

Celia shut the door again, and with silence engulfing her, she stole a glance up at the road.

Standing in the middle of the beams of the headlights was Cyrus in his alien mask, slowly walking forward, a mere 20 or 30 feet from the truck. He had the rifle on his shoulder and pointed into the air when he saw Celia's head peek out. He waved with one hand as he moved the weapon directly toward her with the other.

Celia started shooting before Cyrus got a chance to. Seeing her pull the pistol up, Cyrus broke to the side, out of the glare of the headlights, and she lost him instantly. She yelled a string of profanities, knowing that he would be approaching the cabin door within seconds. With no chance of escape on two flat tires, unable to see her assailant coming at her from either side, and half insane with the adrenaline coursing through her body, Celia did the only thing she could think of in the moment:

She put the truck into reverse and pressed down on the

accelerator with all her might.

The truck barreled backward like a drunken elephant, its wounded front legs preventing any sort of worthwhile navigation. As the headlights momentarily canted to the left, Celia thought she caught a glimpse of Cyrus, but he quickly fell behind, unable to keep pace with the truck, which was now picking up speed as it rumbled ass-first down the hill.

Celia stole a glance in the mirror but was unable to judge how far she was from the squad car. If she could only make it back there, she could live to fight another day. In the truck, though, she was defenseless, no cover from bullets and the machinations of men who wanted her dead.

She turned to the right, looking out the tiny passenger side window that allows the driver to see any cars that might be lined up alongside it. Rather than look out for cars, Celia was using it to gauge where she was in alignment with the road, nudging the wheel slightly in either direction so that she stayed relatively in the middle of the two lanes.

Her own squad car zoomed past in the window space and Celia let go of the gas, the speed of the truck already taking the car out of view. She pressed down on the brakes, but it took the truck much longer to stop than she would have liked.

The truck finally ground to a halt, but just as Celia righted herself in the cabin and prepared to dash for her car, something struck the semi from behind, rocketing her forward to smash her face against the steering column, her nose striking the wheel and immediately gushing blood. Bright circles swam in and out of her vision, and Celia suddenly had a hard time seeing anything directly in front of her.

Celia pushed her knuckles into her eyes, willing the circles to go away, and when she opened them back up, she was able to look in the left-hand rearview mirror. A pickup truck was back there, its front hood all sorts of smashed in. The driver had hurtled directly into the motionless semi.

But it wasn't the pickup that truly frightened her. A tall man in an alien mask, likely the Giant, was running toward the driver's side of her prone vehicle, his weapon drawn and ready to fire. Celia looked on the right-hand side mirror to see another man approaching from that way. This man had gauze shoved into one of the eyeholes of the mask.

The assholes I hurt earlier.

     PERSISTENCE

Not wanting to wait for them or anyone else to reach the door, Celia brandished her pistol and lurched forward, through the shattered windshield, trying to ignore the shards of glass as they dug into her hands, arms, and legs. She crawled up the hood of the truck and then rolled herself to the edge, pushing off and landing painfully on her back on the cement at the front of the cab.

The wind was knocked out of her, but Celia sucked in her breath and turned over on her side, aiming her pistol at the feet of the men who were approaching her from either side. She shot the short one first, his toe bursting open in a cloud of red and a scream piercing the background noise of the truck's idling engine. The man fell face first near the tire, and Celia put a bullet in his other eye to match the flare she shoved into the left one earlier.

The Giant must have heard the screams or sensed what Celia was doing, as he then jumped up onto the runner on the driver's side. Celia scrambled to her own feet. Her knees buckled, but she was able to catch herself on the wide front grille of the semi. She forced her left leg to move, and then her right leg, and scampered over with a hobble in her step to the passenger side of the truck, toward the man she had just shot dead.

Their truck. It still works. Run, goddamnit, run.

They had left it idling as its mangled front abutted the back of the tractor trailer, which Celia now saw was an oil tanker. She took two steps and her legs gave out anew, her vision swimming as she struggled to suck in breath.

If you can just make it to the truck, this is over. You win. One foot after the other.

Knowing she would need both hands to prop herself up, she holstered her pistol begrudgingly and took a few more tentative steps, propping herself up on both hands. She began to feel the world balance again, and just as she was working up the will to run, a bullet struck her in the back, hitting the bulletproof vest rather than her spine that lay just behind it.

The man by the squad car. Fuck.

Not taking the time to look back, Celia instead opened the passenger door of the semi's cabin, feeling a sense of twisted *déjà vu* as she pulled herself inside. She crawled across the seat and was positioned above the middle console when the driver's door opened. The Giant stood there, looking bigger than ever from his vantage point on the side runner. He actually didn't see her for a split second, his eyes scanning too high, and that gave Celia all the time she needed to act.

She thrust herself backward, through the center space, and into the sleeping area of the truck cabin.

There wasn't much to work with: a cot, a small closet, no windows, and no protection.

With nothing else to do, Celia spun around while drawing her gun and pointed it toward where she assumed the Giant would be.

She was too late; a fist wrapped around her hand, enveloping it the way a grown adult's would a child's. The fingers squeezed and the gun dropped from Celia's grip. She looked up into the vacant black eyes of the man's mask.

He pointed his pistol at her, and Celia couldn't tell if he was taking his time or if her imminent death had slowed everything down dramatically.

"You could never beat us," it sounded like the man said, although Celia wasn't sure because the mask muffled his voice and things were somehow moving both quickly and in slo-mo at the same time.

The gun barrel turned toward Celia's face, but she took her eyes off it to focus instead on the bandages covering where the man's thumb had been chopped off earlier, his grip on the gun tenuous at best. Although her hand was in his vice-like grip, her head was free. She darted her neck forward like a bird pecking at a cracker and wrapped her teeth around a piece of gauze, pulling with all her might and feeling a burst of warm blood go gushing between her teeth.

"You fuckin' bitch!"

Celia didn't care what he called her, though, because the gun was now on the ground, rolling around their feet. Her hand was free, but just when Celia thought she could make a move, her head was slapped backward and she fell into the cot, her vision going blurry again.

The man hurtled forward, enraged, pinning Celia down. His good hand wrapped around her neck and her range of vision diminished considerably, shrinking into a smaller and smaller tunnel.

She clawed for something, anything, but the last shades of color faded from the world. Now hardly able to see anything but darkness, her hand fell toward her hip…

…and struck a bottle of mace, which had been attached there all day. With a renewed will to live that would buy her seconds at most,

   Persistence

she pulled out the canister, readied the weapon by feel alone, jammed it up under the cowl of the man's hood and let it rip.

His howls were of pure agony, his hands going to his mask and away from Celia's neck. She gasped for air and bright stars replaced the darkness. It was as if the entire universe had been snapped back painfully into focus. She rolled onto the ground, ducking under his feet as he leaned forward over the cot. Celia grabbed the pistol the man had dropped and stood up, pointing the gun at the back of his head as he was about to tear his mask off.

Celia didn't give him the chance. She pulled the trigger execution style, spraying blood and brain across what used to be the home away from home of a lonely trucker. The big man slumped forward, his head on his hunched-together hands, as if praying to some God that was cruel enough to create a world where an Adonis of a man could be killed unfairly by a cunt of a woman.

Knowing that there were at least two other men who could enter the fray at any moment, Celia turned, scooping up her own pistol, and crawled through the windshield once again, firing blindly into the dark to make whoever was out there think twice before shooting.

This time, instead of rolling off the front, she turned her body and climbed up on top of the cabin, making her way onto the tanker full of fuel. If she could just get to the truck behind, this could all end.

She stumbled along its length, forcing herself to move, but the end of the truck seemed unfathomably out of reach.

It was when she reached the halfway point that she heard footsteps up on the hood of the truck. Another set of footsteps joined those. Celia turned, but the motion made her dizzy and she fell on her butt and then lay draped across the tanker, her back curling around the curved metal.

The men near the front of the truck swam in and out of her vision, but they just stood there, their guns raised but apparently not in any hurry to kill her. She must have looked dead already. From their vantage point, her attempts to lift her gun and shoot were failing dramatically, as if the pistol weighed too much for her to even raise her arm. She fired off bullets well before she had them in her sights, the rounds clanging impotently against the metal hull of the tanker, all in the same spot.

Finally, the gun just dropped off the side, falling to the cement below. Celia looked at them and they back at her. One of the men had opted not to wear a shirt. Cyrus. The other appeared to be waiting for a signal.

"It's over, Officer Miller," said Cyrus. "You had a good run."

"I got a lot of you fuckers," said Celia. "You gotta give me that."

"Be proud of yourself. You're more man than any of these pretenders. I don't think anyone will make the mistake of underestimating you again."

Celia laughed, and Cyrus joined in.

"You're wrong," she said.

"Why's that?"

"Because here I am, dead to rights, and you stop to chat like a bitch just because I act like a little girl on death's doorstep."

She slipped the flare out of her back pocket and lit it up, holding it aloft over the hole in the tanker truck she had just shot out with the pistol.

"Go fuck yourself, Cyrus."

Although she couldn't see him through his mask, she imagined his eyes went wide. She dropped the flare into the hole and then rolled off the side of the tanker, a split second before Cyrus and the other man scrambled down themselves.

Celia dropped to the ground, fell, scampered to her feet, and ran into the desert. She didn't know if the tanker would actually explode, didn't know if a flare was hot enough or the petroleum inside combustible enough. She didn't know if it would explode immediately, disintegrating her and the others in an instant. All she knew was that it was her only play.

For a few seconds nothing happened. Celia thought that maybe she had failed, misjudged the effect of the flare on the gas.

She was about to glance back over her shoulder when the sun rose early, the desert illuminating all around her as she was thrust forward into a sudden blinding white light. The sound followed after, a presence more physical than aural.

KA-BOOM.

53

It was the ringing that woke her, a sound she was now becoming far too familiar with on the heels of firing a rifle in the trunk of her car. She tried to open her eyes, could swear she was opening them, but doing so was like a dream where you will something to happen, a part of your body to move, but it absolutely refuses.

She exerted every ounce of energy (which was admittedly not much) toward opening her eyes, yet still she failed, and still that ringing. That damn ringing.

Suddenly she was being lifted. Someone was trying to stand her on her feet.

She panicked at this, flailing her arms in every direction. Her eyes may not have been working properly but her arms seemed to respond. She couldn't see her assailant, couldn't see who was trying to prop her up, so her nails scratched in every direction, and it was enough to cause her to fall back onto the sand, a tuft of dust entering her lungs and causing her to cough.

Firm hands gripped her wrists. She heard yelling through the ringing, yelling that got clearer and clearer.

"…elia, it's me, it's Brian. Please don't fight. Do you hear me? PLEASE DON'T FIGHT!"

Brian must have been shouting in her ear to get her attention. She stopped trying to twist free of his grip and nodded. There was a shape above her coaxing her up and onto her feet. Brian's hands pulled with all their might and Celia let them take her as she tried and failed to get her feet beneath her.

Brian managed to drape Celia's arm around his shoulders and

now moved forward, turning her 180 degrees.

Light filled Celia's vision, causing her to wince. She looked away from the charred remnants of the tanker truck, instead focusing on the shadows dancing beneath her feet, causing her shoes to swim in and out of darkness.

Her shoes. She could see them now, coming into focus, becoming tangible. *She* was becoming more tangible, her thoughts coming back to her. She could remember who she was, where she was.

Emboldened, she planted a tender foot beneath her to assist Brian and immediately screamed in agony, falling back toward the ground. It took all Brian had to keep her held up. She bit down on her lip, forced herself back up to a full standing position with her other leg. Much to her relief, this one did not give.

Brian dragged her through the sand, one foot flopping in the air and the other pushing off the desert.

Where were they going?

Celia looked up and saw that Brian was bringing her back toward the squad car.

She opened her mouth in protest but immediately started hacking up sand and phlegm and bloody sand and sandy blood.

"Try not to talk, Celia."

You don't understand! she wanted to scream. *This is our only chance. There'll be more of them. Get to the truck!*

Celia stole a glance to her left, but was unable to see past the blaze to see if the Illegals' truck was still there or if it had been flung by the blast to some dark corner of the desert where it would never be seen again.

It doesn't matter. We have to try. Brian, please.

But she couldn't get the words out. Instead, Brian continued toward the squad car, drawing closer and closer with every step, bringing Celia toward what had become her prison cell, what might become her tomb.

"Bri—" she got out before the coughing overtook her again, and this time her vision filled with bright spots. The retching brought her low to the ground again, and the moment her toe struck the sand, more pain went shooting up her leg, causing her to cry out.

A rustle of movement caught her eye, and she looked up, forcing the spots to go away. Cyrus was there, trying to stand up like a wrestler who had just kicked out of a nine count. His head lulled to one side and he was able to get an elbow propped beneath his alien mask. Further behind him, another man also began to stir. She saw him tear his mask off and then fall back to the ground, also trying to get his legs back.

Celia pointed, motioning from Brian to Cyrus and then back again.

"I know," said Brian, dragging Celia toward the car now. "I'm getting you away from them. They won't hurt you."

I don't want you to protect me, she thought. *I want you to kill them. Please KILL THEM NOW. This may be our only chance.*

But they were at the car now, and Celia lost sight of the men, and Brian was opening the back-seat passenger door and trying to contort Celia in such a way that would allow her to get inside. He stole a glance over his shoulder and panic filled his eyes. Someone must have been coming down the hill again.

Do they have no end to reinforcements?

Brian ducked and bullets struck the rear passenger window. Thankfully, the door was positioned in such a way as to act like a shield. Hunkered down, Brian was able to get Celia's upper body into the car. She pulled herself in with her arms, biting back on the scream that wanted to emanate from her lips as her foot struck the door frame.

Once she was fully in, Brian closed the door and then dove to the front passenger seat, pulling the door closed behind him.

He immediately moved toward the hole Celia had carved earlier in the metal grille dividing the front and the back and leaned in toward her. He rested a hand on her face and Celia batted it away. She then felt bad about doing so and wrapped her small hand around his larger one and brought it back down, allowing him to brush the grime away from her temple.

"It's okay, Celia," he said. "We're safe now. We made it."

Celia lay on the seat and wept then, harder than she ever had in her life. She wept not from the pain, but from the thought that she would never leave this goddamn squad car ever again.

54

She awoke to light. And heat. It was getting hot again. She squinted her eyes and looked around.

Brian was focused intently on the road in front of him, clouded as it was by the spackling of the windshield where the bullets had hit. Celia's gun sat on the dashboard in front of him.

He must have heard her stir, because he turned around now and immediately moved his face toward hers through the barrier between the seats.

"You're awake," he said, as if he himself barely believed this fact could be true.

"I slept like shit," she said, and was surprised by her own voice, by how strong it sounded.

She sat up in the seat, a dull pain emanating from her foot. Not sharp like before. She looked down and saw that her foot was wrapped in bandages. Scanning her body, she now saw that she actually had various patches covering her where the skin had been broken. She moved her hand up to her temple to feel the wound there, and that too was closed up. She winced as her hand pulled at a thin thread that had been woven there to stanch the flow of blood.

Celia looked at Brian and smiled.

"You've been busy."

"Surprised you don't remember any of it. I was able to coax you awake to give you some water and pain meds. You were out cold during the stitches though."

"How'd you figure out how to do something like that?"

"I learned from the best."

Celia nodded.

"There room for me up there?"

"If you think you can make it."

But she was already leaning forward, pulling herself through the opening she had carved out with the rifle. Brian scooted over to give her room to pass.

She landed on the seat, making sure to not let her tender ankle take any of the weight. Her eyes scanned the desert through the clouded glass.

"Where are they?"

"I don't know," said Brian. "They've been around. The crazy one, Cyrus, he keeps showing up, taking potshots at the car. The other one, the leader, he's been gone since the explosion."

"How many?"

"At least three," he said. "Maybe more. Guess it depends how many they started with. The two on top of the truck, Cyrus and the other one, they were pretty banged up but survived."

"Any cars?"

Brian shook his head. "No, not since last night. You'd think there'd be something since the place lit up like a Christmas tree. And the pizza delivery kid, you'd think they'd send someone after him. But there's been nothing."

Celia furrowed her brow. There was something off about that. The explosion should have brought *someone* out here, whether it be a couple of firefighters or a coot from The Rocks coming to see what all the ruckus was about.

"I suppose they could have killed them," said Brian.

"There is always that."

Celia adjusted her seat and looked around for her keys, spotting them in the center console below the computer terminal.

"You run the car at all?"

"Turned on the lights for about an hour while I patched you up. Didn't want to risk any more than that."

"This desert heat's making you smart."

"Being around you is making me smart."

Celia chuckled and placed her hand on the glass. It couldn't be much later than 7:00 a. m. and the heat was already tangible. The car was going to get hot fast, and they wouldn't be able to run the battery like they did yesterday. And without water, their energy would be zapped quickly.

"We've gotta get out of here," said Celia.

"Sure. You wanna ask the aliens for a ride?"

"Don't be a shit. Hand me my gun."

Brian leaned forward and picked up Celia's gun. He handed it off to her. Celia opened the chamber to see how many bullets she had left.

She stopped short, the gun hovering in midair. Cold sweat formed on her brow despite the rapidly escalating heat.

"Brian, where did you get this?"

"I found it in the desert. A few feet from your body. I figured you dropped it when you went on your little explosion trip."

"I did."

"Then what's the problem?"

"This isn't my gun."

Celia knew her own gun, its precise feel, how many bullets she had in the chamber, the way her thumb had worn the slightest indentation on the side from where she gripped it just a bit too tight when she had to draw on someone. This looked like it, but it was not it.

A shiver went up Celia's spine now, and she felt the gun wobbling in her grip.

"No," she said.

"Celia, what's the matter?"

"It can't be. Please, oh God, it can't be."

Somehow, in her tussle with the Giant in the cabin of the semi, she had confused his gun for her own. It had been his she had picked up off the ground, positioned in her holster, used to open up a hole in the oil tanker. It was the Giant's gun that Brian had found near her body when she was nearly dead to the world.

Celia tossed the gun back onto the dashboard and now reached down around her feet. Once she found what she was looking for, she lifted her head back up and booted up the computer anew.

The seconds ticked by as Celia tapped the severed thumb against the seat. She fidgeted uncontrollably, feeling her teeth chatter in her head.

Please.

The computer kicked on and Celia immediately clicked on the fingerprint database once again. In her rush to get the thumb onto the scanner, she accidentally lost her grip and sent it toward Brian. It dropped on his lap and he scuttled away like it was a particularly gross bug.

     PERSISTENCE

Celia forced herself to take deep breaths, but anxiety gripped her. The ability to take in a steady amount of air proved impossible.

"Brian, the thumb," she said.

"Celia, you already tried this."

"JUST GIVE ME THE THUMB NOW!"

This caused him to get over any compunctions he may have had about handling a severed thumb. He picked it up from the area around his crotch and handed it to Celia. She forced her hands to be as steady as possible (which wasn't very steady at all) as she pressed the thumb down onto the metallic surface of the fingerprint scanner.

Once again, the outline of the digit popped up on the screen, and a green icon gave Celia the option to search.

"We already looked for this guy," Brian said. "There was no record of him."

"Unless we were looking in the wrong place."

Celia tried to move the mouse, but her hand was shaking too much.

"You're going to have to do it," she said, finally giving up after watching her jerky movements on the sensitive touchpad cause the mouse to dance all around the screen.

"Do what? Celia, I don't know what you're talking about."

"Use the trackpad," Celia said.

"Okay..."

"Click on personnel files."

Brian did as he was told.

"Now, run a search on the thumbprint."

Celia pressed her eyes into her hands and slumped over the wheel, chewing the inside of her mouth.

This can't be happening. Please, God, this can't be happening.

"Holy shit," said Brian. "There's a hit. Jared Smalls."

Celia's shoulders slumped. She removed her hands from her eyes and then looked at the name of the man on the screen.

The reason Celia had initially mistaken the gun for her own was because it was an identical type of firearm. There was only one way that you could get them (at least one with a serial number).

You had to be an upstanding member of a law enforcement agency.

Celia double-clicked the name. A photo of a musclebound man in a black hat with a badge in the center filled the screen. Brian gasped beside her.

Jared Smalls was Officer Jared Smalls, six-year member of the Ravencourt Police Department. Otherwise known to all of his fellow officers, except Celia, as Little Red.

The giant in the alien mask that Celia had just executed in the cabin of a semi was an officer of the law.

Which meant that Celia and Brian were well and truly fucked.

55

The megaphone of the Challenger suddenly squawked to life 100 yards away from where Blue Jeans and another Illegal, his finger jammed in his ear to try to deal with the ringing, had positioned themselves to watch the vehicle. Cyrus was closer to the squad car, sitting in the sand and out of sight. With his mask on, Blue Jeans couldn't tell if he was asleep or simply sitting still. He was still breathing, so that was good. Maybe.

"Jason," said Celia.

Blue Jeans's heart dropped when he heard his name over the loudspeaker.

She knew.

All the planning, all the disguises in case something bad happened, all out the window. Somehow, the cunt had been able to put together who they were.

At first a knot of dread filled Jason/Blue Jeans's stomach when he knew he'd been identified, like a lying child being called out by a parent asking who threw the rock through the broken window. Then, something interesting happened: relief. He no longer had to keep up the charade. He didn't have to wear the mask. He could let her see him for who he truly was. She would know that it was him who ended her life.

"Can we talk?" she said from the squad car.

56

This is the story of a boy who loved a girl.

The boy and the girl were inseparable growing up, and everyone told them that they were bound to wind up together, that they were meant to be.

Alas, life got in the way for Celia Miller and Jason Martinez. He wanted to fight for his country and she wanted to meet some city boys. They were like a Ryan Adams song no one remembers.

So the boy gets shipped to the Middle East and fights a war while the girl goes to college to learn all about how to catch criminals. While the girl was studying to do more than what her birthplace suggested was possible, the boy thought of nothing but the girl. Her face filled his mind in moments of tedium, when all there was was the desert and your thoughts. It filled his mind in moments of horror, when you were putting a bullet between the eyes of a man with a beard who looked just like every other man with a beard. It filled his mind when he was having more or less consensual sex with 15-year-olds whose husbands were shepherds who were unable to protect them from even meaner men with weapons.

It filled his mind at all these times, and he assumed that his face filled her mind too.

At one point, the boy met up with another boy and, lo and behold, this boy was from a place that was familiar to the first boy: Ravencourt. Why, they had grown up just miles apart from each other.

This new boy's name was Cyrus Everhaart, and this boy introduced Jason Martinez to the profit that could be made in trafficking hashish overseas and the joy that could be had in killing people from a world you couldn't understand.

When the boys came back from war, they were much changed, although you wouldn't know it from outward appearances alone. The one thing that didn't change was that Celia's face continued to occupy Jason's thoughts, and he dreamed of taking up where they had left off, giving her the ring that they could only talk about but never act upon when they were kids.

But Celia had other ideas.

She had been introduced to a different life, a life that she haughtily assumed was better but that Jason could see right away was just different. It was months before he even got to see her; in fact, Celia had expressed no desire to come back while speaking to him on his many phone calls, and the only thing that had brought her back to Ravencourt was an ailing father.

Ravencourt exerted a type of gravity, like any hometown, calling back those who had left, and Celia was no different. What started as a weekend visit turned to weeks and then months as she sat by her father's side during his last days. At that time, Celia was vulnerable, and Jason lent a shoulder when she needed to cry on it.

Then, one night, they slept together, and Jason remembered the way it had felt like no time had passed at all, but when he looked in her eyes he saw no love. In fact, she had left the room rather quickly, not staying the night as she used to do.

After her father passed, Celia got a job on the same police force as Jason, but try as he might, he could not get close to her. She removed herself from any type of camaraderie, shunning social functions with the rest of the force, but it soon became clear that she was shunning his company.

He tried and tried and yet still he couldn't get her to see that what they had was special, that they belonged together like all of their friends had said, like he himself knew. She refused to recognize this truth, barely making eye contact with him anymore, not letting him inside her heart the way she existed in his.

While Jason tried in vain to woo back Celia, the burgeoning trade that he and Cyrus had initiated upon their return to the States was expanding at a rapid pace. Other cops had been brought in on the trade because, after all, you couldn't survive on a cop's salary alone. Cyrus had provided an avenue for the biggest commodity in all of Ravencourt and Jason's team provided the cover they needed to not have to worry about interference.

It was all working like a peach, until there had been some trouble with some locals. That's when the idea of the Illegals had come about. An urban legend that would allow them to act in a way that cops wouldn't be able to.

And all the while, Celia went about her business, not fitting in with the rest of the gang. Torturing him with her mere presence. He couldn't focus, couldn't convince her to love him, she was clearly miserable being at the station, and yet she didn't leave. She stayed and yet she pushed him away, refusing to fit in yet not willing to cut her losses and carve out a space for herself somewhere, anywhere else.

It was the boyfriend that set him off. He understood at some level that she would have had to date other guys in college, but he wouldn't think about it if she wouldn't talk about it. But to flaunt someone else around his town, the town he bled for, the town that he worked to protect, as if it was nothing?

This he could not abide. He had given her every chance to love him, and barring that, he and the rest of the cops had given her every chance to leave. Jason's love for her hadn't changed, but he himself had changed in fundamental ways. People weren't supposed to look at him with contempt, with loathing; they were supposed to look at him with respect, with fear, with adoration. He was a soldier, and yet she continued to treat him like a mopey teenager that couldn't handle a gun nor a woman.

And when Jason stole into her house late at night, when he had known Celia was busy at a dingy local bar because he had followed her there at a distance, her fate was sealed. For he had discovered that she had been looking into his handiwork, even if she hadn't known it was him.

Celia's investigation was yet one more sign that she thought she was better than him. That she could outsmart him. That she would find something that so many others had missed simply because she had nothing between her legs but a hole that stole into his thoughts in the darkest moments of the night and the surprisingly bright moments of the day.

The meth she had collected, if shown to a man with some actual authority, would trigger a more official investigation. Jason and Cyrus had grown proud, believing themselves untouchable. There were limits to their reach in Ravencourt and surrounding areas. But across state lines? Desert on the Nevada side was identical as on the California side, the Utah side, as were the people. But those states held so

PERSISTENCE

many more of those people, fresh new addicts ready to provide what little welfare money they had for the candy that Cyrus could now create in six trailers within Ravencourt and the surrounding area.

She would not take this from him. She would not ruin his life. He had loved her once, still loved her in fact, in a way reserved exclusively for the grandest poets and the meanest internet trolls in the comments of YouTube videos, yet she had pushed too far.

His extracurricular activity and his team, built of cops looking for extra income and rednecks looking for their only income, had afforded Jason a unique opportunity to both surgically remove Celia from his brain and bring an end to the notoriety of the Illegals. Because when she was dead, Jason, Cyrus, and the other cops would murder the lowlifes and stage everything to make it look like they had been killed in a firefight as the valiant cops swooped in to avenge one of their own. In one fell swoop, Celia and the Illegals would both be dead, and their operation could continue unhindered by state and federal investigations that could flex muscles the Ravencourt PD didn't possess.

Jason wanted to make things quick, orchestrate a break-in gone wrong that very night, but he had been talked out of it. Cyrus was always up for a good time and could be very convincing. Kill her in the apartment, and investigators comb through every inch and find the remnants of her investigation. The Illegals leave any trace behind, they're fucked.

Why not enjoy themselves a little bit? Didn't Jason deserve to have some fun? So instead they came up with a different plan, one that would bring Celia out to the middle of nowhere, so close to the spot where he had first fallen for her. And while she was away? Well, then another of the men responsible for patrolling Ravencourt's streets could take their time cleaning her apartment of every trace of evidence she had compiled.

Jason chose the spot because of what it meant to him. He still held fond memories of that night, the night just over the bluff, just a mile or so further from The Rocks and not a couple hundred yards from here, a stretch of desert you could get to with a four-wheeler or an all-wheel drive that still had its shocks and struts intact. When they were young, you used to be able to drive out there and find beer bottles, broken bongs, all the signs of teens taking their first steps into adulthood.

He and Celia had gone there together, juniors in high school, them and a group of friends. They had talked into the night, drinking beers and even sharing a cigarette, something the normally uptight Celia Miller would never indulge in. The other people just fell away. At one point, they had stopped talking and just looked at the stars, and then Jason had turned his head and looked deep into Celia's eyes. She had smiled at him, the moon making visible every part of her face.

He had kissed her then. Long, deep. They had tiptoed toward each other before, drunken make-outs at parties, a random kiss in a movie, but this was different. Jason knew he was in love, that he would stay with her for the rest of her life.

They had stolen up to that very spot a half dozen or so times more, including the last time Jason had seen her before she left for college. They'd made love, in the back seat, under the stars, Jason looking deep into her eyes as he came while Celia looked out the window and groaned with pleasure, pulling him closer and holding him next to her body for what seemed like hours.

After determining where to bring Celia's life to an end, he let Cyrus do the remainder of the planning. He could be rather...creative about these kinds of things. Cyrus put together the stunt with the coyote, figured out the ringing callbox, picked the positions they could stake out to make her squirm.

But then she had shown up in his squad car. The one with the reinforced armor panels and state-of-the-art bulletproof glass that was capable of taking on a tank, that was itself a tank. The woman who was rightfully his inside the car that was rightfully his. And what's more, her nigger of a boyfriend was inside with her. By some stroke of insane luck, after Jason had cut the gas lines the night prior just to fuck with him after he had run into them at the restaurant, the idiot had wound up on the side of the road that Celia would have to travel to reach them.

An interloper. With his girl. In his car. Jason wanted to kill them both the moment Celia stepped out of the vehicle, but Cyrus insisted on sticking with the plan and having his fun, on tormenting her with the coyote and the masks and the callbox.

After the attack went wrong, after Jason waited for Celia to put the pieces together, to figure out where they were, to call him out on the megaphone for bringing her to their special spot, it became clear that Jason and she had entirely different narratives of when they fell for each other.

The cunt didn't even remember that night.

Not that it mattered. They had her surrounded. She had every reason to give up. No exits, no hope, no reason to live because everything around her reassured her that she was worthless, that the fight was worthless, that men knew better than girls and could do more than them.

Nevertheless, she persisted. She fought, and fought, and refused to die, continued to grind the life out of him like every other woman on this planet seemed intent on doing.

He had lost four men by this point, two of them cops, and now only he and Cyrus and Officer Appleby (about as worthless as they come) remained.

And still she persisted.

57

"You're telling me these guys are all cops?" asked Brian.

"Not all of them," said Celia. "But a lot of them."

"What the hell kind of cops dress up like aliens and try to murder a female officer?"

"The bad kind."

A man in an alien mask appeared from around the bluff and approached the vehicle. He had a rifle slung around his body and a pistol hanging from his blue jeans.

Blue Jeans. Jason. The two were one and the same.

"What did you do to piss these guys off?" asked Brian.

"That guy in the blue jeans? I broke up with him."

"I tell you what, Celia, I've had a couple of girls break up with me in my day, but I never gathered a posse of armed men to engage in psychological warfare topped off by an execution. Thought about it, sure, but never acted on it. How can you be sure?"

"Because I'm thinking clearly for the first time in hours. Their weaponry. The organized nature of their attacks. The fact that no help has arrived. They would be monitoring the calls, making sure we can't get through. Rednecks don't have that kind of technology.

"But cops? Cops have access to all sorts of fun toys that could intercept phone calls, reroute callboxes, and get in touch with any rescue officials who might be tempted to respond to a giant fireball out in the middle of nowhere.

"There would only be one cop who was capable of organizing this type of attack, and it certainly isn't Officer Smalls. He isn't smart enough. He, and all the other officers on the staff, save for the Chief

PERSISTENCE

of Police, they look up to Jason. Blue Jeans. They go where he goes, they do what he does."

"Has Jason been behind the Illegals all along?" asked Brian.

"I may have to accept the fact that my history with him may have clouded my judgment of what he's capable of."

"But why?" asked Brian. "That's still the million-dollar question. Why do all of this? Why buy up the land and risk being caught with a robbery and an attack on one of your own?"

"Maybe it's as simple as Jason sicced his personal hit squad on me just because I broke his heart."

"I suppose, if I did have a personal hit squad at the ready, it might be too tempting to pass up."

"Holy shit," said Celia, looking around.

"What?"

"There's a spot near here. Teens used to go there to drink and make out and do all the dumb shit teens do. Jason and I hooked up there. I'd had way too many beers and barely remember it, but Jason used to talk about how special that moment was. He really has lost it."

"You're telling me that this entire thing is happening simply because you said no to your ex?"

"Have you met men, in general?"

"When you put it that way, yep, it checks out."

Still, it seemed incomplete. There was still Haart of the Sea. Maybe Jason set out to kill her because of a broken heart, but there was a piece she was still missing. She needed answers. And she needed to make it out of this alive to tell the Chief of Police and every media outlet in a three-state area what had happened.

"You should go," said Brian. "They're off-balance, they're not expecting it right now. You could make it to the truck. You need to make your break."

Celia said nothing, just watched as Jason got closer.

"I can cover you."

Celia didn't reply. Instead, she looked behind her shoulder, at the callbox. She looked around the vehicle cabin, conducted a mental inventory of all the tools she had left at her disposal.

Suddenly an idea struck. An idea that was too good to pass up. She pinned her badge, which had been positioned on the dashboard, back to her chest.

"I have a plan," she said.

58

While Jason sauntered down to the car, Celia told Brian her plan and got things ready to make her move. It was now or never.

Jason drew close to the speckled windshield, though he couldn't rightly see in through the pockmarked glass.

At last, he removed the alien mask.

"That's the guy who gave me the tough guy act last night," said Brian.

"It wasn't an act," said Celia.

"Clearly."

Jason propped his foot up on the hood of the car and smiled, the smile that had gotten Celia in trouble back in high school, a smile that promised far deeper trouble now.

"Hi," she said through the loudspeaker.

"Celia," he said. "Never thought you'd see me again."

"Did you think I would just lay down?"

"That's what you always did for me before."

"I'm gonna kill this guy," said Brian.

Celia hushed him with a finger.

"You sure do know how to pick a man," said Jason.

"That's true. I'm thinking of dating Cyrus next."

"So you figured out who we are. It doesn't matter. You have to know that, right? You're never getting out of here alive."

"You can't have that many men left," said Celia.

"You don't know how many men I have. How many I have coming for backup, how many are waiting on the other side of that bluff."

"The bluff where we hooked up? That's what this is about, isn't it? I thought it was some grand conspiracy but all it really boils down to is you not being able to get your dick wet with the girl of your dreams. Did you tell your men that this is what it's really about? How many did you convince?"

"More than you could possibly imagine."

"If that were true, you'd have finished me by now. You would have brought more weapons, better weapons, real tank buster-type shit. You never thought I'd hunker down for this long, take so many of you out."

Jason laughed. "You're still the same girl I fell in love with all those years ago."

"No," she said firmly. "I'm not."

"Maybe not," he said. "The Celia I loved wouldn't act as if I didn't mean anything to her. Wouldn't treat me with disrespect. Wouldn't flaunt men around me as if I was nothing."

"You are nothing."

"Fuck you!" he said, lashing out and slamming the palm of his hand on the vehicle, trying but failing to see inside. "You don't know who I am. I'm not some boy whose heart you can break anymore. I went to war, I deserve you not treating me like the rest of the white trash in this town."

"You're worse," she said.

"I run this city," he said. "I established something that you can't even comprehend. I'm prepared to do things that others won't, and I won't let you or anyone else treat me like a fool anymore. You think you're brilliant because you tracked down some meth in California."

The realization dawned on her.

"You were in my apartment."

"No fucking shit."

"So you're behind it all? And I got too close. That's what this is about? I found out about your land grab and now you have to bring me to an end."

"You give yourself too much credit. You are nothing. You don't belong with us, you haven't seen the things that I've seen. Do you even know how we see you at the station? The way we talk about you? You're a joke. Affirmative action, a soft spot for the Chief of Police who owed a favor to your daddy. I can't wait to see the look on his face when I tell him you're dead.

"And you wanna know a secret? The man you look up to, who you owe everything to? After the initial shock of finding out you're dead, that you're mutilated beyond all recognition? He'll be happy. He'll make a big show of remorse, but deep down you know the truth, and so will he. He'll be grateful for what I've done. Because it means he doesn't have to deal with some stuck-up cunt making things difficult for everyone else. Locker rooms with curtains, always worrying about saying the wrong thing at the wrong time. Equal opportunity bullshit that has no place here."

"You're right," said Celia. "This isn't equal. You've had the odds on me all night and I'm still alive while your soldiers' carcasses litter the road."

"You say soldier like you know the meaning. You don't know what it means to go to war. You're playing dress-up. You are something to be tolerated, not respected, and I will not tolerate you anymore."

"And yet," she said, "Most of you are dead and I'm still alive."

"You're still alive because you have a tank separating you from the bullets. *My* tank. You're just like every other woman, you separate yourself from the real war while the men all die. I will not allow you to leave this desert alive. I will get inside that car if it's the last thing I do. You cannot keep me out. You are not capable."

Celia heard something like madness in Jason's voice. It was nice to know she could still get a rise out of him.

"You're running out of cops," said Celia.

"Proud of yourself, are you? You're proud of being a cop killer? You murdered good men, brave men who were doing whatever they had to do to make this town better."

"I killed boys in a sandbox playing at war."

"NO!" he yelled, pointing the rifle impotently at the Challenger, still unable to see properly through the glass that Cyrus had shot up. "Those were men of honor who would take a bullet for this country and this town. You cannot say the same. You are a selfish cunt, Celia Miller, and you will never see another sunset."

"Aw, you always were so romantic with your talk about sunsets."

He started firing at the vehicle then, as Cyrus had done before. And sure enough, here came Cyrus out from his position hunkered down in the sand, trying to calm Jason down. He put an arm around him but Jason pushed him away.

Celia simply raised the microphone to her lips again.

"You really need to do a better job training these boys of yours. Your cops bled like pussies. Literally."

Jason came around the side of the vehicle now, firing all the while. With the chamber empty, he started bashing at the window, striking the glass repeatedly.

"Goodbye, Jason. Go suck a dead cop's dick."

He roared with rage and brought punches down upon the glass. The window shook repeatedly, but he still couldn't see anything through the clouded glass. He wrapped his hand around the door handle and heaved.

The sudden, unexpected force of the door being opened took him off his feet. His rage was replaced with stupefaction. He raised his head as Cyrus stood next to him, the blank alien face a mirror of his own expression.

The car was empty. Well, not completely empty. There was a canister of gasoline on the driver's seat. With a bunch of rags sticking out the top. And a lit flare in the middle of those rags.

Cyrus tried to slam the door shut as the canister ignited, but he only got it about halfway before it blew up.

Celia and Brian, who had been completely concealed by the clouded glass, jumped up from their spot in the trunk, pushing against the interior hatch as sunlight streamed into the dark crawlspace. Celia dropped the microphone, whose cord had been stretched to its breaking point, and she and Brian immediately set off running toward the remains of the semi.

The explosion and ensuing shockwave sent the door rocketing back into Cyrus's face, drawing blood and sending him crumpling to the ground, but the effect was not quite what Celia had intended. Rather than the inferno set off by the tanker truck in the night, this was more like a few heavy-duty firecrackers piled together.

That meant Celia and Brian did not have the cover she had hoped for when they made their mad dash from the trunk. Still, the die had been cast and Celia was intent to ride this out to the bitter end.

"These cops sure do like to talk," said Brian as they ran away from the car as fast as they could.

"Shut up and run," she said.

They skirted the burnt-out wreckage of the tanker truck, reaching its singed hulk as reports of gunfire shattered the desert. She didn't know which of the remaining three men was shooting at her, but it didn't matter. They had no more ammunition and no other choice but to run without looking back.

As Celia hoped, the husk of the tanker provided cover from the bullets that erupted behind them. She heard Brian's labored breathing alongside her, and focused on that and the sound of pinging bullets so that she didn't have to focus on the pain ripping through her foot. She and Brian had tried to set it as best they could in the car, but the best they could come up with was a makeshift splint, using a nightstick and some gauze they had retrieved from the first aid kit.

"I can't do this much more," said Brian, already growing winded before they even reached the other end of the truck.

"You have a bullet hole in your arm, my foot is hanging off my bloody body. Man up and run faster."

Brian didn't complain after that. They reached the edge of the tanker trunk, Celia's stomach growing tight as she turned the corner.

The truck was still in one piece. Although the pizza delivery guy's car was useless thanks to what the Illegals had done to it, they had not thought to take out the truck that they had driven here. For all she knew (and hoped), it was the only vehicle the Illegals still had on the scene.

Their last hope for salvation was sitting 20 feet away, banged up, covered in soot, tilting at a canted angle in the road, but still in one piece.

She dragged her foot forward, making sure to keep the semi between her and the bullets as best she could. She heard pounding footsteps now, multiple sets, moving along the other side of the semi.

Celia and Brian reached the door of the pickup and she pulled the handle.

It opened. She rushed inside, followed by Brian, and then snuck a glance out the windshield.

Cyrus, Jason, and a newly unmasked Officer Appleby came tearing around the corner. Jason had his gun drawn and immediately aimed it at Celia. She ducked and the bullet went over her head. More gunshots followed, striking the truck's hood and the rearview mirrors and the windshield, which shattered at once.

No bulletproofing here. They would need to act fast or they would die.

She scanned the vehicle for keys but there was no need. In his rush to try to kill her earlier, Officer Smalls had simply turned off the engine and left the keys in the ignition. There was a mermaid with large breasts and the logo of an American beer company hanging off the key ring.

The engine started right away, and after throwing the truck into gear, Celia hit the gas. She looked up to see where she was going.

The men had nearly closed the distance, standing a mere ten feet away from the truck when Celia gunned the vehicle forward. Jason yelled "FUCK!" and then dove to his right, while Cyrus, his alien mask still on, rolled beneath the trailer.

Appleby thought he could get a shot off before Celia reached him. She decided to make him pay for that mistake.

She lowered her head below the steering wheel and plowed forward, but before she reached her target, she raised her eyes once more so that she could lock them with Appleby's.

The truck plowed through him with a perversely satisfying *thunk*, and Celia was somewhat alarmed by her own glee as she watched his eyes widen in the split second before his body fell beneath the grill of the accelerating truck.

Celia felt the truck shudder beneath her and then cant toward the right, and at first she thought that Officer Appleby's body had been the cause. Then she heard the gunshots and cursed her bad luck, as either Cyrus or Jason had just used a bullet to puncture a hole in one of the truck's right tires.

"You've got a flat," said Brian.

"You're not helping!"

Celia jammed the wheel to the left and pushed her foot down on the brake, pulling the vehicle around 180 degrees. She needed to get back to town, not farther into the desert on a flat tire, and the road that brought her here was the only path that led to Ravencourt.

She gunned it past the vehicles strewn on the road, and even felt a pang of remorse at having to leave the squad car behind. It had protected her throughout this whole sordid affair and she felt like she owed it more than to let it be penetrated by the men the way it was. Still, to become who she needed to be, to survive, she needed to move on.

Another bullet, another tire. The steering wheel wobbled from side to side and Celia tightened her grip, willing it to keep straight. She gunned the truck past what remained of the tractor trailer, and though she couldn't see Cyrus or Jason anywhere, she could hear the potshots they were taking, and she kept her head down as a result.

Then, after all the tumult, the gunshots, the shouting and the shattering glass, the sounds were gone. In a not-quite silence, all she could hear was the revving of the engine and the rattling of tires. The truck continued straight, the scene falling farther and farther behind them.

For the first time, she allowed herself to hope. The ordeal was almost over. All she had to do was get close enough to Ravencourt proper to pick up a signal on a cellphone. She could drive to the station on two wheels if she had to, tell the Chief what had happened, get her and Brian to the hospital. It was almost over.

And then her eye caught the gas gauge, which was rapidly dwindling.

"Fuck me," said Celia.

"What?" asked Brian.

"They hit the gas tank," she said.

59

Cyrus and Jason stood, stunned, and watched Celia drive off with their truck back toward Ravencourt.

"We're fucked," said Jason.

"No we're not," said Cyrus. "I hit her gas tank."

"Why couldn't you hit her head?"

"She was ducking. Gas tanks can't duck."

"C'mon. We need to get the other car and finish this."

Together they took off running toward the hill that led to the bluff, where a squad car, the last vehicle they had, sat empty.

They passed Appleby, a quick glance all it took to confirm that he was dead. Yet another victim to a bitch who refused to die. She would take out a dozen good men if it meant saving her own skin.

"If we don't kill her…" said Jason between deep breaths as he ran past the truck.

"We will, brother," said Cyrus. "You have my word."

They ran on.

60

"We're not gonna make it," said Celia.

The truck was wobbling, the engine was stuttering, and they were still miles outside of town.

"How far are we?" asked Brian.

"Too far."

The truck finally gave out, rolling to a stop as Celia pulled it onto the shoulder. They had made it a couple miles down the road, but Ravencourt still remained a good five miles off. They wouldn't be making it in the truck.

"Are you getting a signal?" she asked.

Brian, who had kept his phone held up throughout their ride, shook his head.

"Fuck!"

She glanced around the front of the truck's interior, all discarded junk food bags and flecks of sand, then looked behind her, into the rear passenger seats, for the first time.

"Holy shit."

Boxes. Three of them, pressed in next to each other. And tumbling out the tops of those boxes were items she recognized: alien masks, reports about criminal activity, maps, a bag of meth plopped haphazardly atop a pile of paperwork.

"That's my stuff," she said. "They're covering it all up," she said.

"What? How?"

"They brought me out here so that they could get inside my home without being noticed. To clean up everything I'd put together."

"Is there a phone in one of those boxes?"

She shook her head, then turned back around. Something caught her eye, lodged deeper within the center console, barely visible underneath a bundle of Burger King breakfast sandwich wrappers.

"Try that," she said, pointing down at the flip phone stashed there.

Brian picked it up and flipped it open.

"Who still uses a flip phone?"

"It's a burner. Untraceable. Any signal?"

He tried a few buttons and shook his head.

"Hold onto it," she said. "And keep trying while we run. We need to go."

She opened the driver's side door and Brian followed her lead, taking tentative steps away from the truck as if afraid to exit its protection.

"Go where?" asked Brian. "You just said we were too far."

"Too far from Ravencourt," said Celia. "But not from there."

Celia pointed at a jagged gash in the desert, large enough for an ATV, that wound its way up a steep hill toward a flat piece of land that seemed to jut straight up from the desert. You could just make out weathervanes, satellite dishes, and the tops of metal trailers peeking out from the precipice overlooking the rest of the area.

She opened the door and started running, and Brian, not really having much choice in the matter, followed Celia up the ATV track, leaving the truck behind.

61

Jason and Cyrus drove in silence, following the only road that led back to Ravencourt, but making sure to keep an eye out for tire tracks in case Celia tried to evade them.

"Put your mask back on," said Jason as they drove.

"Fuck I am," said Cyrus. "Can't see half a shit out of that thing."

"We don't need to see half a shit. If she gets back to town and we have to put her down in public, people can't know who we are. The Illegals can execute people in public. I can't investigate the crime as a cop if people see me commit the crime."

"Fuck," said Cyrus. He put on an alien mask and Jason did the same. There were three in the glove box and a couple more under the seat; they kept themselves stocked, getting rid of them as needed after a job was done.

Cyrus spotted the truck first as they rounded a corner. It was pulled off to the shoulder, seemingly empty. He cradled a rifle like it was a child he would never sell for meth money.

"Is she hunkering down again?" asked Jason.

Cyrus didn't reply. They pulled up well short of the vehicle and then got out, each drawing their weapons and then moving cautiously toward the truck. Neither wanted to be hit with a bullet, or a flare, or an exploding gas can rigged like some asshole kid defending his home on Christmas.

Jason approached the car first, Cyrus staying slightly behind to cover him. He pulled even with the door and pointed his rifle inside.

Nothing. They were gone.

"Jason," said Cyrus.

Jason came around the other side of the car. Cyrus was pointing his weapon up a trail that led slightly up and to the left.

"Holy shit," said Jason. "She's hiding out at The Rocks."

62

Celia and Brian moved as fast as they could, which truly wasn't very fast at all, crawling their way up the path that was designed chiefly for ATVs. Celia had known about this spot from one of her many patrols of the area. The locals would catch it and then race down to the bottom until they caught the unflagging expanse of the Mojave Desert. They would go for hours until they drove back up to whatever existence they had carved out among the trailers, hovels, and dark corners of The Rocks.

She half walked, half crawled her way up the gravelly slope, every once in a while dealing with a rock that dug into her palm and drew fresh blood from a wound she barely even felt. The pain meds she had taken were beginning to subside, and with that came a return of the pain in her ankle, slowing her down and forcing her to catch Brian's shoulder a couple times so that she didn't stumble.

They heard the sound of an engine down below, and though a series of boulders along the path obscured them from view, there was no mistaking what path they had taken. They were about three quarters of the way up the slope, but by the time they reached the top in their current state, Jason and Cyrus would be right behind them.

"I guess they had a car," said Brian between heaving sobs. He tried to spit but nothing came out.

"Just keep going up. Once we get up top they'll help us."

Celia doubted whether this statement was true. The Rocks could be welcoming to a methhead or an out-on-parole pedophile or a prostitute willing to turn tricks for a pittance, but cops weren't high up on their list of desired guests. But she couldn't exactly tell Brian (or herself) that they might get away from the paramilitary threat only to have a single mother with a sandwich in her hand shoot them for disturbing her wrapping a joint for her boyfriend.

"Check your cellphone," said Celia. "We're up high, you might have a signal."

"No luck," he said as he tried to catch his breath.

"What about the burner?"

He looked, clearly not expecting to be met with good news, but Celia saw his eyes widen.

"I've got one. I'm calling 911 now."

"No," screamed Celia. "I just killed three quarters of the police force. We don't know that the rest weren't in on it."

"What then?"

"Chief Burton. He's the only person we can trust. Give me the phone."

Brian handed it to her as they continued their trek upward. She dialed the Chief's personal cellphone number, her hands shaking. Twice she messed up, but after a few tries, she was able to get the entire number keyed in.

She leaned on Brian, using him to support her weight while she pressed the phone to her other ear. It rang. Once. Twice. Three times.

Then, just when she had about given up, figuring the Chief was probably at Sunday Mass with his wife or a car show or taking a nap in his big comfy easy chair, a voice picked up on the other line.

"Hello?"

"Chief," said Celia. "It's me."

"Celia," he said, his voice immediately growing concerned, "Celia, are you alright? You sound out of breath."

"Jason Martinez is trying to kill me. He and a man named Cyrus Everhaart."

"What are you talking about?"

"You have to trust me," said Celia, howling with pain as her foot scraped against a particularly large rock. "I'm at The Rocks hiding with a friend, but we won't last long. The Illegals, those guys in the alien masks, Jason was behind it all, and they tried to kill me. We got away but there's not much time."

"Celia…"

"Please. I'm in trouble, Henry."

It was probably speaking his first name that did it. She didn't even call him that when they were outside work. Celia could almost hear Henry Burton switch from lazy Sunday mode to Chief of the Ravencourt Police mode.

"What do you need?"

"We'll be somewhere in The Rocks. I don't know where. But you cannot trust Jason if you see him. He's behind everything, you have to believe me."

"I do, Celia. Hang tight. I'll have every available officer, fire-fighter, and EMT in the city out there."

"Ok, but I'll only hand myself over to you. There might be other cops in on this. You can't trust anyone else in the department."

"Roger that. I have to let you go now to send out the call. Celia?"

"Yeah?" said Celia, feeling every bit like the little girl she still suspected he perceived her to be. She just wanted, needed, someone to come in and make all the bad things go away.

"You be careful. I'll be there in 15 minutes."

He hung up the phone and Celia did likewise. She stuffed the burner in her back pocket as they reached the top of the ATV trail, a jumble of trailers surrounding them on all sides.

"They're coming," said Celia.

"Good," said Brian, before looking back over his shoulder, "because so are they."

63

Now that they had her in their sights, out in the open, it was amazing how quickly Cyrus and Jason fell into the old patterns. They had met each other as soldiers and now were chasing a quarry as soldiers, each with weapons at the ready, deftly pointed toward the goal of putting an end to this once and for all. They scaled the incline with speed and efficiency, gaining ground with every step.

Finally, the lip of The Rocks was in sight, and Jason held his hand up in a clenched fist. Cyrus stopped in his tracks, his automatic weapon pointed forward. Jason turned his masked face slightly, locked eyes with Cyrus, and nodded.

Jason scaled the remainder of the hill and looked out at the series of trailers spread out in front of them.

A pair of feet darted behind one trailer and out of sight, about fifty feet ahead. A crack addict smoking a cigarette watched those feet go and then saw Jason and Cyrus striding forward with guns drawn.

The crack addict didn't bat an eyelid, just pointed in the direction that Celia and the other one had fled.

God bless The Rocks, thought Jason.

64

As Celia and Brian passed the old-timer, she placed a finger up to her lips, hoping that the man with the cigarette hanging lazily from his lips would catch her meaning.

A quick look behind her shoulder confirmed that he did not.

She could barely walk at this point. Whatever was keeping her on her feet before, adrenaline, pain meds, some combination of both, she had been depleted of everything. She let Brian support her full weight, leaning on the arm that hadn't had a bullet tear through it earlier in the evening. If they didn't find shelter, Jason and Cyrus would be on them in seconds.

"Where are we going?" asked Brian, his breath growing more labored with each step. "Let's just hide out in one of these trailers."

"No," said Celia. "Take a right here."

They reached the end of a double-wide and Brian steered them to the right. A small wading pool sat in front of a decrepit trailer. A scrawny Chihuahua stood on the front step, yelping hysterically.

Celia didn't wait. She pulled the door of the trailer open and led her and Brian inside. Brian closed the door behind them.

The scrawny girl sitting on the mattress started upright. Her eyes were glassy, scratch marks ran up her arms, and recognition dawned on her face.

"Billy," said Celia. "I need your help."

Jason and Cyrus reached the double-wide and turned the corner, just as Celia and Brian had done mere seconds before.

A trailer with a wading pool in front of it lay directly in front of them. People were arguing inside of it, their voices carrying over the relative silence of The Rocks. Now that two men with armed guns had stormed their shitty little desert community, most of the people they passed had stopped their conversations and activities and simply watched them go by. Some had slunk back into their trailers and tents.

The Illegals' reputation held sway up here.

"What's she doing in there again?" Jason asked as he pulled up to the trailer.

Cyrus shook his head. "This bitch just can't stop meddling."

Back in the trailer, Brian had knocked the small kitchen table over at Celia's urging so that it blocked the front door. It wouldn't hold for long but it was something. He looked out the window as Celia attempted to negotiate with the woman whose trailer she had visited a month ago to find a pile of methamphetamine and cash sitting in the microwave.

"Get outta my trailer!" yelled Billy, already moving the blinds from the window and looking around with a panic.

"Billy, listen to me," said Celia. "We're going to die if you don't help us."

"Fuck do I care. Get out! Hoyt nearly killed me last time you rolled in here fucking up our shit."

"Hoyt's dead," said Celia. "Dirnt too. But there are much badder men than them about to come bursting through that door."

"That ain't my problem. All's you're gonna do is get my ass shot up too."

Celia marched forward and grabbed Billy by the shoulders.

"Listen to me," Celia said, looking her in the eyes through the shafts of sunlight that streamed in through the trailer. "You do not need to live in fear. Whatever's going on here, it's over. But if they kill me, they'll kill you too just because you saw me. So now that you're in this, you can either work with me to help me kill them, or you can die in this trailer in the next 30 seconds."

"Fuck, man," said Billy, looking down at her shoes.

"Fuck is right," said Celia.

"Celia," said Brian, "they're here."

Celia didn't break eye contact with Billy.

"Now I need you to answer me a question honestly, which will be tough because what I'm about to ask you is something that your every instinct will tell you should not be answered honestly when asked by a cop. But do you have meth in this trailer?"

Billy looked Celia in the eyes. She nodded.

"Do you have a lot of meth in this trailer?"

Billy nodded again.

"Get it. Now."

"Billy!" shouted Cyrus from in front of the trailer. "Billy, it's your pal Cyrus. I need you to come on out of there."

He got no response. The trailer had gotten quiet, and Jason was getting tired of surrounding vehicles with his weapon drawn worthlessly.

"Forget it," said Jason. "I'm sick of this. Let her die too. It'll be on Celia, not us."

Cyrus shrugged. "She brings in good business. Lotsa the boys like her and she don't complain much when they get rough."

"The boys are dead and you can get another hooker. We're ending this."

Inside, Celia was directing Billy and Brian toward the hatch in the floor of the trailer when the door started to buckle inward. The table was propped up against it, but after the second kick, it was already splintering apart.

She took one last look around the trailer and felt like laughing. She was getting pretty good at this.

Celia slammed the hatch shut and made her retreat just as Jason kicked down the door and swept his rifle around the trailer.

He saw nothing. She had somehow eluded him. Again. He turned from one side of the room to the other, until he saw the door to the bathroom slightly ajar.

He didn't waste another second. He marched over to the door and threw it open.

It took him a second to register what he was seeing, simply because it didn't make sense. On top of the toilet tank, with a cord extending to an outlet on the wall, was a microwave set on high.

If Jason could have seen inside that microwave through the cloud of smoke flowing around it and spewing out its sides, he would have feasted his eyes on six stacks of already cooked meth, a set of forks and knives, and three separate and highly combustible chemicals, all of which Billy had been able to grab with relative ease.

The idea that had occurred to Celia one month ago as she stood trapped in this very same trailer and dismissed as too outlandish and dangerous to try, she had now put into action as her only option.

Jason's eyes widened as the microwave door exploded outward...

...and a small gust of smoke and a terrible odor emanated from the microwave. Rather than the trailer-rocking explosion Celia had expected, the burst was more akin to a small gust of smoke that a stage magician might use when showing how a bird had transmogrified into a rabbit.

Jason chuckled to himself.

"Dumb bi..."

The "itch" portion of that word would have to remain unscratched, as two metal prongs were now shooting bursts of electricity directly into Jason's testicles.

Jason slumped to his knees, dropping his weapon, his hands immediately groping at his crotch. Celia momentarily lost sight of him from her vantage point directly below, where she had just pushed open the hatch.

Celia really thought there would be a bigger explosion than that. Good thing she had a Plan B: lie in wait beneath Jason's feet, using the one weapon she had thus far not been able to deploy — her department-issued taser.

Rather than follow Brian and Billy out into the tangle of trailers that made up The Rocks, Celia had elected to stay behind. Brian protested separating at this juncture, but Celia told him she had to make sure her stunt had worked and that the cabinet would protect her from the blast.

In reality, she didn't want to be with Brian anymore. Or Billy, for that matter. Enough people had gotten caught in the crossfire today, and she wanted to give them the opportunity to escape from this in one piece.

She crawled out of the hatch, simultaneously dropping the taser while picking up the door of the microwave. Jason must have heard her feet shuffling, as he fought against the electricity and started to turn.

Celia was quicker. She immediately brought the displaced door of the microwave around in a batter's arc and drove it into the back of his head. Jason fell all the way to the ground this time, his face mashing against the crusted carpet of the trailer.

Celia stood over Jason's body, clutching the busted and charred microwave door in her hands. She could see blood smacked onto the remarkably resilient glass plating on the front.

Jason rolled over now, pulling off the alien mask as he did. His eyes locked with Celia's as she stood above him. He brought a hand up to the back of his head and pulled it away covered in blood.

"I think you…"

But he never got another word out. Celia brought the cover of the microwave down on his skull. Then again. And again and again and again, feeling his temple crack and then feeling and hearing the glass of the microwave door crack and then shatter as Jason's skull pushed up against it.

Once again, the only way to identify the leader of the Illegals was by his Blue Jeans.

Celia dropped the door of the microwave and then slumped over, taking deep breaths. She would have thought she would feel something for the man who had once loved her, but there was nothing but exhaustion.

"Jay, what the fuck's going on in there?" came Cyrus's voice from outside.

No rest for the wicked.

Celia reached for Jason's rifle and slung it over her shoulder. She sat there with it pointed at the partially opened door, waiting for Cyrus to stick his mask-covered head in so she could tear it from his body.

But Cyrus didn't come. She sat there, her finger poised over the trigger, yet more seconds ticked by and still nothing.

"Get outta there man, it's going up fast."

Going up fast?

Celia felt heat now, and turned to her right to see flames engulfing the bathroom area and slowly spreading to the rest of the trailer. It was only then that she realized her right eye was half shut, preventing her from seeing that far over. She couldn't even remember at what point it had been struck.

The flames crept closer and Celia stood up. As she did, her foot brushed against the alien mask, which was inches away from the flames. Her first thought was to kick it into the fire, but instead she picked it up and placed it on her head so that it covered her face.

She strode to the door, limping all the way, and then stuck her head into the opening.

Cyrus, wearing an identical mask, spotted the alien face staring back at him.

"Shit man," he said, "tell me you got them."

He lowered his weapon toward the ground for just a moment, but it was all Celia needed. She swept her gun, and in turn her entire body, into the doorframe and leveled the weapon at Cyrus.

"Oh, fuck," said Cyrus.

He lifted his weapon and Celia fired off a couple shots to the right of him.

"Don't," she said.

Cyrus dropped the weapon and held his hands in the air. Celia walked forward, putting the burning trailer at her back.

"I'm defenseless," said Cyrus.

Celia stopped in front of him, two people in alien masks staring each other down with about a foot between them. Denizens from all around The Rocks had gathered in a circle to watch. The flames crept higher behind Celia, and the smell of smoke and singed meth sullied the air.

"You wouldn't kill an unarmed man, would you?"

The butt of the rifle smashed into the side of Cyrus's alien mask with a satisfying thud.

He crumpled to the ground. Celia kept the weapon pointed at him.

That's when she first heard the sirens. They carried across the desert, but they weren't far off judging from the distance. More sirens joined them. Chief Burton had made good on his promise.

Celia tore off the alien mask, suddenly feeling like she might suffocate. She tossed it on Cyrus's chest.

"I'm not going to kill you," she said, "because you're going to talk. About today. About the operation you've been running. About everything that you and Jason put together under the guise of the Illegals. And most of all, you're going to talk about how a squad of corrupt cops and redneck assholes was gunned down by a pissed-off bitch with nothing more than a plate of bulletproof glass and some moxie. You're under arrest, asshole."

Cyrus laughed from behind his mask, and the laughter picked up momentum. He continued to laugh even when Celia pulled his mask off and then shoved the gun in his face.

Finally, the laughter subsided, and Celia now heard the engine of the police car coming closer. Not far behind it were more sirens, likely the firefighters and maybe the EMTs. Celia had told the Chief not to bring more officers, so he had brought others in the rescue crew. That was fine. She doubted Jason had recruited anyone but cops into his little group.

"Your ride is here," said Celia.

People had gathered around by now to take in the sight. Their desert-beaten leathery faces peered at her not from behind windows, but out in the open, getting a good look at the lady cop in the alien mask who had a gun pointed at a man who lorded over this section of the town like a redneck slumlord.

From around the corner of the trailer came Brian and, a few feet behind him, Billy. Brian smiled at Celia, but she didn't smile back. She had been through too much. Instead she just nodded, and then shifted her eyes to Billy and did the same. Billy nodded back and then scurried away somewhere. Celia made a silent promise to thank her once she got patched up.

The police car entered through the gravel road that poured itself into the center of The Rocks in a circle. It was followed closely by a fire truck and an ambulance.

Chief Burton got out of the car and surveyed the scene. With the arrival of the authorities, those gathered around retreated back into the trailers from which they came.

Before they did, though, Celia heard one of the residents of The Rocks murmur to her baby daddy.

"Ain't never seen a response time like that. One cop shows up and they're here in seconds."

The firefighters ran off to try to douse the trailer, while the EMTs moved toward Celia.

Chief Burton got there first. Celia's hands shook even with the gun still pointed at Cyrus.

"We got him," he said, looking down with contempt at the criminal who lay at Celia's feet. "You don't need to worry anymore, Celia."

Celia allowed herself to be wrapped in his arms.

"Let's get you home," the Chief said.

65

The EMTs had shuffled Celia into the back of an ambulance to take a look at her and pump her full of morphine. Her foot had suffered the worst damage. The technician thought she probably had a fracture. She also had two broken fingers in her left hand, and she didn't even remember how that had happened.

A car pulled up. It had the insignia of the State Police on the side.

Where were you when I was stranded on the road for 24 hours straight?

Sergeant Haddock, the State Police investigator, exited the vehicle and stormed over.

"What the hell is going on?"

"I found the men you've been investigating," said Celia. "They're not doing so well."

"They attacked you?"

Celia laughed. The morphine had swept its way through her body and suddenly everything seemed just a little more funny.

"Clearly."

Chief Burton was walking over now. He looked pissed.

"What the hell do you think you're doing?" he asked.

"Trying to find out why my private investigation just became massively public."

Burton jabbed a finger in Haddock's chest.

"Let's talk about your investigation," he said. "It's because of you that my officer got into this whole mess. You brought the state in when we could have handled everything. You turned up the heat and it almost got my best officer killed!"

The Chief was riled up. And even though Haddock hadn't done anything to her personally, it felt good to see someone finally standing up for her.

His best officer.

She knew she shouldn't need the approval of anyone, but damn if that didn't feel good.

"I need to talk to her," said Haddock, not standing down. "To find out what happened."

"Look," said Chief Burton, catching himself. "I can read the writing on the wall. After tonight, I wouldn't be surprised if the Ravencourt Police Department doesn't even exist. I can look forward to being absorbed by County and being out of a job. There's a lot to sort through, but it can wait a few hours. My officer just went through absolute hell, and I'll be damned if I'm going to let some random prick from the state put her through the wringer."

"Was I talking to you?" asked Haddock.

His eyes turned to take in Celia, sitting in the back of an ambulance on a gurney, conscious but with pain medication coursing through her system.

"I'd like to rest, Sergeant. Can we talk later?"

Haddock looked like he was about to speak, then thought better of it and nodded.

"The hospital," he said. He reached into his back pocket and produced a wallet, fishing around for a moment. "You get patched up and I'll talk to you there. I need to know everything."

He removed a slick, templated business card with his name and contact info, the details embossed upon thick card stock with the name and logo of the Nevada State Police. Celia took it from him and pocketed it.

"Call me the moment you're feeling up to it," he said. "I have some calls to make in the meantime. Holy hell, this is fucked."

He turned to address Chief Burton.

"We'll talk later."

Haddock walked away, getting into his vehicle and pulling away from The Rocks. The Chief watched him the entire time.

"I'm sorry about that, Celia," said Burton, finally, turning toward her and looking every bit his age.

"It's okay," she said. "He's just doing his job. It's a lot to take in."

"I'm worried it's more than that."

"Chief?"

He sighed then.

"I've been looking into Haddock. His independent investigation? Maybe it's not as independent as we thought. Turns out he's been buying up land using some shell company. Hell, we might be standing on his property right now."

"Wait, Haddock is the one buying up land? What's the name of the shell company?" she asked. Her voice sounded weak to her ears.

"Haart of the Sea," he said. "Apparently he's one of the top investors along with that scumbag."

Chief Burton extended a thumb back to his own squad car. Cyrus Everhaart sat in the backseat, his alien mask off, blood dripping from where Celia had cracked him in the forehead.

"But that means..." her voice trailed off.

"I know what it means," he said. "He's going to be waiting there for you at the hospital. And we need to be prepared."

She tried to control her breathing. The morphine made it easier than she expected. It made sense. Someone had to have been pulling the strings, helping the Illegals avoid prosecution. Who better than the very investigator charged with looking into them?

Haddock had shown up in Ravencourt out of the blue. And now she knew why. So he could control the investigation. So he could make sure no leads ever turned up that could point to him or his men.

"What do we do, Chief?"

"Come with me back to the station," he said. "You and Brian both. Clean up and tell me everything that happened. Then we'll go to some other hospital outside the county lines, somewhere he can't find you. We don't know if any other of my guys..."

His voice caught and he punched his fist against the ambulance.

"Jesus, my own fucking men did this."

"It's okay," said Celia. She steadied his arm with her palm. He was shaking.

"I need to know which of my guys I can trust," he said. "And frankly, I can't give you a protective detail at a hospital if Haddock or some other officer decides you're still a threat. Tell me, Celia: whose families am I breaking the news to? Who did this you?"

"Jason's inside the trailer. He's dead."

"Who else?"

"Little Red. Appleby. One more I think. Wilson maybe? Plus a couple assholes from The Rocks. I didn't see all their faces."

"Jesus, Celia. Six people dead?"

"She didn't have a choice," said Brian. He had walked up without either one noticing, having received fresh bandages and stitches for his bullet wound. The new stitches were holding up better than what Celia had been able to provide. "They did everything they could to kill us. She wouldn't let them."

"They're all out on the stretch of road by the callbox," said Celia, "along with a pizza delivery boy and a long-haul trucker who happened to be at the wrong place at the wrong time."

She was numb. What emotion she may have felt before at the death of two people who did nothing more than show up to work was gone. It'd probably come back later, washing over her in waves of guilt, but for now she was too exhausted.

"There's going to be media," said Chief Burton, disbelieving, but resigned to what had happened. "And inquiries. This may even bring the Feds in. The press is gonna have a field day. After we talk, we'll need to get you good and rested up for your Brokaw interview."

Celia smiled now. "I don't think Brokaw does those types of interviews anymore."

"What do I know?" he said. "I'm old. Do what you kids do for attention. Go on the internet, do a blog."

"Facebook Live tell-all?"

"We're going to pretend like I know what that means and just say yes," said the Chief. "So what will it be, Celia? I can let this ambulance take you to the hospital, where Haddock will be. Or we can go to the station. Clean yourself up, answer a couple questions, only as much as you're able. I need a debrief before the shitshow starts. Then we put miles between us and Haddock and make sure everyone responsible faces justice."

Celia thought about it. She looked at the back of Burton's squad car, where Cyrus looked at her. He smiled.

It was really no choice at all.

"If it means that I get to be there when he gets put in a cell," said Celia as she looked in Cyrus's direction, "then I think I can push through just about anything."

They gave her new bandages and a slew of fantastic-feeling pain medications and sent her on her way. Brian came along, Chief Burton saying he would be safer and things would go a lot smoother with the media if his testimony corroborated with Celia's before they had time to chat about it.

Now they drove on, Cyrus in the back, Celia crammed between Brian and Henry Burton, truth be told the only men left in her life, leaving The Rocks behind and approaching the outer reaches of Ravencourt, which just hours ago had seemed impossibly far away.

Cyrus's alien mask lay between her feet.

"You got spunk, kid," said Cyrus. "I'm impressed. First time a woman's ever really impressed me with anything other than her pussy."

"Shut up, you coward," said Burton.

"Let him talk," said Celia, looking back. "It's all he has now."

Cyrus smirked. "You really fucked things up for your ex and I, you know? We had a business going. A good one too."

"You muscled people out of their homes to buy up the land underneath their feet. You're a slumlord. Nothing more than that."

"We could have done a great thing for this city," said Cyrus. "Brought it back from the dead."

"Do you ever stop?" asked Brian.

"Tell me one thing," said Celia. "What did you need the land for?"

His gaze looked out the window, taking in the scenery as they drove down the road leading away from the Rocks and toward Ravencourt itself.

"You wouldn't believe me."

"Illegal casino? Brothel? Distribution warehouse?"

"A water park," Cyrus said suddenly.

"A water park?"

"My mother took me to a water park when I was a kid. I splashed around, swam from one end of the wave pool to the other, ran up the steps to the slides, the desert so hot you'd be dry by the time you got to the top. Then I'd go down, holding my breath in ice cold water for as long as I could and pop back up into 100-degree desert heat. Hot and cold, hot and cold, over and over again.

"It was the best day of my life. Until I met you, Officer Miller. You know, I'm still holding out hope you'll come around and kiss me before this is all over. Real sloppy like. You and I both know you want it."

"I'm flattered."

Cyrus got quiet then, looking out the window as they got nearer and near to town.

"Thank you," said Celia, turning her attention to Chief Burton. "For everything."

     Persistence

He smiled and nodded, eyes focused on the road.

Celia looked over at Brian now as the blue and red lights up at The Rocks receded in the rearview mirror. They were just a few minutes away from the police station.

"We did it," said Celia. "We're alive."

"<u>You</u> did it," said Brian.

She leaned her head on his shoulder then, and for the first time in what seemed like a long time, Celia felt good.

66

"What the fuck is going on?" said Officer Hilcox as Chief Burton led Cyrus Everhaart in through the front doors of the vacant police station. "There's calls going out over the radio, a trailer's up in flames, shots fired, officers down. What the fuck, Chief?"

Celia and Brian walked in a few steps behind, Celia using Brian like a crutch.

"Celia, what are you doing here?"

"Were you in on it?" asked Celia.

A look of befuddlement appeared on his face. "I'll repeat again, what the fuck is going on?"

"Officer Hilcox," said Chief Burton. "You're relieved for the rest of your shift. Please go home immediately and tell no one what you've seen here."

"Shouldn't I stay and..."

"You should not," said Burton. "Go. Now."

Hilcox heard the steel in Burton's voice then and decided to shut up. He tore the 911 headset from around his skull and set it down on his desk before heading toward the locker room.

"That's not the way to the door," said Chief Burton.

"I've gotta get my keycard..."

"Now!" said Chief.

Hilcox walked out, Celia staring daggers at him as he passed. Brian's hand dug deeper into Celia's shoulder.

The people Celia thought were her compatriots – the ones still living – could be murderers too, no different from Jason and the others whose bodies now littered the highway. She could never trust any of them again. She would always be wondering if they were just waiting for their time to finish what the Illegals had started out in the desert. She'd always be looking for someone who might sink a knife into her back.

A change of scenery may be in order, she thought.

Celia heard the closing of the front door as Hilcox exited the station. They were in the station alone now, the four of them, no one else able to gain access unless they had the proper clearance. And Celia had just killed almost everyone who had that clearance.

They marched Cyrus Everhaart to his cell in silence. Ravencourt didn't have much in way of prison cells, just a large holding area for petty offenders and drunks who just needed to sleep off a bender, and two other cells reserved for lowlifes who didn't play well with others. Cyrus qualified for that distinction.

"May I?" asked Celia.

Chief Burton, who was about to shut the cell door and then lock it, stepped away.

Celia took his place, her hands gripped around the cell door. She slid it on its squeaky hinges and clanged it into place. She took immense satisfaction from the sound the key made as she turned it in its lock.

"See you in court," said Celia.

"I'll see you long before then," said Cyrus. "Goodbye for now, my love."

He sneered, and Celia turned away in disgust. She handed the keys to Chief Burton as they walked out of the small hallway that contained the jail cells.

Celia turned to approach Chief's office, but he placed a hand on her elbow.

"Why don't you get cleaned up first? Take a nice cool shower, change clothes, and then come in."

"Okay," said Celia. She turned to Brian. "Will you be alright?"

"I will be now," he said. He grabbed Celia's hand in his palm and squeezed. She smiled at him.

"I'll take good care of him," said Chief Burton.

Celia nodded. "Thank you."

She turned and walked to the locker room, leaving Brian and the Chief behind.

She walked to her locker and leaned on it, savoring the feel of the cool metal on her forehead. It was cold, and kinda painful on the cuts on her face, but it meant she was alive. After everything, it was finally over.

She didn't cry. She supposed she would later, but instead she got an urge to scream. And she did so, albeit silently. Her mouth opened wide and she voicelessly let out the curses and the rage that had built up inside her all day, and it didn't matter that no sound came out. It felt good nonetheless.

She closed her mouth and then looked around at the lockers. She allowed herself to smile. Not a wide smile, not a smile like a maniac, but more like a smirk she just couldn't suppress.

After everything, she had won.

She walked to her shower, the one with the curtain, the one that all the male officers had bitched about, and then stopped. Rather than get in behind the curtain, she walked to a nozzle in the main shower, the communal one, and turned it on. She might as well experience what it was like, just for once, to be treated like all the other officers. Tonight, she had proved that she deserved that and much, much more.

67

Brian had just taken a seat in Chief Burton's office, letting the weight of the day push him into the chair that sat opposite the Chief's. He couldn't believe he was alive. After everything, Celia had somehow delivered him to this point, this point where he would be able to continue with the rest of his life.

"Can I get you something to eat? Drink?" Chief Burton asked.

Brian said sure. Any soda would do. The Chief walked out, leaving Brian to his visions of a brighter future with Celia by his side.

A couple minutes later, Chief Burton came back into the room and handed Brian a Coke and a bag of chips. Brian tore open the soda and let the cool liquid flow down his throat.

Damn it felt good. He never thought a sugary drink could taste like such heaven.

He took the soda from his lips and wiped his mouth with the back of his hand. The sound of water flowing through pipes had started as Celia had apparently stepped into the shower.

"So, how does this work?" asked Brian.

"You just tell us everything that you know. We need to get a better picture of what happened so that you two don't get in trouble. Your accusations are pretty bold."

"Bold but true," said Brian. "I saw half your damn police force try to kill her with my own eyes."

Once he began the story, the words were unstoppable, Chief Burton listening and nodding as Brian told the story of how Celia Miller single-handedly took on a corrupt police force and its redneck stooges.

68

Celia sighed heavily, trying to will the stress away, to make her hands go steady. She cracked her knuckles against the cool metal of her locker then unbuttoned the top button of her shirt, which stuck to her body from the blood and sweat and sand.

Before going further, Celia sat on the bench, intending to remove her boots.

THUNK.

She sat down unevenly, as if there was a rock in her back pocket. She tilted to one side and reached behind her.

The burner phone from the Illegals' truck. In the scuffle at The Rocks, she had forgotten all about it. She was about to set it aside but then her hand stopped.

If there were numbers on there, that could be evidence. Forensics could match them with the other cops' and any conspirators who were involved with the Illegals.

Celia opened the phone and navigated to Call History, something that took longer than she expected considering she hadn't used a flip phone since she was in middle school.

Jason's number was the earliest outgoing call of the day, placed just after midnight, prior to a few random calls to numbers she didn't recognize. Then nothing for the next few hours until, finally, the two most recent calls. These were to Chief Burton's number, from when Celia had grabbed the phone and called him for help while she and Brian made their escape to The Rocks.

Wait a second, Celia thought. *Look again.*

Chief Burton's number. *Twice.*

But you only called him once.

Yet there it was. The first call to Chief Burton was at 5:50 a. m. — three hours *before* she had the phone.

Her hands stopped shaking and her body turned cold.

Why would one of the Illegals have called Chief Burton at 6 in the morning?

69

Brian continued speaking while Chief Burton looked on. He had just wrapped up his story.

"It was quite a sight to behold," said Brian as he tilted his head back to take another sip of soda, his eyes still pointed upward as he pulled it away from his lips. "Watching her pick them off one by one. They must have thought it would be easy but she made them..."

The bullet passed through the can of soda and into Brian's brain, cutting him off mid-sentence and sending Coca Cola, blood, and brain matter splattering to the floor in equal measure, the soda fizzing up around the viscera. Brian's body slumped back in the chair. He was dead instantly.

Chief Burton lowered the gun and ran a shaky hand over his gray, balding scalp. He holstered the gun as he stood, wincing from the weight of years of hard work for the town of Ravencourt. He picked up the alien mask that lay on his desk, the one Cyrus had worn, and walked past Brian's dead body without haste, plodding as he would on any normal day. He left his office and then turned, toward the jail cells, pulling out his ring of keys from his back pocket.

Cyrus sat on the cot that acted as the only furniture in the sparse cell. Chief Burton tossed the alien mask inside and then unlocked the door, throwing it open as he walked forward, ignoring the mask and addressing Cyrus.

Chief Burton handed him the pistol he had just shot Brian with.

"How hard is it to kill a little girl in the middle of the fucking desert?" asked Chief Burton.

70

This is the story of a man who loved his town.

He loved the streets he patrolled when he was just starting out, loved the people he interviewed once he became a Lieutenant, loved the perks of the job once he became the Chief.

He loved Ravencourt. But he hated what it was becoming.

The reverberations of the economic dive bomb were felt even in a place as small as Ravencourt. A town that always struggled to create an industry in the middle of a desert that had no resources to speak of found itself filled to bursting with people collecting food stamps, Medicaid, and the various other trappings and creature comforts of a welfare society on the verge of collapse.

The Rocks exemplified the disease that had taken hold of Ravencourt. It was like a hemorrhoid that insisted on bleeding and pulsing and giving Ravencourt grief whenever it took a shit, that shit being the latest parolee who had been found guilty but had served their time and was now allowed to congregate in a pedophiliac, drug-addled, lecherous community that insisted on sucking the life out of the town the Chief had once loved.

As the population of The Rocks steadily climbed while the population of the rest of Ravencourt steadily dwindled, the people the Chief cared about the most, the officers he had pledged his life to work alongside, began to lose their jobs. The Town Council and the Mayor, they saw no need for good men, for men who had served the town their whole lives, and so they forced the oldest officers into retirement. Good men who planned to work for another ten years suddenly had to go work at grocery stores and gas stations and lawn-mowing services that would ensure a heart attack some five years later. The police force was drained of the old, replaced by the young, who didn't have 25 years of benefits and vacation days and 401(k)s to price them out of the market.

The town the Chief had loved so much was being left to rot, and unless someone intervened, Ravencourt would die.

Chief Burton could not allow that to happen, and his solution came from the last place the Chief would have thought to look: The Rocks.

A man named Cyrus Everhaart, pulled over for a minor traffic infraction, had put up a fight and been arrested. In his trunk was enough methamphetamine to put him away for the next decade. Mr. Everhaart's address placed him at The Rocks.

Everhaart had been brought in and sat in a cell, the very cell he had just been unlocked from in point of fact. While there, a former army buddy named Jason Martinez had seen him and had come in to talk to the Chief. He had explained that Cyrus had just gotten mixed in with the wrong folks, that he was reeling from PTSD, that he was just a courier for someone out of state.

No doubt Jason was lying, but that didn't matter, because the Chief had an epiphany then. If The Rocks was turning his town into a cesspool, then The Rocks could be its salvation as well.

If Chief Burton used Cyrus Everhaart to oversee the meth trade, he could control that meth trade. He could direct it wherever he wanted. Instead of making the drugs available throughout Ravencourt, the town he loved, he could divert shipments to The Rocks.

Everhaart would not only supply the citizens with a product they craved, he'd provide Chief Burton with valuable intel. He thus had a means of arresting and sending away the competitors and assorted three-strikers who were tearing his town apart.

But there was a problem of some significance. The shitheads at The Rocks, the recidivists pushed along their downward spiral by Burton and Everhaart and an ever-willing Jason Martinez, popped up like weeds. Clear one trailer of the filth, and another sex offender or drug user or plain white trash with a couple burglaries and assaults to his name would move right in, flaunting a welfare or disability check or putting up a paycheck advance they received from one of the many loan sharks in the state.

It was Cyrus who came up with the Big, Bold Idea: They could buy the land right out from under the feet of the criminals hauled in on a weekly basis. Buy them under the guise of a shell corporation

 Persistence

owned and operated by Cyrus Everhaart.

They would gentrify the fuck out of The Rocks.

But to do so would take cash flow, and so Cyrus expanded the operation. He sent his product outward, into the greater Nevada area as well as California and Arizona and Utah. And he could collect money that was then invested into The Rocks, trailer by trailer, Chief Burton making sure to upgrade his officers' equipment and set aside some portion as an emergency fund for the cops who were out of jobs and struggling to get on.

The sheer amount of money that came in boggled Chief Burton's mind. He had lived on a peace officer's salary for going on 40 years, but the amount of money that could be made from meth addicts astounded him, especially seeing as how his customers had to scrounge just to pay an electric bill.

At this point, the crew had been expanded beyond Jason Martinez to include other like-minded officers who could easily be cajoled into helping. Once you framed the operation as being about doing what was right, the mental gymnastics of each individual would do the rest. It was surprisingly easy to get officers who swore to uphold the law to break that law.

The money those other officers got for helping out with the endeavor didn't hurt either.

Unfortunately, problems arose. The meth trade was as volatile as the stock market even if it was slightly more honest. There would always be someone trying to skim product or a competitor attempting to muscle in on your turf. Most criminal enterprises could afford to use intimidation, coercion, and illicit means to see to certain unsavory needs of the business, but Chief Burton could not take that risk himself. He couldn't have his men acting like a Ravencourt Gestapo, sent out to do his bidding, smashing skulls with aplomb. While you wore the badge, you had to uphold the law. At least, in public.

It was, of course, Cyrus Everhaart who came up with the idea of the masks. So simple yet so effective. The Illegals would be the boogeyman that Ravencourt needed, that hushed voices would gossip about whenever something bad happened.

The test run of the Illegals had been the liquor store. A clerk had decided to supplement his income with drug money earned off of selling OxyContin brought in from Colorado.

Burton had made it clear to Cyrus and Jason that no one was to die. But Everhaart had other ideas. And, to Chief Burton's surprise, his own men were more than happy to comply.

After that came the church, the fire that so dismayed and shocked the sleepy town. Everyone believed Father Wallace to be a faithful man, proselytizing the Good Word of God to the townsfolk every day and reciting his own prayers every night.

The truth was that kindly Father Wallace had lost his faith right around the time his wife's throat was torn apart by cancer and God refused to answer a single one of his prayers to save her (never mind that she and her husband had both smoked like holier-than-thou chimneys their entire lives). He was more than open to the idea of using the church collection plate as a means of laundering money for Chief Burton's own holy cause.

But after a couple months, the take coming from the church basement was not adding up to what was brought in. And, as Cyrus explained, there could be no warnings in this game. So the church went up in flames with Father Wallace and two others still in it.

They now owned almost half of The Rocks, yet, to the Chief's dismay, they were no closer to doing anything to snuff out the worst parts of humanity that lived there. They'd been clearing out trailer after trailer, but not everyone at The Rocks fell back into their criminal ways. They couldn't get those truly dedicated to cleaning up their acts to break the law, and thus the straight arrows held onto their land and trailers and even began to prosper. Sure, you could plant evidence and cajole them into falling into old habits, but that had its own risks, and it still wouldn't be fast enough.

When Chief Burton voiced his frustration over a half dozen empty bottles of Miller Lite far from town, Cyrus just smiled, looked across at the Chief, and said, "I thought you'd never ask."

As the Chief listened, Cyrus explained how he had been amassing enough money to simply buy out those who refused to break the law. Then they could build something of their own, something real.

Chief Burton felt his gut clench as he thought about what Cyrus would propose putting at the former site of The Rocks. A brothel? A seedy motel? A money laundering operation of the highest order, no doubt.

So Burton was somewhat shocked when Cyrus made his actual proposal: a goddamn water park.

Cyrus had almost seemed sheepish when he talked about his plan. Here was this hardened criminal, drawing on a napkin the different waterslides and food stands and characters that would greet children.

A water park could bring in families. It could bring in tourism dollars. They could expand out with a golf course, and revitalize the drive-in, real attractions that would even bring in people used to sticking close to The Strip.

For the first time in a long time, Chief Burton smiled. He saw the end in sight. It just might work. They could buy out the rest of The Rocks, consolidate their holdings into one company, a legitimate company, and open a water park and other attractions that would turn the entire town around.

They needed money, of course. Even more than they had currently. They'd have to do something major, something that they'd never done before.

Cyrus offered up his solution: they would need to rob a casino.

Chief Burton had certain conditions. First, they would have to do their research. They couldn't come at this without careful planning. Second, they couldn't kill anyone. They would use beanbag guns instead; he would be damned if he would let fellow badges, even if they were security badges rather than police badges, get killed. And third, they would not be doing this again. This would be the most high-profile job the Illegals had ever pulled off, and thus it would be the last.

When the day of the operation arrived, Chief Burton waited with bated breath. But his concern was all for naught; the robbery turned out to be a rollicking success, the men making off with $342,096.37 without a single casualty.

Now all they had to do was wait while the money was laundered into their corporation, buy up the rest of The Rocks, and begin construction on the project that would save Ravencourt once and for all.

Everything was going great. Ravencourt was back on course, and Chief Burton could look forward to a little extra bonus in his retirement. He was ready to put everything behind him.

But all good things must come to an end. And in this case, that end proved to be a pretty young blonde named Celia Miller.

Chief Burton had never brought Celia into the fold. She wasn't the type. You had to have a certain willingness to see the gray in things, but Chief Burton had known Celia her whole life and it was obvious that she only viewed the world as black and white. She would rather let the city die than have it profit off the back of the drug trade. And so she had been kept in the dark.

Until she wasn't.

Celia stumbled right into the middle of it that day out at The Rocks. That was a problem, because she was like her father and had a tendency not to let things go.

Still, he wouldn't let her be killed, despite Cyrus warning him about what she could do, the threat she posed. She hadn't talked to anyone yet, figured the Chief. She gave no signs that she suspected anything more than what was on the surface.

That is, until two nights ago, when Jason Martinez had broken into her home and discovered that Celia had looked far deeper into their crimes than anyone suspected, far deeper than even the State Investigator. Haddock was a nuisance, but he had nothing of any real consequence. Grasping at straws, not even sure where to point his flashlight in the dark.

But Celia? She had almost everything. The real estate holding corporation. The various side operations. The meth they had sold across state lines, enough to trigger a federal investigation and bring everything crashing down upon them.

Chief Burton had defended her until then, but he wouldn't defend her against this. She could destroy everything. If she went to Haddock or, worse, the Feds with what she knew, it would be hard to cover up. He had covered his tracks well, certainly, but not well like you see in the movies. He didn't use dead drops and voice modulators, his officers' squad cars could be tracked with GPS, he had even written Cyrus a few emails for chrissake.

Jason initially wanted to do it quick, make it look like an accident. Except it was more complicated than that. Jason hadn't worn gloves because he hadn't expected to find what he found, and he couldn't remember what he had and hadn't touched while he was inside. If they killed her in her own home, investigators, real investigators with real resources, would turn the place upside-down. Any shred of evidence that linked back to the cops would be their undoing.

Instead, they came up with another solution. One that would allow them to end Celia's life and solve the notoriety problem of the Illegals all at once, pinning the crimes on The Rocks lowlifes Cyrus was ready to put behind him to become a legitimate businessman. And paint the cops as the heroes who avenged the death of one of their own. Celia's memory would be honored. In a way, it would be her final act as an officer to save her town.

Chief Burton didn't think the other officers would have gone for it, but there wasn't a dissenting vote among them. None of them cared much for Officer Miller, and they would be glad to see the interloper removed once and for all.

When Celia Miller left the station that morning, Chief Burton fully expected never to see her again.

Except something went wrong out there in the desert. Somehow, against all odds, this little girl whom Chief Burton watched grow up had somehow managed to murder every single member of his organization save for Cyrus Everhaart.

They could still make things right. The town could still be saved. He had the money, and with it, he would soon have all the land they needed to break ground on the water park that would ensure the future of Ravencourt for years to come.

But first, they had to bury the past once and for all.

Chief Burton felt somewhat bad killing the black kid, as he certainly hadn't known what he had gotten himself into.

He would not, though, feel bad about putting a bullet in Officer Celia Miller. Not anymore. After all the pain she had caused him, all the headaches, all the lies that would have to be spun to make it look like a drug bust had gone awry and a maniac like Cyrus broke loose in the police station, it was all her fault. After taking Celia onto the force, after looking out for her, she had ultimately betrayed him, and she would bring the whole of Ravencourt down if allowed to live.

Celia Miller would not leave this police station alive.

71

Celia scrolled through the call history on the burner phone. If there was one mystery call to Chief Burton…

There. Yesterday. An outgoing call to Chief Burton. Then an incoming one. Multiple times. Spaced out irregularly throughout the preceding day.

Progress reports. To the man in charge of everything. To the man you trusted…

BANG!

The shower was loud, but whatever sound Celia had just heard was louder, loud enough, in fact, to interrupt her thoughts, which had grown more and more panicked.

She waited and listened some more, but a similar noise didn't follow.

Get your gun. Now.

She stepped to her locker opposite the door and dialed the familiar combination. But when she reached to where she typically stashed her personal firearm, there was nothing to grab.

I must have taken it with me, she thought.

But *you didn't.*

Celia placed her hands on either side of the locker and looked inside. She picked up the empty holster and examined it from every angle.

Did I put it in my squad car?

No.

Leave it at home?

You have a gun *at home, but not this one.*

   PERSISTENCE

Did it wind up out in the desert?

Wrong again.

Celia liked to prepare. Overly so. It was one of the things that drove Jason nuts about her. In her locker, at home, and in the glove compartment of her squad car, she kept a set of clothes, various cosmetics and toiletries, a pack of gum, some type of candy (the fruitier, the better), and assorted first aid supplies. But she also kept a pistol, nothing huge, just something that could be strapped to the hip or even the ankle in case of an emergency.

But now it was gone.

Why would it be gone?

None of the men who had surrounded her in the desert had come back to town at any point, as far as she could tell, and if they did, it certainly wouldn't be to remove a dead girl's gun from her locker. And even if they wanted to get into her locker, they'd have no way to access it.

Steam began to filter into the locker area from the shower, but she paid scant attention to it. The sweat that was on her brow, far from being hot, was ice cold.

Each officer had their own individual locker, the combination changed when a unit was shuffled from one to another. Many of the men on the force simply left theirs unlocked, but Celia never did. The last thing she needed was some idiot officer taking a pair of her panties and stringing it up on a CPR mannequin's head (something that had happened on numerous occasions to other rookies, albeit with boxer briefs).

No one would have had access to her locker unless they could pick locks.

No one except for the Chief of Police.

Officers were not permitted access to each other's lockers, but in the event of an "officer down" situation, the Chief of Police needed access to the contents of the locker and thus was required to keep a skeleton key that could open any lock in the room.

There was only one person who knew you might make it out of there alive.

She forced herself to take deep breaths as the last of the pieces fell into place.

You called him. He was the only one you trusted. And you gave him everything. He said exactly what he needed to get you here. He played on your mistrust by pointing the finger at Haddock. That's all

*it took to make it seem like the most logical thing in the world to make
a quick stop-off at the station to make a statement.*

*The station. Where you'd be alone. Alone in a building with Cyrus
Everhaart and no weapon that wasn't behind lock and key. Where he
would have time to come here and remove the gun from the locker
so that you couldn't put up a fight when he and Cyrus came bursting
through the door. And Brian...*

Celia winced when she thought of his name, and of the sound
that was far too close to a gunshot to her liking.

He was gone.

Her body got real still then. The only person on her side through
all of this, the only person who believed in everything she was capable of, was gone. She had no doubt of that. The gunshot had been
his execution, and now they were coming for her. Chief Burton was
coming for her.

She raised up the burner phone, dialed 911 and was about to hit
Send, but then she stopped. The 911 call would kick straight over
to the desk in the bullpen, not 30 feet from where she stood right
now.

Instead, she fumbled in her back pocket and removed the only
other object she had on her.

Haddock's business card.

She dialed the number. It rang, once, twice, three times.

"Come on, fucking fuck, come on..."

"Haddock here."

"Haddock! It's Celia Miller."

"You're not at the hospital. What's going on?"

"It's Chief Burton," she said, struggling to catch her breath as she
jogged to the shower area. "He's behind it. All of it. The drugs, the
robberies, the murders, everything. I'm at the station and he's coming to kill me. I have minutes at most."

"Christ, Celia, I can't get there in that time. The nearest cops are
the next town over, a 20-minute drive, minimum."

"I know," she said. She approached the first shower head and
cranked up the hot water as far as it would go. Then did the same
to the next one, moving down the line to repeat the action. They had
left her unarmed and with few options, but the steam might serve
to obscure their vision. It wasn't much, but it was all she had.

"Listen, you need to follow the ownership of Haart of the Sea LLC.
Two A's. You can trace it all back to Burton and that scumbag

Everhaart. They've been buying up land for a fucking waterpark. Fucking hell, Burton probably thought it would turn his broke-ass city into a tourist destination."

"Save all that for later, Celia. Fight them. Get somewhere safe."

"There is nowhere safe. And I have nothing to fight them with. Get here soon. If I don't make it, burn these motherfuckers to the ground."

She hung up the phone and finished turning up the last shower-head. And then she thought of something as she ran back toward the lockers. Maybe they hadn't left her unarmed after all.

72

Although Chief Burton was armed with a shotgun and his pistol, Cyrus had insisted on hitting the armory to obtain a pistol for each hip, a piece of body armor, and a helmet.

"Don't you think that's overkill?" asked Chief Burton as Cyrus put on the body armor. "She's a naked, defenseless girl wiping the dirt and blood from her tits in the shower."

"You can underestimate her if you want," said Cyrus. "But that's a mistake I'll not make again."

"I should never have let it come to this. Any of this."

"She was more resourceful than we thought."

"I don't just mean her," Burton yelled, trying to control his breath. "I mean all of it. You and Jason. I could have put an end to it."

"But you didn't. You wanted to save your town. You looked the other way while we did the bad things as if that would absolve you."

Cyrus strapped his helmet into place then pointed at the newly fired pistol in Burton's shaking hand.

"Now you don't have to pretend anymore," said Cyrus. "Now you're truly one of us."

There was a banging at the front door. Cyrus looked up from strapping on a pair of combat gloves.

"Expecting company?"

Chief Burton was in the process of stepping out of the room when he called back.

"The last member of the Celia Miller Survivors Club."

The Chief walked through the bullpen through the rows of desks and then opened the front door to the reception area. Standing in the foyer was Officer Wilfred, pushed into retirement, forced to work in a grocery store, and the beneficiary of supplemental income directed his way from Chief Burton, who would never let it be said that he didn't take care of his own.

"What the fuck happened?" asked Wilfred, a kindly-looking man who Chief Burton knew had been a mean sonofabitch who acted with more brutality than necessary during his days on the force.

"Celia Miller happened," said the Chief, handing Wilfred a shotgun.

"Sweet girl," said Wilfred. "So she found out about the operation?"

"Things got out of control. She killed four of my men."

"Jesus Christ, that's almost your entire police force!"

"You have a problem helping me end this?"

Former Officer Wilfred who worked at the Wheel-Loo grocery store stared down the sights of the gun with the kind of experience taught by age.

"The cunt that took my job? Just point me in the right direction."

And so it was that Chief Burton and Wilfred the grocer strode back into the bullpen, where a thoroughly armored Cyrus Everhaart stood waiting, his face obscured by a face shield. He brandished a pistol in one hand and a riot shield in the other.

"What's his deal?" asked Wilfred.

"My daddy was a scout leader."

"And he told you to be prepared?"

"No. He used to beat the shit out of me on camping trips and I learned to never go into a fight without adequate protection."

The three men walked toward the door of the locker room. They could hear the water running inside. Cyrus hesitated.

"What are you afraid of?" asked Wilfred. "That you're gonna slip on the soap coming off of her bush?"

Cyrus gestured toward the closed door.

"Be my guest."

Wilfred cocked the shotgun, his considerable paunch jiggling considerably.

"With pleasure."

Wilfred pushed the door open with one hand, raising the shotgun as he did so.

A report rang out, and the top of his skull splatted away before the shotgun even got hoisted above his waist. The gun, and Wilfred himself, crumpled uselessly to the ground.

"Like my daddy also once told me," said Cyrus. "When a woman gets to throwing shit, never underestimate her ability to find more shit to throw."

73

Celia darted back into the steam, which had obscured the locker room considerably but now was drifting out the open door. She needed someplace to hide.

The gun wasn't hers, but Chief Burton had made a mistake when he only cleared her locker out. True, he had thought to lock every other locker so that Celia couldn't get a hold of some other police-issued firearm and possibly use it against him, but there was one locker she had always known the combination to.

Jason Martinez's. He wasn't the type to accept change in life, certainly not in his relationship with Celia, and she prayed that resistance extended to his locker combination. Celia had it memorized in high school: The date of their anniversary.

It worked.

Celia popped open Jason's locker, and sitting right there was a Ravencourt PD firearm and a clip just waiting to be unloaded into a corrupt cop and a redneck who liked to wax poetic.

When they had opened the door, Celia had simply fired. She hadn't expected Wilfred to be there, but fuck him. It wouldn't surprise Celia to find out that the entire City Council and the Mayor and the mudfucking Governor were on Chief Burton's payroll, coming through the door in matching alien masks to murder her.

She was done thinking about the consequences of any action she needed to survive.

Celia Miller was going to leave this police station alive if it killed her.

74

Cyrus Everhaart, replete with all manner of riot control garb, walked into the locker room with the shield held frontward and the pistol peeking out from behind it. There were only two rows of lockers, with a partition of smaller lockers in the middle not unlike a tall kitchen island. The showers stood off to the side, a lump of sweaty towels in the corner.

The steam clouded his riot mask and made it exceedingly difficult to see where he was going. Chief Burton followed him inside, his pistol drawn and ready to fire.

Cyrus moved to the other side of the locker island, stopping at the corner before swiveling out. He aimed his gun down the row of lockers but there was no one there.

He gave an all clear signal to Chief Burton, who stood watch at the door. Cyrus walked to the showers and turned off the one closest to the lockers. He then went through and shut them off one by one, the sound of flowing water and the shroud created by the steam diminishing with each shutoff.

The final shower trickled to nothing, and with the last *drip drip drip*, all Cyrus could hear was his breath in his own ears.

She wasn't hiding behind the curtain that partitioned the corner shower from everyone else, as Cyrus had already looked there.

Which left only one place: the lockers.

Cyrus turned around and peered into the unit closest to the showers. He wiped the moisture off the front of the riot gear and scanned the lockers that ran the length of the wall.

"Which one's hers?" he asked.

“Fifth one down.”

Cyrus moved to that locker and peered inside. There was no one.

“Celia,” said Chief Burton. “I don’t know what you think is going on, but I want to help you.”

“She’s not an idiot, Henry.”

Chief Burton glared at Cyrus. “You look in the lockers. I’ll stand by the door. There’s only one way out of here and she isn’t getting out.”

Cyrus walked down the rows of lockers, peering into each one. Celia was thin, but he didn’t know if she was this small. Still, there wasn’t anywhere else that she could be.

Unless…

Cyrus pivoted and then stood on the bench that lined the lockers, aiming his gun up above the tops of the lockers, where he thought Celia might hide to gain an advantage.

Except there was no one there either. Celia Miller seemed to have disappeared into thin air.

Cyrus walked back to Chief Burton and shrugged his shoulders.

“You sure there’s only one way out of here?”

That’s when Chief Burton saw the stack of towels piled in the corner move ever so slightly.

“Cyrus, down!”

75

Celia held her breath while Cyrus wove his way past each shower head, sure she would be spotted, but the steam must have limited his vision. He walked right past her, and Celia would have shot him right then, but she wasn't sure it would do the trick given all the armor he was wearing. And even if she did, Chief Burton would have had her in his sights.

So she waited, her breath held, as Cyrus's steps took him right past the towels she hid beneath. Cyrus had checked the lockers and then peered above them before climbing down.

He stood in front of Chief Burton, away from Celia, partially blocking his view with his body.

She wouldn't get another chance. She made her move.

"Cyrus, down!" yelled Burton.

Celia lurched forward, the towels falling off of her as she ran. She fired off shots toward Cyrus but couldn't tell if they hit home, because she was already diving forward.

Cyrus was in the middle of turning when Celia's body struck his with all of her might. He tumbled forward, into Chief Burton, and the three of them went sprawling through the door and in a heap on top of the dead body of Wilfred.

Unfortunately, the gun went flying out of Celia's hand and she lost sight of it. On top of the heap, she tried to push up and off of the other's bodies. Her feet struggled to find purchase on the wet ground, and then hands were wrapping around her arms and waist.

But they were Burton's arms, and he had Cyrus's heavily armored body between him and Celia. She swatted his hands away and then

 PERSISTENCE

was able to use the frame of the door as leverage to peel herself off of the ground and into the small hallway. She pivoted, grabbing a flash of black that she rightfully determined to be the gun, and with her leg threatening to give out, she ran down the stub of a hallway.

As she ran, she caught a glimpse of Brian's body lying dead in Burton's office at the end of the hall. She looked away quickly.

Celia turned into the bullpen, and not a moment too soon, because someone was already shooting at her.

They would be on their feet in a second or two and around this same corner in a second more. She moved on pure instinct now, weaving through the desks that made up the bullpen, sliding over one to give herself some cover as Burton came through the door.

She fired off a couple potshots and Burton retreated. Unfortunately, a few seconds later, it was Cyrus coming through the door with the riot shield held in front of him. Burton followed him a few steps behind and then darted in another direction.

The two were trying to flank her.

Cyrus was moving forward through the desks while cutting off the left side of the room and the front exit, while Chief Burton worked his way along the wall to the right, moving closer and closer to the door that led to the garage and the only other way out.

The choice was simple. Cyrus had a riot shield; Chief Burton had a paunch.

She fired a shot at the wall near Burton to cause him to duck and then grasped both hands around the chair that sat next to her behind the desk. She lifted it into the air and threw it at Cyrus, who was closer and the more serious threat. His reflexes caused him to bring up the riot shield, his weapon momentarily lowered.

Burton was already readying his next shot, but Celia was running and firing at the same time. He was forced to duck behind a desk. Celia fired until there were no more bullets and then leapt over the desk that Burton was crouched behind, the two of them tumbling into a metal file cabinet.

She dug her right hand into his eyes while fending off the shotgun, his selection of which proved to be a critical error. He tried to bring it up toward Celia's chin but she wouldn't allow it.

He fired off a shot, and with her left hand wrapped around the muzzle, intense burning pain flared through her palm. She screamed and let her hand fall off. Burton used the opportunity to bring the shotgun around, but Celia reached with her other hand

and opened the middle section of the file cabinet while simultaneously using what little strength she had left to pull the entire thing forward, creating an upside-down V with Burton stuck in the nook formed between the desk and the metal cabinet. The scattershot bullets of the shotgun reverberated against the metal.

A bullet tore through Celia's shoulder and she dropped to the ground. As she fell, the room spinning madly, she saw Cyrus with his pistol pointed forward. His shot had hit home, but he had dropped the riot shield for the moment, so there was that little moral victory.

Burton, unable to turn the shotgun in a way that would get it pointed toward Celia, scooted his way out from under the file cabinet. Celia, lying on her back on the ground now, kicked him full in the face, using her hands and the heels of her feet to push backward, toward the door that led out to the garage.

She reached it and, using the desks as cover, crouched down to open the door, bullets pinging above her head as Cyrus ran to meet her, firing all the while.

She got to the other side of the door, but instead of going for one of the cars, for which there would be no time, she grabbed the first thing she saw that could be used as a weapon: a large wrench from the tool bench positioned by the door.

Cyrus's pounding footsteps were unmistakable, but as he got to the door frame, he slowed down. When he was right at the door that Celia was holding open, she brought the wrench around on the pistol-clutching arm that appeared in the doorway.

The pistol clattered to the floor and Cyrus screamed. Liking the sound and wanting to hear more, Celia now brought the wrench around and smashed it into the face of the riot mask.

The shield splintered inward and Cyrus fell backward, clutching his face mask.

She looked at the three squad cars parked inside the garage, and the keys that lined the wall that went to each of those cars. She took a step toward those keys now.

No.

She planted her foot but then turned back to the doorway Cyrus had just fallen through.

Finish this.

She swung the door wide open again and marched toward Cyrus, who was leaning back against a desk and had torn the riot mask from his face. He pushed himself up to confront Celia and she met his bared teeth with a sickening and satisfying cracking sound that sent him backward and then to his knees.

She turned then and set her sights on Burton, who was getting his feet beneath him as he struggled to get up. He raised the shotgun anew and Celia swung the wrench upward this time, connecting with the fingers that were wrapped beneath the barrel of the gun, breaking two fingers instantly and causing the shotgun to drop.

Chief Burton screamed in pain and fell back to his knees. Celia did a backhand like a tennis swing and caught him in the windpipe. He fell against another file cabinet, trying to suck in breath and failing, his airway making a bizarre sucking sound like a thick chocolate shake through a straw.

She swung the wrench and hit him in the temple. His face, the other side propped up flat against the metal cabinet, simply collapsed. She swung two more times to make sure she finished the job.

He was unrecognizable by the third swing.

Celia gasped for breath now, but turned slowly when she heard laughter.

Cyrus was splayed out on the desk. His mouth and nose bled profusely yet he continued to laugh. She shuffled forward like a zombie, the wrench dripping blood on the stucco floor.

"Why are you laughing?

Cyrus spit blood and what looked like a piece of a tooth up into the air.

"I was hoping I might finally get that kiss now."

Celia wrapped her hand around Cyrus's throat as she raised the wrench above her head. That was when the punchline to an inappropriate joke came to her.

"Not until you brush your teeth, bitch."

The wrench came down once, twice, and a few times more, ending Cyrus's laughing and his life.

Celia looked around the bullpen, which, besides one banged-up corner, looked about as it did before the shootout.

She let the wrench clatter to the floor, vaguely aware of the pain in her leg, her ear, and now her shoulder. She staggered ahead, using her hand to support her weight on the desks.

She grew weaker and weaker as she moved forward. Finally, unable to stagger any further, she sank into a chair.

Celia picked up the phone that set on that desk and dialed the direct number for the hospital, which was mercifully only a couple blocks away. The phone rang twice and a voice answered. Celia didn't let that voice get any further than "Ravencourt County Hospital, this is…" before she spoke.

"This is Officer Celia Miller. I've been injured. You need to send an ambulance to the police station. And then you need to call the county police and the State Troopers and have them send officers."

"Miss, I…"

"There's been a massacre. I'm the only one left alive…" Celia gasped at this point and struggled to choke back the tears. She collected herself. "My name is Celia Miller and I am the only one left alive. Send ambulances and the county and state police. Can you do that?"

"You're saying there are people dead?"

"Lots. Now make the calls."

Celia hung up the phone and slumped back in the seat. She realized then that she was sitting at the 911 desk. Except, rather than taking an emergency call, she had just sent one out. Had to be something ironic in that, she just couldn't think of what. She couldn't think of much of anything right now.

Jason was dead. Brian was dead. Cyrus Fucking Everhaart was dead. And Chief Burton was dead.

Would she go to jail? She didn't think so. The squad car had a camera. It would have recorded much of what happened. And there was sure to be an investigation, probably by the FBI. They would comb through the property and electronic fingerprint of everyone Celia had killed today. And that would reveal the truth.

But that would be later.

For now, Celia closed her eyes and was drifting into sleep when the phone rang. Her eyes flicked open and alit on the caller ID. The name there said Marsh.

She recognized the name, but in her foggy state, she couldn't think of from where. Whoever it was, they needed help. Celia doubted she could give it in her current state, but maybe she could relay things to the right people.

Confident for the first time in a long time that she would be alive to see another sunset and many more sunsets after that, Celia reached for the phone. She winced as the muscles in her wounded shoulder stretched taut.

She picked up the line and raised the phone to her ear.

"911, what's your emergency?"